P9-DYZ-285

Raves For the Work of
DONALD E. WESTLAKE!

"Dark and delicious."
— *The New York Times*

"A pleasure…Westlake's ability to construct an action story filled with unforeseen twists and quadruple-crosses is unparalleled."
— *San Francisco Chronicle*

"Ingeniously twisted plotting."
— *Cleveland Plain Dealer*

"[A] book by this guy is cause for happiness."
— *Stephen King*

"Brilliant."
— *GQ*

"I thoroughly enjoy his attitude."
— *Elmore Leonard*

"A wonderful read."
— *Playboy*

"Westlake is one of the best crime writers in the business."
— *Los Angeles Times*

6-17-17

"Westlake remains in perfect command; there's not a word…out of place."
— *San Diego Union-Tribune*

"Energy and imagination light up virtually every page, as does some of the best hard-boiled prose ever to grace the noir genre."
— *Publishers Weekly*

"Tantalizing…The action is non-stop."
— *The Wall Street Journal*

"A brilliant invention."
— *New York Review of Books*

"A mystery connoisseur's delight. His plot delivers twists and turns…A tremendously skillful, smart writer."
— *Time Out New York*

"Crime fiction stripped down — as it was meant to be…oh, how the pages keep turning."
— *Philadelphia Inquirer*

"Donald Westlake's…novels are among the small number of books I read over and over. Forget all that crap you've been telling yourself about *War and Peace* and Proust—these are the books you'll want on that desert island."
— *Lawrence Block*

I took the bus uptown and checked a car out and got my first fare half a block from the garage, a good-looking girl in an orange fur coat and black boots and pale blond hair. "2715 Pennsylvania Avenue," she said.

I said, "Brooklyn or Washington?" I kid with good-looking female passengers whether I'm worried about money or not.

"Brooklyn," she said. "Take the Belt."

"Fine," I said, and dropped the flag, and headed south. My luck was finally in. Not only a good-looking blonde in the rear-view mirror, but a long haul at that, and it would end not too far from Kennedy.

The highways were all cleared, and carried way below their usual midday load of traffic. We got up on the West Side Highway at twenty to four and left the Belt Parkway at Pennsylvania Avenue in Brooklyn at just four o'clock. In between I'd made a couple of small attempts at conversation, but she was the strong silent type, so I let it go. I'm content to look, if that's the way they want it.

The first half mile of Pennsylvania Avenue is through filled-in swampland. There's no solid ground at the bottom, just dirt piled into a swamp, so the road is very jouncy and bouncy, full of heaves and holes, and even though there's little traffic at any time there and no housing or pedestrians around, you can't make very good time. The snow plows, probably because of the uneven road surface, hadn't been able to do much of a job here, so that slowed me even more.

Which meant I was doing about twenty when the girl stuck the gun into the back of my neck...

SOMEBODY
Owes Me Money

by Donald E. Westlake

A HARD CASE CRIME NOVEL

A HARD CASE CRIME BOOK
(HCC-044)
June 2008

Published by

Dorchester Publishing Co., Inc.
200 Madison Avenue
New York, NY 10016

in collaboration with Winterfall LLC

*This book is a work of fiction. Names, characters, places, and
incidents either are the products of the author's imagination or
are used fictitiously, and any resemblance to actual events or
persons, living or dead, is entirely coincidental.*

ISBN 0-8439-5962-2
ISBN 978-0-8439-5962-8

Cover design by Cooley Design Lab

Typeset by Swordsmith Productions

The name "Hard Case Crime" and the Hard Case Crime logo
are trademarks of Winterfall LLC. Hard Case Crime books are
selected and edited by Charles Ardai.

Printed in the United States of America

Visit us on the web at www.HardCaseCrime.com

I bet none of it would have happened if I wasn't so eloquent. That's always been my problem, eloquence, though some might claim my problem was something else again. But life's a gamble, is what I say, and not all the eloquent people in this world are in Congress.

Where I am is in a cab in New York City. Fares frequently ask me how it is somebody as eloquent as me is driving a cab, and I usually give them a brief friendly answer which doesn't really cover the territory. The truth is, my eloquence comes from reading rather than formal higher education, which limits the kind of job open to me. Besides, driving a cab gives me a chance to pick my own hours. Day shift when the track is closed, night shift when it's open. If there's a game somewhere I'm particularly interested in, I skip a night and nobody cares. And if I'm broke, I can work as many hours as I want till I make it up.

Also, driving a cab is a lot more pleasant than you might think. You're dealing with the public all day long, but only as individuals, one or two at a time. People are best one or two at a time. Also, economics being what they are, you're generally dealing with a better class of customer. You get to talk with lawyers, businessmen, actors, tourists from Europe, all sorts of that kind of people. You get to look at a certain number of pretty girls, too, and sometimes have nice friendly conversations with them, and on rare occasions make a date with one. Like the girl I went with last year, Rita, the one where it looked serious for a while, until the Big A opened and it turned out she didn't want to go to the track with me. She was down on gambling, is what it was, and the funny thing was she worked for a stockbroker. She kept wanting me to put money in the stock market. "Aerospace is undervalued right now," she'd say, and things like that. Then I'd tell her I'd rather play the races than the market because I knew the races and I didn't know the market, and she'd get mad and start claiming that horse-racing and the stock market weren't the same thing, and I'd say of course they were and give her analogies, and she'd get madder and insist the analogies were false, and so it went until finally we gave the whole thing up and she went her way and I went mine, and that was about the last steady girl I had up to the time of which I wish to speak.

The time of which I wish to speak began with a customer I took from Kennedy Airport to Manhattan. He started the whole mess I got into, and I never saw him again after that one time. He started it indirectly and inadvertently, but he did start it.

He was a heavyset red-faced guy of maybe fifty, he smoked a really rotten cigar and had two expensive suitcases, and he went to an address on Fifth Avenue below 14th Street. With a doorman. It was January and a snowstorm had been threatening for three days without yet showing up, and also he'd just come back from somewhere warm, so naturally we got into a discussion of New York City weather and what should be done about it. I cracked a few jokes, made some profound statements, threw in a few subtle asides about politics and scored a few good ones off the automobile industry, made a concise analysis of the air pollution problem around the city, and all in all I would say I was at my most eloquent.

When we got to his address the meter read six ninety-five. I got out and unloaded the suitcases from the trunk while the building's doorman held the cab door open. The fare got out and handed me a ten, I gave him change from my pocket, and then we just stood there on the sidewalk together, luggage on one side of us and doorman on the other, my customer smiling as though thinking about something else, until finally he said, "Now I give you a tip, right?"

"It's the usual thing," I said. It was cold outside the cab.

He nodded. "That paper I noticed on the seat beside you," he said. "Was that the *Daily Telegraph?*"

"It was," I said. "It is."

"Would you be a horseplayer?"

"I've been known to take a chance," I said.

He nodded. "How much of that six ninety-five do you get to keep?"

"Fifty-one percent," I said.

"That's three fifty-four," he said, faster than I'd have been able to. "All right. I like you, I like the way you talk, you gave me a pleasant ride in, so here's your tip. You put that three fifty-four on Purple Pecunia, it will bring you back a minimum of eighty-one forty-two."

I guess I looked blank. I didn't say anything.

"Don't thank me," he said modestly, smiled and nodded, and turned away. The doorman picked up the luggage.

"I wasn't going to," I said, but I don't think he heard me.

It happens every once in a while you get beaten out of a tip for one reason or another, and my philosophy is, you have to be philosophical about it. It also happens every once in a while you get a really big tipper, so it all evens out. So I just shrugged and got back into the cab in the warm and went looking for a really big tipper.

This was at about nine in the morning. Around eleven-thirty I went over to my usual diner on 11th Avenue and had coffee and a Danish even though I'm supposed to be on a diet. Sitting in a cab all the time there's a tendency to spread a little, so every once in a while I try to take off a few pounds. But after a while you begin to get hungry, you don't want to take the time for a whole meal, so you stop for a quick coffee and Danish. It's only natural.

Anyway, I brought the paper in with me and looked it over and my eye got caught by this horse Purple Pecunia, the one I got stiff-tipped on. I'd thought he'd said Petunia, like the flower, but it was Pecunia, which was peculiar. He was running down in Florida, and judging from past performance he'd be lucky to finish the race the same day he started. Some hot tip.

But then I got to thinking about it, and I remembered how the guy had been friendly all the way into town, how he obviously had money, and how fast he'd been at fig-uring my fifty-one percent of the meter, and I wondered if maybe I should listen to him after all.

I remembered the numbers. Three fifty-four was my percent, and eighty-one forty-two was what he'd said I would make if I bet that amount. At *least* eighty-one forty-two.

I did some long division on the margin of the *Telegraph* and it came out at exactly twenty-two to one. To the penny.

A man who can do numbers that fast in his head, I told myself, has got to know what he's talking about. Besides, he was obviously not hurting for money. And further be-sides, what was the point in giving me a bum steer?

If there's one thing a horseplayer or any other kind of player learns early in his career it is this: Play your hunches. Get a hunch, bet a bunch, that's what the poker players say. And all of a sudden, I had a hunch. I had a hunch that fare of mine—who had just come up on a plane from some place warm, let's not forget that—knew what he was talking about, and Purple Pecunia was going to romp home a winner, and some few people on the inside were going to walk away twenty-two times richer than they started. A *minimum* of twenty-two times.

And I could use the money. There's a couple of regular poker games I'm in, and for about five weeks I'd been running a string of bad cards to make you sit down and cry. The only thing to do with a run like that is wait it out, and I know it, but in the meantime I was spreading a lot of paper around, there were half a dozen guys with my marker in their pockets now, one of them for seventy-five dollars, and frankly I was beginning to get worried. If the cards didn't turn soon, I didn't know what I was going to do.

So if I was to put some money on this Purple Pecunia, and the tip should turn out to be good, it would be a real lifesaver and no fooling. The only question was—how much did I want to risk? Just in case, just in case.

It seemed to me I should leave that up to Tommy. Tommy McKay, my book. I was going to have to do it on credit anyway, so I might just as well go as steep as he'd let me.

I finished the coffee and Danish, paid my check, and went to one of the phone booths in the back. Tommy works out of his apartment, so I called there and got his wife. "Hi, Mrs. McKay," I said. "Is Tommy there? This is Chet."

"Who?"

"Chet. Chet Conway."

"Oh, Chester. Just a minute."

"Chet," I said. I hate to be called Chester.

She'd already put the phone down. I waited, thinking things over, having second thoughts, and so on, and then Tommy came on. His voice is almost as high-pitched as his wife's, but more nasal. I said, "Tommy, how much can I put on the cuff?"

"I don't know," he said. "What are you in to me for now?"

"Fifteen."

He hesitated, and then he said, "I'll go to fifty with you. I know you're okay."

Second thoughts came crowding in again. Another thirty-five bucks in the hole? What if Purple Pecunia didn't come in?

The hell with it. Get a hunch, bet a bunch. "The whole thirty-five," I said, "on Purple Pecunia. To win."

"Purple Petunia?"

"No, Pecunia. With a *c*." I read him the dope from the paper.

There was a little silence, and then he said, "You sure you want to do that?"

"I got a hunch," I said.

"It's your dough," he said. Which was almost true.

After that I was very nervous. I went back to work, and I even began to let the midtown traffic get to me. I never do that, I'm always insulated inside my cab. The way I figure, I'm in no hurry, I'm *at* work. I'll go with the flow of the traffic, I'll take it easy, I'll live longer. But I was very nervous about that thirty-five bucks on Purple Pecunia, and the nervousness made me edgy with other drivers. I kept hoping for a fare out to one of the airports, but it never happened. Nothing but short hops through the middle of the mess. Eighth Avenue and 53rd Street. Then Park and 30th. Then Madison and 51st. Then Penn Station. On and on like that.

I keep a transistor radio on the dashboard, so in the afternoon I turned it on for the race results, and at ten minutes to four in came the word on Purple Pecunia. She won the race. I had an old lady in the cab at the time. She had a hundred packages from Bonwit Teller's and she kept looking out the window and saying, "Look at that, just look at that. Look at that black face. It's a disgrace, right on Fifth Avenue. Look at that one, walking along as nice as you please. They ought to stay down South where they belong. Look at that one, with a *tie* on if you please!" She was a ten-cent tip if there ever lived one, but I no longer cared.

She got out at a townhouse in the East Sixties. I switched on the Off Duty light and headed for a phone booth. Using her dime I called Tommy, and he said, "I thought I'd hear from you. That was some hunch."

It sure was. At twenty-two to one, that hunch was going to bring back eight hundred and five dollars.

I said, "What does it pay?"

"Twenty-seven to one," he said.

"Twenty-*seven*?"

"That's right."

"How much is that?"

"Nine eighty," he said. "Less the half yard you owe me, that's nine thirty."

Nine hundred and thirty dollars. Almost a thousand dollars! I was rich!

I said, "I'll be over around six, is that okay?"

"Sure," he said.

I couldn't turn the cab in before five, so I headed uptown to try to stay out of the midtown crush, so naturally I got flagged down right away by somebody wanting to go to the PanAm Building. What with one thing and another, it was twenty after five before I clocked out at the garage over on Eleventh Avenue. I immediately became a fare myself, hailing a cab for one of the first times in my life, and headed down to Tommy's apartment on West 46th Street between Ninth and Tenth. I rang the bell, but there was a woman coming out with a baby carriage, so I didn't have to wait for the buzz. I held the door for the woman and went on in. There still hadn't been any buzz when I got into the elevator.

He must have heard the bell, though, because the door was partly open when I got to the fourth floor. I pushed it open the rest of the way and stepped into the hall and said, "Tommy? It's me, Chet."

Nothing.

The hall light was on. I left the front door partly open like before and walked down the hall looking into the rooms as I went by. Kitchen, then bathroom, then bedroom, all lit up and all empty. The living room was down at the end of the hall.

I went into the living room and Tommy was lying on his back on the rug, arms spread out. There was blood all over the place. He looked like he'd been shot in the chest with antiaircraft guns.

"Holy Christ," I said.

2

I was on the phone in the kitchen, trying to call the cops, when Tommy's wife came in with a grocery bag in her arms. She's a short and skinny woman with a sharp nose and a general look of disapproval.

She came to the kitchen doorway, saw me, and said, "What's up?"

"There's been an accident," I said. I knew it wasn't an accident, but I couldn't think of anything else to say. And at just that minute the police answered, so I said into the phone, "I want to report a— Wait a second, will you?"

The cop said, "You want to report what?"

I put my hand over the mouthpiece and said to Tommy's wife, "Don't go into the living room."

She looked toward the living room, frowning, then came in and put the bag down on the counter. "Why not?"

The cop was saying, "Hello? Hello?"

"Just a *second*," I told him, and said to Tommy's wife, "Because Tommy's in there, and he doesn't look good."

She took a quick step back toward the hall. "What's the matter with him?"

"Don't go there," I said. "Please."

"What's the matter, Chester?" she said. "For God's sake, will you *tell* me?"

The cop was still yammering in my ear. I said to Tommy's wife, "He's dead," and then to the cop I said, "I want to report a murder."

She was gone, running for the living room. The cop was asking me my name and the address. I said, "Listen, I don't have much time. The address is 417 West 46th Street, apartment 4-C."

"And your name?"

Tommy's wife began to scream.

"I've got a hysterical lady here," I said.

"Sir," said the cop, as though it was a word in a foreign language, "I need your name."

Tommy's wife screamed again.

"Do you hear that?" I said. I held the phone toward the kitchen doorway, then pulled it back and said, "Did you hear it?"

"I hear it, sir," he said. "Just give me your name, please. I will have officers dispatched to the scene."

"That's good," I said, and Tommy's wife came running into the kitchen, wild-eyed. Her hands were red. She screamed at the top of her lungs, *"What happened?"*

"My name is Chester Conway," I said.

The cop said, "What was that?"

Tommy's wife grabbed me by the front of my jacket. It's a zip-up jacket, dark blue, two pockets, it's comfortable for driving the cab all day in the winter. *"What did you do?"* she screamed.

I said to the cop, "Wait a second," and put the phone down. Tommy's wife was leaning forward to glare in my face, her hands on my chest, pushing me backward. I gave a step, saying, "Get hold of yourself. Please. I got to report this."

All at once she let go of me, picked up the phone, and shouted into it, "Get off the line! I want to call the police!"

"That is the police," I said.

She started clicking the phone at him. "Hang up!" she shouted. "Hang up, this is an emergency!"

"I'm supposed to slap you now," I said. I tugged at her arm, trying to get her attention. "Hello? Listen, I'm supposed to slap you across the face now, because you're hysterical. But I don't want to do that, I don't want to have to do that."

She began violently to shake the phone, holding it out at arm's length as though strangling it. *"Will—you—get—off—the—line?"*

I kept tugging her other arm. "That's the police," I said. *"That's* the police."

She flung the phone away all at once, so that it bounced off the wall. She yanked her arm away from me and went running out of the kitchen and out of the apartment. "Help!" I heard her in the hall. "Help! Police!"

I picked up the phone. "That was his wife," I said. "She's hysterical. I wish you'd hurry up and dispatch some officers."

"Yes, sir," he said. "You were giving your name."

"I guess I was," I said. "It's Chester Conway." I spelled it.

He said, "Thank you, sir." He read back my name and the address and I said he had them right and he said the officers would be dispatched to the scene at once. I hung up and noticed the phone was smeared with red from where Tommy's wife had held it, so now my hand was smeared, too. Red and sticky. I went automatically to wipe my hand on my jacket, and discovered the front of my jacket was also red and sticky.

A heavyset man in an undershirt, with hair on his shoulders and a hammer in his hand, came into the kitchen, looking furious and determined and terrified, and said, "What's going on here?"

"Somebody was killed," I said. I felt he was blaming me, and I was afraid of his hammer. I gestured at the phone and said, "I just called the police. They're on their way."

He looked around on the floor. "Who was killed?"

"The man who lives here," I said. "Tommy McKay. He's in the living room."

He took a step backward, as though to go to the living room and see, then suddenly got a crafty expression on his face and said, "You ain't going anywhere."

"That's right," I said. "I'm going to wait here for the police."

"You're damn right," he said. He glanced at the kitchen clock, then back at me. "We'll give them five minutes," he said.

"I really did call," I said.

A very fat woman in a flowered dress appeared behind him, putting her hands on his hairy shoulders, peeking past him at me. "What is it, Harry?" she said. "Who is he?"

"It's okay," Harry said. "Everything's under control."

"What's that stuff on his jacket, Harry?" she asked.

"It's blood," I said.

The silence was suddenly full of echoes, like after hitting a gong. In it, I could plainly hear Harry swallow. *Gulp*. His eyes got brighter, and he took a tighter grip on the hammer.

We all stood there.

3

When the cops came in, everybody talked at once. They listened to Harry first, maybe because he was closest, maybe because he had the hammer, maybe because he had his wife talking with him, and then they told him to take his wife and his hammer and go back across the hall to his apartment and take care of the bereaved lady over there and they, the cops, would stop in a little later. Harry and his wife went away, looking puffed with pride and full of good citizenship, and the cops turned to me.

"I didn't do it," I said.

They looked surprised, and then suspicious. "Nobody said you did," one of them pointed out.

"That guy was holding a hammer on me," I said. "*He* thought I did it."

"Why did he think so?"

"I don't know. Maybe Tommy's wife told him I did."

"Why would she say a thing like that?"

"Because she was hysterical," I said. "Besides, I don't even know if she said it. Maybe it was because of the blood on my jacket." I looked at my hand. "And on my hand."

They looked at my jacket and my hand, and they stiffened up a little. But the one who did the talking was still soft-voiced when he said, "How did that happen?"

"Tommy's wife grabbed me," I said. "That's when it got on my jacket. She'd gone in to look at Tommy, and I guess she touched him or something, and then she got it on me."

"And the hand?"

"From the phone." I pointed to it. "She was holding the phone."

"Is she the one who called in the complaint?"

"No. I did."

"You did. Who did Mrs. McKay call?"

"Nobody. She was hysterical, and she wanted to call the co—police, but I was already talking to them. It got kind of confusing."

"I see." They looked at one another, and the talking one said, "Where's the body?"

"In the living room," I said. I made a pointing gesture. "Down the hall to the end."

"Show us."

I didn't want to go down there. "Well, it's just—" I said, and then I saw what they meant. They wanted me with them. "Oh," I said. "All right."

We went down the hall to the living room, me in the lead, and Tommy was still there, spread out on the floor, sunny side up. With the yolk broken.

I'm sorry I thought that.

I stood to one side, and the cops looked. One of them said to me, "Use your phone?"

"Sure," I said. "It's not mine."

The phone was over by the windows, which looked out on the street. While the silent cop went over and made his call the other one said to me, "Why didn't you use that phone there? Why the one in the kitchen?"

"I didn't want to be in the same room with him," I said. I was not looking at Tommy, but I could still see him out of the corner of my eye. "I still don't," I said.

He looked at me. "You going to be sick?"

"I don't think so."

He pointed near the hallway entrance. "Just wait there a minute," he said.

"All right," I said. I went over there and waited, looking down the hall toward the entrance. Behind me I could hear the cops talking together and talking on the phone, low murmurings. I wasn't interested in making out the words.

After a couple minutes the talking cop and I went across the hall to Harry's apartment. Harry seemed surprised to see me walking around free, surprised and somewhat indignant, as though he was being insulted in some obscure way. Tommy's wife was lying on her back on a very lumpy sofa in an overcrowded and overheated living room. She had one forearm thrown over her face, and I saw she'd washed the blood off her hands.

The cop sat down on the coffee table and said softly, "Mrs. McKay?"

Without moving her arm so she could see him she said, "What?"

"Could I ask you a couple questions?" He was even more soft-voiced than before. A very nice corpse-side manner.

I said to Harry, "Can I use your bathroom, please?"

Harry frowned in instant distrust. He said to the cop, "Is it okay?"

The cop looked over his shoulder, nettled at the interruption. "Sure, sure," he said, and went back to Tommy's wife.

Harry's wife, being polite because now I was a guest in her house, showed me to the bathroom. I shut the door with my clean hand, turned on the water in the sink, and washed my hands. Then I used a washcloth to try to wash off the front of my jacket. I got it pretty well, then rinsed the washcloth, dried my hands, and went back out to the living room.

The cop wasn't alone any more. There were three plainclothesmen there, all with hats on their heads and their hands in their overcoat pockets. They looked at me, and the uniformed cop said, "He's the one made the discovery."

One of the plainclothesmen said, "I'll take it." He took his hands out of his pockets and came over to me, saying, "You Chester Conway?"

"Yes," I said. In a corner I could see Harry and his wife both sitting in the same armchair, blinking at everything in eager curiosity. They'd happily given up the participant roles and drifted into their real thing, being spectators.

"I'm Detective Golderman," the plainclothesman said. "Come along."

Sensing Harry and his wife being disappointed that I wasn't going to be questioned—grilled—in front of them, I followed Detective Golderman out and across the hall and into Tommy's apartment. We went into the bedroom now, and I could hear murmuring in the living room. It sounded like a lot of men in there, a lot of activity.

Detective Golderman, notebook in hand, said, "Okay, Chester, tell me about it."

I told him about it, that I'd called Tommy at four, that I'd said I'd be over at six, that when I got here I came into the building without his buzzing to let me in, that the apartment door was open, that I found him dead and started to call the police and his wife came in and everything got hysterical. When I was done, he said, "McKay was a friend of yours, is that right?"

"That's right," I said. "Sort of a casual friend."

"Why were you coming over today?"

"Just a visit," I said. "Sometimes I come over when I quit work."

"What do you do?"

"I drive a cab."

"Could I see your license?"

"Sure."

I handed it to him, and he compared my face with the picture and then handed it back, thanking me. Then he said, "Would you know any reason anybody would do a thing like that to your friend?"

"No," I said. "Nobody."

"He didn't sound frightened or different in any way when you talked to him on the phone this afternoon?"

"No, sir. He didn't sound any different from usual."

"Whose idea was it you should come over at six?"

I had a problem there, since I didn't feel I should tell a cop that my relationship with Tommy was customer to bookie, but on the other hand I felt very nervous making up lies. I shrugged and said, "I don't know. Mine, I guess. We both decided, that's all."

"Was anybody else supposed to be here?"

"Not that I know of."

"Hmm." He seemed to think for a minute, and then said, "How did Tommy get along with his wife, do you know?"

"Fine," I said. "As far as I know, fine."

"You never knew them to argue."

"Not around me."

He nodded, then said, "What's your home address, Chester?"

"8344 169th Place, Jamaica, Queens."

He wrote it down in a notebook. "We'll probably be getting in touch with you," he said.

"You mean I can go now?"

"Why not?" And he turned around and walked out of the bedroom as though I'd ceased to exist.

I followed him out. He turned right, toward the living room, and I went the other way. I went out to the street, which seemed much colder now, and walked over to Eighth Avenue, where I got my subway to go home. I sat in the train thinking about things, and I was all the way to Woodhaven Boulevard before it occurred to me I hadn't collected my nine hundred thirty dollars.

4

My father had papers all over the dining-room table again. He had the adding machine out, ballpoint pens scattered here and there, and lots of crumpled sheets of paper on the floor around his chair. When he's thinking hard he tends to scratch his face, scratching his nose or his chin or his forehead, and frequently he forgets he's holding a ballpoint pen at the time, so after a session at the dining-room table he winds up looking like the paper they use for dollar bills, with little blue lines an inch or so long wig-wagging all over his face.

"I'm late," I pointed out. "It's after seven."

My father looked at me in that out-of-focus way he has when his mind is full of numbers. Pointing a pen at me he said, "The question is, are you going to have any children?"

"Not right away," I said. "Did you put anything on for dinner?"

"If you would just get married," he said, "it would make it simpler for me to figure these things out."

"I'm sure it would," I said. "Maybe I will some day. What about dinner?"

He glared at me, meaning I'd broken his train of thought. "Dinner? What time is it?"

"After seven."

He frowned and pulled out his pocketwatch and lowered his brows at it. "You're late," he said. "Where've you been?"

"It's a long story," I said. "Did you start dinner?"

"I got involved in this," he said, waving his hands vaguely at all the paperwork. "Another insurance man came by today."

"A new one?"

"Same old stuff, though," my father said. He threw the pen on the table in disgust. "The math still works out against me."

"Well," I said, "they've got computers." I went out to the kitchen and got out two turkey TV dinners, put them in the oven, lit the oven.

My father had followed me out to the kitchen. "They'll make a mistake some day," he said. "Everybody makes mistakes."

"Not computers," I said.

"Everybody," he said. "And when they do, I'll be ready."

It is my father's idea that he is going to beat the insurance companies. As the years have gone by, the insurance companies have competed with one another by presenting more and more complicated insurance packages, the packages getting steadily more intricate and unfathomable, with expanding this and overlapping that and conditional the other. Of course, whatever the package the odds are still with the company. Insurance companies, like the casinos in Las Vegas, are in business to make money, so the edge is always with the house. Except that my father is convinced that sooner or later one of the companies is going to come out with a package with a flaw in it, that the complexities are eventually going to reach the stage where even the company isn't going to be able to keep up with the implications of the math, and that some company is going to put out a policy where you don't have to die ahead of time to win. My father's hobby is looking for that policy. It hasn't showed up yet, and I don't believe it ever will, but my father has all the faith and obstinacy of a man with a roulette system, and more often than not I come home to find him and his papers and his adding machine all over the dining-room table.

Actually, it's a harmless enough hobby and it does occupy his mind. He's sixty-three now, and he was forcibly retired from the airplane factory when he was fifty-eight —he worked in the payroll office—and if he didn't have this insurance thing I don't know what he'd do with himself. Mom died the year my father retired, and naturally he didn't want to go off to Fort Lauderdale by himself, so we kept on living at home together, and it's pretty much worked out. My parents were both thirty-four when I was born, and I was also an only child, so I never knew either of my parents when they were very young and we never did have much of a lively, exuberant household, so things aren't so much different from the way they always were, except Mom is gone and I'm the one who goes out to work.

Anyway, while we waited for dinner I told my father

about my day, and every once in a while he'd put his head on one side and squint at me and say, "You wouldn't be telling me tales, would you, Chester?"

"No," I'd say, and go on with the story. I finished by saying, "And the upshot of it is, I didn't collect my nine hundred thirty dollars."

"That's a lot of money," he said.

"It sure is," I said. "I wonder who I collect from, now that Tommy's dead."

"I wonder where you go to get the money now," he said.

"That's what I said," I said.

He raised his head and sniffed. "Aren't those dinners ready yet?"

I looked at the clock. "Five more minutes. Anyway, I'll call Tommy's wife tomorrow and ask her. She should know."

"Ask her what?"

"Where I go to collect my money," I said.

He nodded. "Ah," he said.

We went on in and had dinner.

5

I got up late the next morning, and decided not to go to work till the afternoon. I called Tommy's wife around noon and she answered the phone on the second ring and I said, "Hello, Mrs. McKay? This is Chet."

"Who?"

"Chet," I said. "You know, Chet Conway."

"Oh," she said. At least she didn't call me Chester. She said, "What do you want?"

I said, "I'm sorry, Mrs. McKay, I know I shouldn't disturb you at a time like this, and I wouldn't under normal circumstances, but the fact of the matter is I'm sort of strapped for cash right now."

"What is this?" she said. She sounded irritable.

I said, "Well, the fact is, Mrs. McKay, I went over to your place yesterday to pick up the money from a bet I made that came in, and naturally I didn't get to collect. So I was wondering if you could put me in touch with whoever I should see now to get my money."

"What? What do you want?" Now she sounded as though I'd just woken her up or something and she couldn't comprehend what I was talking about.

I said, "I want to know where to go to collect my money, Mrs. McKay."

"How should I know?"

"Well—" I was at a loss. I floundered for a second or two and then I said, "Don't you know who Tommy's boss was?"

"His what?"

"Mrs. McKay, Tommy worked for somebody. He worked for a syndicate or somebody, he didn't run that book of his all by himself."

"I don't know what you're talking about," she said.

I said, "Is it because I'm asking you on the phone? Listen, could I come by later on? Are you going to be home?"

"You'd better forget it," she said. "Just forget it."

"What do you mean, forget it? It's almost a thousand dollars!"

Suddenly a different voice was on the line, a male voice, saying, "Who's calling?"

A cop. It had to be a cop. I said, "I'll talk to Mrs.

McKay later," and hung up. So that was why she hadn't
wanted to tell me anything.

I wondered how long it was going to be before I could
find out. I needed that money in the next couple of days.

I hung around the house till about two in the afternoon,
then finally got up the energy to go to work. I read about
myself in the *News* on the subway, under the headline
BOOKIE FOUND SLAIN IN APARTMENT. It said Tommy
was a known bookmaker with a long history of arrests; it
said he'd been shot three times in the back with dum-
dum bullets, the kind of bullet that has been creased on
the nose so it'll expand when it hits something, which was
why his chest had been so smashed up from where the
bullets had come out the other side; and it said the body
had been found by "Chester Conway of 8344 169th Place,
Jamaica, Queens. Mr. Conway stated he was a friend of
the dead man."

That made me feel a little odd. It's one thing to gamble
a bit, put down a bet with a bookmaker from time to
time, but it's another thing to read about yourself in the
Daily News, listed as the friend of a murdered bookie. All
of a sudden I felt like a Mafia hoodlum or something, and
I imagined friends of mine reading that in the paper, and I
was both embarrassed and—I hate to admit this—secretly
pleased. We all of us would like a dramatic secret life that
nobody knows about, that's the whole idea behind Super-
man and Batman and the Lone Ranger, and here the *Daily
News* was giving me one for free, by implication. All of a
sudden I was the kind of guy who knew secret entrances
to apparently abandoned warehouses, unknown passage-
ways in the very walls of the apartment itself, meetings at
midnight, people who wore masks and never gave their
right names. It made me feel very special, sitting there on

the train, surrounded by people reading the *News* and little knowing that in their midst was the very man they were reading about, the ubiquitous Chester Conway, 8344 169th Place, Jamaica, Queens.

Nobody at the garage had read the paper, apparently, or they hadn't made the connection, or maybe they were just being very cool. Anyway, nobody said anything. I went in, signed out my car, and took off.

The first place I went was Tommy's place. I threw on the Off Duty sign as soon as I was out of sight of the garage and went straight down to 46th Street. There weren't any police cars stopped out front, so I parked by a hydrant—there are no parking places in New York, the last one was taken in 1948, but a cab stopped for a short time by a hydrant is usually left alone—and I went over and rang the bell, but there wasn't anybody home, so I went back to the cab and at last to work.

I tried a couple of the midtown hotels and jackpotted right away with a fare to Kennedy. Unfortunately, the only thing to do after that is take another fare back to Manhattan, which I did, and then hacked around the city the rest of the afternoon and evening.

I tried Tommy's place again around seven and there still wasn't anybody home, and there kept on being nobody at home when I tried for the third time around eleven.

I turned the cab in a little after midnight and took the subway home. I got to the house shortly before one, seeing the light in the kitchen that my father leaves for me when I'm out late, and I went up on the front porch, stopped in front of the door, put my hand in my pocket for my keys, and somebody stuck something hard against my back. Then somebody said, in a very soft insinuating voice, "Be nice."

6

I was nice. I stayed where I was, facing the door a foot from my nose, not moving any parts of my body, and the hard thing stopped pressing against my back, and then hands patted me all over. When they were done, the voice said, "That's a good boy. Now turn around and go down to the sidewalk."

I turned around, seeing two bulky guys in bulky winter clothing and dark hats on the porch with me, and I went between them and down the stoop and down to the sidewalk. I felt them behind me, coming in my wake.

At the sidewalk they told me to turn right and walk toward the corner, which I did. Almost to the corner there was a dark Chevrolet parked by the curb, and they told me to get into the back seat, which I did. I was terrified, and I didn't know who they were or what they wanted, and all I could think of to do was obey their orders.

One of them got into the back seat with me and shut the door. He took out a gun, which glinted dark and wicked in his lap in the little light that came in from the corner streetlamp, and I sat as close to the other door as I could, staring at the gun in disbelief. A gun? For *me?* Who did they think I was?

I wanted to say something, tell them some sort of mistake was being made, but I was afraid to. I had this conviction that all I had to do was make a sound, any sound at all, and it would break the spell, it would be the signal for carnage and destruction.

If you spend much time driving a cab around New York City, especially at night, sooner or later you'll find yourself thinking about anti-cabby violence, and what you would do if anybody ever pulled a gun or a knife on you to rob you in the cab. A long time ago I decided I was no hero, I wouldn't argue. Anybody with a knife or a gun in his hand is boss as far as I'm concerned. It's like the old saying: The hand that cradles the rock rules the world.

One time a guy who works out of the same garage as me had a knife pulled on him by a rider, and he turned around and disarmed the guy and handed him over to the nearest cop. The police department thanked him, and on his identification displayed on the dashboard they rubber-stamped a notification about how he'd been given this special police citation, but all I could do was look at him and wonder what he'd been thinking of. The guy with the knife had been a junkie wanting money, and this cabby had eighteen dollars in the cab at the time. Eighteen dollars. Frankly, I think my life is worth more than eighteen dollars and a rubber stamp.

Life. I suddenly wondered if these were the guys who killed Tommy. Were they going to kill *me*?

Maybe nobody was supposed to bet on Purple Pecunia. Maybe they're killing all outsiders that bet on that rotten horse. But that couldn't be, it didn't make any sense at all. Think of all the hunch betters, all the people that bet horses by their names. "Oh, look at this one, Harry, Purple Pecunia! Ain't that cute, Harry? Let's put two bucks on this one, Harry! Aw, come on, Harry!"

But these two still could be the guys that killed Tommy, maybe for some other reason entirely. I might not know why they did it, or why I was involved in whatever they were up to, but I wouldn't have to know why. Maybe Tommy hadn't known why either.

When the second one opened the door to get in behind the wheel, the interior light went on and I got my first look at the one with me in the back seat. He looked like the sadistic young SS man in the movies, the blond one that smiles and is polite to ladies but his face is slightly pockmarked. He was looking at me like a butterfly collector looking at a butterfly, and I looked away quickly without memorizing his features, not having any need or desire to memorize his features. I faced front, and the driver had black hair between hat and collar. That was all I wanted to know about him, too.

We drove away from my neighborhood, and quickly into neighborhoods I didn't know, and through them, and beyond. They never took the car on any of the parkways, they stayed on the local streets, and for a while we were under an El. Now and again something would look vaguely familiar, but not enough for me to be sure. An occasional car passed us, minding its own business, or sometimes an empty bus went blooping along all lit up inside like a diner, but mostly the streets were dark and empty all around us.

Snowflakes began to drift down, one at a time, fat and lacy, in no hurry to land anywhere. So maybe we were going to get that big snow after all, the one that was four days overdue already. Here it was the middle of January and so far this winter we hadn't had even one monstrous horrible snowstorm to tie up traffic and give people heart attacks.

I found myself wondering whether I'd be able to work tomorrow or not, there being no point hacking around New York in the middle of a snowstorm, and then I realized that was a ridiculous thing to be wondering about. I might not work tomorrow, but it wouldn't be the weather's fault.

Should I try to make a run for it? Should I leap from the car one time when it was stopped at a red light? Should I go running zigzag under the streetlights, looking for alleys, maybe an open tavern, some place to hide and wait for these guys to give up and go away?

No. It seemed to me if I were to reach out and put my hand on the door handle beside me, it would more than likely be the last thing I ever did on this earth. And although it was possible these two were taking me for a one-way ride, there wasn't any point rushing the finish.

Besides, how could I be sure they wanted to kill me? Grasping at any consolation at all, I told myself if all they wanted was to kill me they could have done it back at the house and gone on about their business in perfect safety. If they were bringing me with them, it must mean they had something else in mind.

Maybe they wanted to torture me to death.

Now why did I have to think a thought like that?

Trying to think of other thoughts to think, I sat there while the car continued down one dark anonymous street after another until it suddenly made a right turn in the middle of a block. An open garage doorway in a gray concrete block wall loomed before us, blackness inside it, and we drove through and stopped. Behind us I could hear the garage door rattling down, and when that noise stopped, the lights abruptly went on.

We were in a parking garage. Rows of black low-nosed four-eyed automobiles gave me the fish-eye. Iron posts painted olive-green held up the low ceiling, in which half a dozen fluorescent lights were spaced at distances a little too far apart to give full lighting. Shadows and dim areas seemed to spread here and there, like fog.

There was nobody in sight. The driver got out of the car and opened the door beside me. The other one said, "Climb out slow."

I climbed out slow, and he followed me. The driver pointed straight ahead and I walked straight ahead. It was a wide clear lane with a rank of cars on each side, the cars facing one another with all those blank headlights, me walking between them down the gauntlet. I kept feeling eyes on me, as though I were being stared at, but I knew it was only the cars. I couldn't help it, I had to terrify myself even more with an image of one of those cars suddenly leaping into life, all four headlights blaring on, the engine roaring, the car slashing out of its slot to run me down like an ant on a racetrack. I walked hunched, facing only front, blinking frequently, and the cars remained quiet.

At the end there was a wall, and a flight of olive-green metal steps against the wall going upward to the right. As I neared it, I was told, "Go up the stairs."

I went up the stairs. Our six feet made complicated echoing dull rhythms on the rungs, and I thought of Robert Mitchum. What would Robert Mitchum do now, what would he do in a situation like this?

No question of it. Robert Mitchum, with the suddenness of a snake, would abruptly whirl, kick the nearest hood in the jaw, and vault over the railing and down to the garage floor. Meantime, the kicked hood would have fallen backward into the other one, and the two of them would go tumbling down the steps, out of the play long enough for Mitchum either to (a) make it to the door and out of the building and thus successfully make his escape, or (b) get into the hood's car, in which the keys would have been left, back it at top speed *through* the closed garage door, and take off with a grand grinding of gears, thus successfully making his escape and getting their car in the bargain.

But what if *I* spun around like that, and the guy with the *gun* was Robert Mitchum? What would he do then? Easy. He'd duck the kick and shoot me in the head.

I plodded up the stairs.

At the top was a long hall lined with windows on both sides. The windows on the left looked out on a blacktop loading area floodlit from somewhere ahead of me. The windows on the right, interspaced with windowed doors, looked in on offices and storage rooms, all in darkness except for one room far down at the end of the hall. Yellow light spilled out there, angled across the floor. There was no sound.

I stopped at the head of the stairs, but a hand against the middle of my back pushed me forward, not gently, not harshly. I walked down the hall toward the yellow light.

It was an office, the door open. Inside, a heavyset man in an overcoat with a velvet collar sat at a scruffy wooden desk and smoked a cigarette in an ivory holder. His head seemed too large for his body, a big squared-off block matted with black fur everywhere but in front. His face shone a little, as though he'd been touched up with white enamel, and his heavy jaw was blue with a thick mass of beard pressing outward against the skin. He sat half-turned away from the desk, a black velvet hat pushed back from his forehead, his one forearm resting negligently on the papers on the desk top, as though to imply this wasn't his office really, he was above scraggly offices like this, he'd just borrowed this one from some poor relation for the occasion.

He looked over at me when I stopped in the doorway, his eye a pale blue, blank and unblinking. It was as though that wasn't really his eye, his actual eye was hidden behind that one, was looking through that one at me without giving me a chance to look back.

The hand in my back again sent me into the room. I stopped in front of the desk, looking at the man sitting there. The other two stayed behind me, out of my sight. I heard the door close with a little tick of finality, like the last shovel-pat over a filled-in grave.

The man at the desk took the cigarette and holder from his mouth and pointed with them at a wooden chair beside the desk. "Sit down." His voice was husky, but emotionless, not really threatening.

I sat down. I put my hands in my lap, not knowing what to do with them. I met his eye—his eye's eye—and wished I could control my blinking.

He glanced at one of the papers littering the desk, saying, "How long you been working for Napoli?"

I said, "Who?"

He looked at me again and his face finally took on an expression: saddened humorous wisdom. "Don't waste my time, fella," he said. "We know who you are."

"I'm Chester Conway," I said, struck by the sudden hope that this whole thing could be a case of mistaken identity.

It wasn't. "I know," he said. "And you work for Solomon Napoli."

I shook my head. "Maybe there's another Chester Conway," I said. "Did you look in the phone books for all the boroughs? A few years ago I used to get calls—"

He slapped his palm on the desk. It wasn't very loud, but it shut me up. "You pal around with Irving Falco," he said.

"Irving Falco," I repeated, trying to think where I knew the name from. Then I said, "Sure! Sid Falco! I'm in a poker game with him."

"Irving Falco," he insisted.

I nodded. I was suddenly and irrationally happy, having something I knew about to deal with at last. It didn't change things, it didn't explain things, but at least I could join the conversation. "That's the one," I said. "But we call him Sid on account of a movie with—"

"But his name's Irving," he said. He looked as though he was starting to lose his patience.

"Yes," I said.

"All right," he said. "And Irving Falco works for Solomon Napoli."

"If you say so. I don't know him well, just at the poker game, we don't talk about—"

He pointed at me. "And *you* work for Solomon Napoli," he said.

"No," I said. "Honest. I'm a cabdriver, I work for the V. S. Goth Service Corporation, Eleventh Avenue and—"

"We know about that," he said. "We know all about you. We know you got a straight job, and you lose twice that much at the cards every week. Plus you play the ponies, plus—"

"Oh, now," I said. "I don't lose *all* the time. I've been having a run of bad cards, that could happen to any—"

"Shut up," he said.

I shut up.

"The only question," he said, "is what you do for Napoli." He made a show of looking at his watch, a big shiny thing with a heavy gold band. "You got ten seconds," he said.

"I don't work for him," I said. The young blond SS man came into my line of vision on the right.

Nobody said anything. We all looked at the heavyset man looking at his watch, till he shook his head, lowered his arm, looked over at the SS man, and said, "Bump him."

"I don't work for anybody named Napoli," I said. I was getting frantic. The SS man came over and took my right arm, and the other guy came from behind me and took my left arm, and they lifted me out of the chair. "I don't even *know* anybody named Napoli!" I shouted. "Honest to *God!*"

They lifted me high enough so only my toes were touching the floor, and then they walked me quickly toward the door, me yelling all the time, not believing any of this could possibly be happening.

We got through the doorway and then the man at the desk cut through all my hollering with one soft-voiced word: "Okay."

Immediately the other two turned me around and brought me back to the chair and sat me down again. My upper arms hurt and I was hoarse and my nerves were shot and I figured my hair was probably white, but I was alive. I swallowed, and blinked a lot, and looked at the man behind the desk.

He nodded heavily. "I believe you," he said. "We checked you out, and we saw where you buddied up with Falco, and we figured maybe we ought to find out. So you don't work for Napoli."

"No, sir," I said.

"That's good," he said. "How's Louise taking it, do you know?"

I experienced a definite sinking feeling. Here we go again, I thought, and very reluctantly I said, "I'm sorry, I don't know who you mean."

He looked sharply at me, frowning as though this time I was telling a lie for no sensible reason at all. "Come on," he said.

"I'm sorry," I said, and I really meant it. "I don't want to get in trouble with you or anything, but I don't know anybody named Louise."

He sat back and smirked at me, as though I'd just made a lewd admission. "So you were having a thing with her, huh? That's what it is, huh?"

I said, "Excuse me, but no. I don't have a girlfriend right now, and I can't remember ever going out with a girl named Louise. Maybe in high school one time, I don't know."

The smirk gradually shifted back to the frown. He studied me for a long minute, and then he said, "That don't make any sense."

"I'm sorry," I said again. My shoulders were hunching more and more. By the time I got out of here, they'd probably be covering my ears and I'd never hear again.

He said, "You knew McKay well enough to go around to his place, but you don't know his wife's first name. That don't make any sense at all."

"Tommy McKay? Is that his wife?" I suddenly felt twice as nervous as before, because obviously I *should* know Tommy's wife's name, and anything at all I could think of to say right now would have to sound phony.

The man at the desk nodded heavily. "Yeah," he said. "That's his wife. You never met her, huh?"

"Oh, I *met* her," I said. "Sometimes she'd come to the door when I went over there, or she'd answer the phone when I called. But we never talked or anything, we never had any conversation."

"McKay never said, 'Here's my wife, Louise'?"

I shook my head. "Usually," I said, "I wouldn't even go into the apartment. I'd hand him some money, or he'd hand me some, and that'd be it. The couple of times I was in there, his wife wasn't home. And he never introduced us. I was a customer, that's all. We never saw each other socially or anything."

He seemed dubious, but no longer one hundred percent disbelieving.

Another part of what he'd been saying abruptly caught up with me, and I said, "Hey!"

Everybody jumped and looked startled and wary and dangerous.

I hunched some more. "I'm sorry," I said. "I was just thinking about what you said, that's all."

They all relaxed.

I said, "About me having a thing with Tommy's wife. I mean, that's just impossible. She's not—I mean, she and me—it just wouldn't—"

"Okay," he said. He looked tired and disgusted all of a sudden. "You're clean," he said.

"Well, sure," I said. I looked around at them all. "Is that what you wanted to know? Did you think *I* killed Tommy?"

They didn't bother to answer me. The man at the desk said, "Take him home." What beautiful words!

The SS man said to me, "Up."

"All right," I said. I got quickly to my feet, wanting to be out of there before anybody changed anybody's mind. Up till a few seconds ago I hadn't counted on getting out of here at all.

This time they didn't grab my arms. I walked of my own accord to the door, and as I was stepping through, the man at the desk said, "Wait."

Run for it? Ho ho. I turned around and looked at the three of them.

The man at the desk said, "You don't talk to the cops. About this."

"Oh," I said. "Of course not. I mean, nothing happened, right? What should I talk to the cops for?"

I was babbling. I made myself stop, I made myself turn around, I made myself walk down the hall and down the stairs and down the gauntlet of cars and over to the Chevrolet. I got into the back seat without anybody telling me. Looking at the dashboard, I saw the keys had been left there after all, so maybe Robert Mitchum does know best.

The other two got into the car, same seating as before, and behind us the door rattled upward. We backed out, and they drove me home. The trip seemed shorter, through streets that were now even emptier.

The snow was increasing. It was still slow and lazy, but there were more flakes, and they were starting to stick. A thin white coating of confectioners' sugar covered the black streets. They let me off in front of the house. "Thank you," I said as I got out, as though they'd just given me a lift home, and then felt foolish, and then was afraid I'd slammed the door too hard, and then walked quickly into the house while they drove leisurely away.

Usually I'm a beer man, but my father is a Jack Daniel's man, and this was a Jack Daniel's moment. Two ice cubes and some Tennessee mash in a jelly glass, a few minutes of sitting quietly, sipping quietly, at the kitchen table, and slowly my overwound mainspring began to relax its tension a little.

Now that I could think it over, in safety and solitude, I saw what had happened. Those three guys had to be from the gambling syndicate Tommy worked for. The syndicate, not itself having had Tommy killed, had wanted to know who had done for one of its employees. Apparently they suspected a man named Solomon Napoli, God alone knew why, and they must have read in the *News* about me finding the body, and they decided to check me out, and they saw the poker game connection with Sid Falco —I hadn't known *he* was involved in anything shady— and the rest followed.

But then to think I was having an affair with Tommy's wife. Louise? Louise. I mean, there's nothing wrong with the woman, she's not bad-looking or anything, but she's skinny as a telephone pole and about ten years older than me and every time I've seen her she's worn bargain-basement dresses and heavy shoes, and her hair is usually wrapped up in so many huge pink plastic rollers she looks like a refugee from a science-fiction movie.

Well. The man at the desk, the important one, had seemed convinced at the end there that I was innocent, so that should finish it. I downed the last of the Jack Daniel's, put the glass in the sink, switched off the light, and went upstairs in the dark to my bedroom, where it occurred to me I could have asked those people tonight who I should see now about collecting my money. Damn. Well, tomorrow I'd go see Tommy's wife. Louise.

7

Except I didn't. When the alarm rousted me out after four and a half hours' uneasy sleep, the world was white and muffled and socked in. The snow was still lazy, still drifting down the air, but now the flakes were coming down in the millions and the ground was already three or four inches thick with it. Our first snowstorm had finally arrived.

I didn't say anything to my father about last night's incident because he'd only get excited and want to call the police, and it seemed to me if I called the police I would run a real risk of meeting those guys from last night again, the which I was in no hurry to do. My whole feeling was of being a little fish floating around in the water, living my little life, and then suddenly being yanked up at the end of a fishing line, caught by powers too strong for me to fight and too big for me to understand, with terrible immediate oblivion all of a sudden staring me in the face, and then the reprieve coming and being tossed back into the water because I'm too small. I didn't want to hang around and make a fuss, all I wanted to do was go quickly away by myself somewhere and forget the whole thing. So I didn't tell my father a thing about it.

We had breakfast, and I kept looking out the kitchen window at the snow, and it kept being there. I'd gotten up early in order to work the day shift, since my regular

Wednesday night poker game was tonight, but with all that snow out there it was hopeless. After breakfast I called the garage and told them I saw no point adding myself to the snarl-up Manhattan was undoubtedly in the middle of, and the dispatcher said fine by him, and then I had the day in front of me.

My father went back to his percentages at the dining-room table, leaving me essentially alone with myself, so I called a few guys to see if enough were staying home to get a game up, but half of them had gone to work and the other half wouldn't leave the house. "If you want to play over here, Chet, it's fine by me." I didn't call Sid Falco, feeling very weird about him since knowing what I now knew. I phoned in today's number—214, don't ask me why—to the stationery store and promised to drop by tomorrow with the quarter, and then there was nothing to do but read the sports pages of the *News* and wait for tomorrow.

When the doorbell rang a little after eleven it was a godsend. I was reduced to watching an old horse-race movie with Margaret O'Brien on Channel 11, and I hate that kind of picture. I know the races are rigged, and they never give you enough information on the entries anyway, but there I sit trying to handicap the damn things.

I switched off the set right away, went to the door, opened it, and in came a swirl of snow and the detective who'd questioned me at Tommy's apartment. Detective Golderman. The amount of snow I could see through the open doorway was unbelievable, but a plow had been down the street recently, so it was possibly passable. A black Ford was parked out front.

I shut the door, and he took off his hat and said, "Remember me, Chester?"

Why do policemen call everybody by their first names? "Sure," I said. "You're Detective Golderman."

My father called from the dining room, "Who is it?"

Detective Golderman said, "You didn't go to work today."

"Who did?" I said.

"I did," he said.

My father called from the dining room, "I'm expecting an insurance man."

Detective Golderman said, "Do you have a few minutes?"

"Sure," I said. "Come on in the living room."

My father bellowed, "Chet! Is that my insurance man?"

I led Detective Golderman into the living room and said, "Excuse me."

"Certainly."

I crossed the living room to the dining-room doorway and said, "It's a policeman." I said "policeman" instead of "cop" because Detective Golderman was in earshot.

"Why didn't you say so?" my father said. He was irritable, which usually meant the math was being too tricky for him. Sooner or later he always worked the policies out, but some of them were very tough, and when he had one of the really tough ones he tended to get irritable.

"We'll be in the living room," I said, and went back over to Detective Golderman. I asked him to sit down, he did, I also did, and he said, "You knew Tommy McKay pretty well, did you?"

I shrugged. "Pretty well," I said. "We weren't really close, but we were friends."

"You knew what he did for a living?"

"I'm not sure," I said doubtfully.

He grinned at me. We were just guys together, I could come off it. He said, "But you could guess."

"I suppose so," I said.

"You want me to say it first?"

"If you don't mind."

"Tommy McKay was a bookie."

I nodded. "I believe so," I said.

"Mm. Would you say you knew him best as a friend or as a customer?"

It was me doing the grinning this time, nervous and sheepish and out in plain view. "A little of each, I guess," I said.

"Don't worry, Chester," he said. "I'm not looking for gamblers."

"That's good," I said.

"Our interest is the homicide, that's all."

I said that was good, too.

"Have you got any ideas on that, Chester?"

I suppose I looked blank. I know I felt blank. "Ideas?"

"On who might have killed him."

I shook my head. "No, I don't. I didn't really know him that well."

"Did you see anybody else in the apartment or in the building that day?"

"No, I didn't."

"Did McKay ever express worry to you, any fear that he thought somebody might be after him?"

"No."

"Was he ever slow in paying off on winnings?"

"Never. Tommy was always straight about things like that."

He nodded, thought for a second, then said, "Do you know anybody else in that building?"

"Tommy's place? No."

"Does the name Solomon Napoli mean anything to you?"

Until last night I could have given that question a straight no with no qualms. Trying to figure out what such a denial would have sounded like and then imitate it, I furrowed my brow, scratched my head, shook my head, stared out the window, and finally said, "Solomon Napoli. Noooo, I don't think so."

"You seem doubtful."

"Do I? I don't mean to. I really don't know the name, I just wanted to be sure before I said anything. Who is he?"

"Somebody we're interested in," he said, making it clear it was somebody he didn't want me being interested in.

I said, "Does he live in the same building as Tommy?"

He frowned, as though confused. "Of course not. Why?"

"Well, you asked if I knew anybody in that building, and then right away you wanted to know if I—"

"Oh," he said, interrupting me. "I see what you mean. No, it's two different questions."

"Oh," I said.

"Did you ever hear of Frank Tarbok?" he asked. "And he doesn't live in McKay's building either."

"Tarbok? No."

"You don't want to think about that one first?"

"Well," I said. "Uh. It's just, I just knew right away he—"

"Okay," he said. "How about Bugs Bender?"

"That's a name? No, if I'd ever heard that one I'd remember it."

"What about Walter Droble?"

I was about to say no when the name did ring some sort of distant bell. "Walter Droble," I repeated. "Did I read about him in the papers or some place?"

"That would be the only way you know him?"

"Yeah, I think so. It's like I've heard the name some-where, a long time ago."

"All right." He seemed to consider things for a minute, and then said, "How well do you know Mrs. McKay?"

Him, too? "Not very well," I said. "Mostly I just had dealings with Tommy."

"Ever hear any rumors about her? Running around with another man, anything like that?"

I shook my head. "Not a thing," I said.

"Did she ever make a play for you, flirt with you?"

"Mrs. McKay? Have you ever seen her? Sure you have, the other day."

"She wasn't looking at her best the other day," he said. "You don't think she's good-looking enough to flirt?"

"Well, she's not *bad*-looking," I said. "I don't know, I never saw her dressed up or anything, I don't know what she'd look like."

"All right," he said, and got to his feet. "That's about it. Thank you for your cooperation."

"Not at all," I said.

"You're going to be around town?"

"Sure."

"You'll be notified about the inquest."

"I'll be here," I said, and led the way to the front door. He buttoned up his coat and put his hat on and then I opened the door and he slogged out into all that swirling snow. There were little puffs of wind, this way, that way, with still places in between, so when you looked out, it was like looking at a photograph full of random scratches.

I watched him go down the stoop, then shut the door and went back to the living room, but this time I left the television off. I sat there thinking, and it seemed to me if there was anybody in this world I didn't want to be right now it was probably Solomon Napoli. The cops obviously thought he might have had something to do with Tommy's death, and so did Tommy's bosses, and that seemed to leave Napoli square in the middle.

Who was Napoli? Maybe the boss of some other gang that was trying to muscle in. Maybe all this was part of some kind of gang war. There still are gang wars, only they don't get as much publicity as they used to. Mobsters just disappear these days, they don't get blown up in barber-shops or machine-gunned in front of nursery schools any more. But still every once in a while something will get into the papers, usually when something goes wrong. Like the guy a couple of years ago that was attacked in a bar in Brooklyn and two cops just happened to walk in while he was being strangled with a wire coat hanger. He was known to be a member of one of the mobs down there, and the cops figured the killers had to be with some other mob. They got away, both of them, and the victim naturally insisted he didn't know who they were or why they were after him.

But if Tommy's death was a gang killing, how come he didn't disappear? He was very visible, his murder made the newspapers and everything. (There hadn't been any-thing about it in today's paper, but that's because nothing new had happened.)

Well, it wasn't my problem. My problem was collecting my money, and losing a day's work today was making that collection even more urgent than before.

Of course, if 214 came in today my twenty-five cents would bring me back a hundred fifty dollars, but I wasn't going to hang by my thumbs till it happened. In all the years I've played the numbers I've never won spit, and sometimes I wonder why I even bother. I treat it like dues, not like a bet at all. Once or twice a week I hand over a quarter at the stationery store. But what the hell, the return is six hundred to one—the odds are a thousand to one, so nobody's doing anybody any favors—and I figure at a quarter a throw it can't hurt me to try.

In the meantime, back in the real world 214 was not going to come in today, so the question was how to get my nine hundred thirty dollars, and for that I was going to have to go see Mrs. Louise McKay.

If she knew.

Did she know? Did Tommy tell his wife his business, enough for her to know who I should see now? Some husbands do, some don't, and thinking about Tommy now it seemed to me he could best be described as the close-mouthed type.

Listen, I had to have that money. If Mrs. McKay couldn't tell me how to get it, who could?

I remembered those other names Detective Golderman had mentioned—Frank Tarbok and Bugs Bender and Walter Droble. Maybe one of those guys was in the same syndicate with Tommy, and could tell me who to see now.

But I'd prefer to get it from Tommy's wife. It struck me as easier, maybe safer, and all around better.

Just to be on the safe side, though, I went to the dining room and borrowed a piece of paper from my father and wrote down the three names, so I wouldn't forget them. Frank Tarbok. Bugs Bender. Walter Droble.

8

By three, I couldn't stand the house any more. The snow had finally sighed to a stop around one, the plows had continued to rattle their chains down the street for a while after that, and the radio said we'd had eight inches and it was now definitely over. The day was white, tending to gray at the edges, and there was a sort of muffled feeling everywhere, as though I were walking around with cotton in my ears.

I'd made some Campbell's pea soup for lunch, since my father was still multiplying and dividing in the living room, and after lunch I played myself some solitaire for a while, betting a hypothetical dollar a card against a hypothetical house and quitting in disgust when I owed a hypothetical seventy-six dollars. I hadn't run the cards once.

So at three o'clock I decided to go try for Mrs. McKay. I put on my overcoat and overshoes and hat and gloves and told my father, "I'll probably be home for dinner. If not, I'll call."

"What's one-thirteenth of seventy-one?" he said. His face was covered with little blue ink squiggles, and his eyes were a little out of focus.

"See you later," I said, and left.

No walks were shoveled yet, of course, so I walked down the plowed street to Jamaica Avenue, where I stopped in at the stationery store, paid my quarter dues, bought the *Telegraph* and then went on to the subway. Down underground in the station there was that clammy coldness the place has every year from November till April, and I stood alone on the platform, stamping my feet and reading my paper, till the train came.

The train, too, was almost empty, and when I emerged at Eighth Avenue and 50th Street in Manhattan the city had a weirdly deserted look to it. There were only a few cars and trucks crunching up 8th Avenue, only a few over-coated people walking around the streets, and some of the stores I could see were shut, the gratings drawn across their windows and entrances. It was one of those rare days when Manhattan did not contain more people than it could contend with.

The sidewalks were impassable, of course, so I joined the trickle of pedestrians in the street. Mountain ridges of snow as tall as a man lined the street on both sides, shoved there by the plows, with here and there the hood or side window of a buried car glinting through. Big old green trucks with dirty snow piled high in their backs clankety-clanked up Eighth Avenue.

I walked down to 47th and turned right. The side streets were worse, not having yet been cleared. Traffic had kept one wavering lane open, two deep black ruts in the dirty snow down the middle of the street, and when there was no car coming, the few pedestrians moved like tightrope walkers along these ruts. When a car did come along, there was nothing for the pedestrians to do but stand knee-deep in snow at one side and wait till the rut was clear again.

Some of the snow in front of 417, Tommy's place, was more than knee-deep. I flumphed through it, lifting my knees almost up to my earlobes at every step, and went into the entranceway and rang the bell of 4-C. No answer.

While waiting, I read a hand-written notice about a stolen baby carriage, asking anybody with information to get in touch with apartment 1-B, and then I rang the bell again and there still wasn't any answer.

Where the hell was she? Maybe gone to stay with relatives or something, maybe she didn't want to be around the apartment so soon after Tommy's death. I had to admit it would be only natural, if that's the way she felt, but at the moment it was nothing to me but a swift pain. I needed that money.

There was no point hanging around in here, though, so I left, and outside, standing in two of my inbound footprints, was Detective Golderman. His hands were in his pockets, his hat on his head, his eyes on me, his expression skeptical. "We meet again," he said.

"Oh," I said. "Hello, there."

"I thought you were staying home today," he said.

"Well, the snow stopped," I said. I was feeling very guilty, and afraid I was looking very guilty, and I was trying like crazy to find some reason I could give him for being here, but there didn't seem to be any. "I was going to work," I said, "and I thought I'd stop by here and, uh…" I shrugged, and moved my feet around in the snow, waiting for him to stop waiting for me to finish the sentence.

But he wouldn't. He just kept looking at me, and the unfinished sentence hung in the air between us like a snake hanging down from a tree branch, and I finally said, "To offer my condolences."

He moved his head slightly, but he kept looking at me. "To offer your condolences," he said.

"To the widow," I explained. "Mrs. McKay," I explained further. Then, beginning to warm up to the lie, I said,

"The last time I saw her, she was pretty hysterical, I didn't get much of a chance to say anything to her."

"I see," he said, and it was pretty plain he didn't believe me. He looked past me at the building front, then up at the upper-story windows, then at me again. "Was she home?"

"No," I said.

"You'll probably try again," he said.

"I don't know," I said, trying to be casual. "If I'm in the neighborhood, I guess."

"It isn't all that important," he suggested.

"Not really," I said. "It's just sort of a nice gesture, you know?"

"Uh huh," he said, in the flat way of a man who doesn't believe a word you're saying.

I considered telling him the truth, but it was just impossible. Gambling is against the law, and it didn't matter if this was a homicide cop or not, I just couldn't come right out and admit to him that I made off-track bets. I mean, he *knew* I did, he knew the whole thing anyway, but I couldn't *say* it. All I could do was stand there and act stupid and feel guilty and make him suspicious of me.

I broke an uneasy silence that had settled down between us by saying, "Well, I guess I better get going now, if I want to get some time in today. In the cab."

He nodded.

"I'll see you," I said.

"See you around, Chester," he said.

9

I really did go to work. I went over to Eleventh Avenue
and took the bus uptown to the garage and checked a car
out and got my first fare half a block from the garage, a
good-looking girl in an orange fur coat and black boots
and pale blond hair. "2715 Pennsylvania Avenue," she
said.

I said, "Brooklyn or Washington?" I kid with good-
looking female passengers whether I'm worried about
money or not.

"Brooklyn," she said. "Take the Belt."

"Fine," I said, and dropped the flag, and headed south.
My luck was finally in. Not only a good-looking blonde in
the rear-view mirror, but a long haul at that, and it would
end not too far from Kennedy.

The highways were all cleared, and carried way below
their usual midday load of traffic. We got up on the West
Side Highway at twenty to four and left the Belt Parkway
at Pennsylvania Avenue in Brooklyn at just four o'clock.
In between I'd made a couple of small attempts at conversation, but she was the strong silent type, so I let it go.
I'm content to look, if that's the way they want it.

The first half mile of Pennsylvania Avenue is through
filled-in swampland. There's no solid ground at the bottom,
just dirt piled into a swamp, so the road is very jouncy and
bouncy, full of heaves and holes, and even though there's
little traffic at any time there and no housing or pedestrians around, you can't make very good time. The snow

plows, probably because of the uneven road surface, hadn't been able to do much of a job here, so that slowed me even more, which meant I was doing about twenty when the girl stuck the gun into the back of my neck and said, "Pull over to the side and park."

I immediately froze, my hands gluing themselves to the wheel. Fortunately my foot hadn't been on the accelerator at that instant, so it stayed paralyzed in mid-motion and the cab began at once to lose speed.

My first thought, when I finally had a thought, was: Did she have to run up six bucks on the meter first? Thinking, naturally, that I was about to be robbed.

But then I had a second thought, scarier than the first, and this was: This girl is no mugger.

Tommy again? Something more?

The cab was down to about three miles an hour now, but until I touched the brake or shifted out of drive it would go on doing three miles an hour forever. Across the entire United States and into the Pacific Ocean, at three miles an hour. I put my foot on the brake and shifted into neutral.

There was a cab coming from way behind me, there was a little traffic going the other way on the other side of the center divider, but for all practical purposes I was alone in the world with a girl with a gun.

A little over half the cabs in New York are equipped with bulletproof clear plastic between the driver and the passenger, but naturally this was one of the times when the long shot came home, because I had nothing between me and my passenger but extremely vulnerable air.

Yes, and there's another thing some cabs have, that when the driver presses a button with his foot a distress light flashes on top of the cab. Most people probably have never heard of it and wouldn't know what it meant if they saw one, but still I bet it's a comfort to any cabby who has a hack equipped like that. The V. S. Goth Service Corporation, the cheap bums I work for, wouldn't even equip their cabs with brakes if there wasn't a law about it, so you know I didn't have any distress light to comfort me right now.

When I had stopped the car at last, the girl said, "Turn off the engine."

"Right," I said, and turned off the engine.

She said, "Leave both hands on the wheel."

"Right," I said, and put both hands on the wheel. I couldn't see her in the rear-view mirror any more, which meant she was directly behind me. From the sound of her voice she was probably sitting forward on the seat. The gun was no longer pressing its cold nose into my neck, but I could sense that it hadn't gone very far away.

Well, Robert Mitchum? What now?

The girl said, "I want to ask you a few questions, and you better tell me the truth."

"I'll tell you the truth," I said. "You can count on that." I didn't know what she could possibly want to know, but whatever it was I was primed to tell her.

"First," she said, "where's Louise?"

"Oh, God *damn* it," I said, because all of a sudden there I was back in that office with the hoods again, being asked questions I couldn't answer because the assumptions were all wrong, and by God enough was enough. Forgetting all about how a sudden movement might make today's nut get excited and shoot me in the head, I turned around in the seat and said, "Lady, I don't know who you are, but at least I know it. You don't know who I am either, but you think you know who I am, and that screws things up entirely because I'm not him. Whoever he is. I'm me."

She was sitting there in the back seat with her knees and ankles together, shoulders hunched a little, gun hand held in close to her breasts, the little pearl-handled automatic pointing approximately at my nose. She continued to look at me for a few more seconds, and then a frown began on her face, first with a vertical line in the middle of her forehead, then spreading out to curve down her eyebrows, and finally covering her entire face. She said, "What?"

"I don't know where Louise is," I said. "If by Louise you mean Tommy McKay's wife, I don't know where she is. If you mean any other Louise, I don't know any other Louise."

"Then what were you doing at the apartment?" She didn't ask that as though she wanted an answer, she asked it in the style of somebody zinging in the irrefutable proof that I'm a liar.

I said, "Looking for Louise."

"Why?"

"None of your business."

"She killed him, you know," she said, acting as though she hadn't heard my last answer. Which was just as well, since I hadn't intended it. It just popped out. With those hoods last night I'd never for a second lost my awareness of their guns and the threat and the danger, but with this girl it was hard to keep in mind. She was pointing a gun at me and all, but it was almost irrelevant, as though it wasn't really what we were doing at all.

My belated remembrance of her gun obscured what she'd said for a few seconds, so my take on that was belated too. Then I said, "You mean Mrs. McKay? She killed her husband?"

"You mean you don't know it?" Said sneeringly, as though I was being a really obvious liar now.

"She didn't act it," I said. "I found the body, you know."

"I know." Full of menacing overtones.

I rushed on. "And Mrs. McKay didn't act like any murderess," I said. "It would have been tough for her to put on an act like that."

"So *you* say."

"Well," I said, "I was there." Gun or no gun, I was finding it possible to talk reasonably to this girl now that I was facing her.

"That was very convenient, wasn't it?" she said. "You being there."

"Not very," I said. "I didn't think it was convenient at all."

"You and Louise could cover for each other, lie for each other."

"Oh, come on," I said. "Me and Louise? Me? Louise? Look at me, will you? Have you ever seen Louise?"

"Of course I have," she said. "She's my sister-in-law."

"You're Tommy's sister?"

"I'm the only one he has," she said. Her face began to work, as though she was fighting back tears. "There's nobody else any more," she said. Biting her lower lip, blinking rapidly, she looked away out the side window. She'd obviously forgotten all about the gun.

I don't know why I did it. Because she'd forgotten about the gun, I suppose. And because there's a touch of Robert Mitchum in all of us, or anyway the desire to be Robert Mitchum is in all of us. Anyway, I made a grab for the gun.

"Oh!" she said, and jumped a foot, and for a few sec-

onds there were four hands on the gun and we were both
squirming around, trying to get it, and then it went off.

You talk about loud. Inside that cab, with all the windows shut except the vent on my side, that noise had
nothing to do but ricochet, which it did, forever. It was
ten times worse than having some clown explode a blown-
up paper bag next to your ear, which up until then I'd
always thought of as the world's loudest and most obnoxious noise.

Well, it isn't. Shooting off a gun in a closed car takes
the palm, hands down. It immobilized the two of us for
maybe half a minute, both of us staring, both of us open-
mouthed, neither of us moving a muscle.

Happily, I recovered first. I grabbed the gun away
from her, pointed it at myself, pointed it at her instead,
and said, "All right, now. All right."

She blinked, very slowly, like a mechanical doll coming
to life, and said, in a tiny voice, "Are you hurt?"

That hadn't occurred to me. Only the noise had occurred to me, not the fact that in conjunction with the
noise a bullet had left this stupid gun and gone very rapidly
through the air of the automobile to somewhere. To
lodge in me? I looked down at myself, saw nothing any
redder than usual, looked at her to see if she was dead
and we hadn't noticed, looked up, and saw a smudge in
the top of the cab. The cloth up there had a dirty smudge
on it, an inch or two across. Looking closely at it you
could see a burned-looking tiny hole in the middle of the
smudge.

"You put a hole in the cab," I said.

She looked up at the smudge. "Somebody could have
gotten killed," she said.

"How am I going to explain that?" I asked her. "I signed this cab out, you know."

"You've got the gun!" she screamed, staring at it as though it had just popped into existence this second. Then she threw her arms around her head, stuck her pressed-together knees way up in the air, and cowered back on the seat, rolling herself into as much of a ball as possible in the space available.

I stared at her. I couldn't figure out what she was up to. She was acting as though she was afraid of me. What the hell for?

I looked at the gun, seeing it myself for what was in some ways the first time. The first time I'd ever seen a gun in my hand, that was a first. And also it was the closest to me I'd ever seen a gun. I'm not counting the ones poked into my back, because I didn't see them when they were against my back. But this one I'd been holding high enough over the top of the seat so the girl could see it and not do anything crazy. I had the butt resting on the seat top and the barrel pointed generally out the back window, which made it only a couple of inches from my nose. I had to look a little cross-eyed to get it in focus.

How small it was. Handy for pocket or purse, I suppose, a small flat silver metal gun with what I guess was a pearl handle. It was an automatic, I knew that because it looked like the baby brother of Colt automatics you see in the movies. It looked about big enough to shoot spitballs, but it had sure put a hole in the cab roof.

I looked back at the girl and she was still crunched up against the back of the seat, nothing but black-booted knees and orange-furred elbows, with here and there a glint of blond hair peeking through. I said, "What are you doing?"

She said something, so muffled it took me a few seconds to make it out: "You're going to kill me."

"I am not," I said. I was insulted. I said, "What would I do a thing like that for?"

Arms and legs shifted a little, enough for a blue eye to be seen way down in there. With a sort of brave but hopeless defiance she said, "Because I know too much."

"Oh, come on," I said.

Legs lowered, arms shifted some more, and her head emerged like a beautiful turtle. "You can't fool me," she said, still with that scared defiance. "You're an accomplice and I know it. I'd give twelve to one on it."

"Done," I said, and without thinking I reached my hand over for a shake, forgetting the gun was in it. Immediately the turtle popped back into her orange shell. I said, "Hey! I'm not going to shoot you. I was just taking the bet."

She inched out again, mistrustful. "You were?"

I switched the gun to my left hand and held the right out for her to shake. "See? You give me twelve to one odds on a lock, you've got yourself a bet. How much? Ten bucks? Make it easy on yourself."

The legs this time slowly lowered all the way to the floor. She kept looking at me, studying me, very doubtful and mistrustful, as though wondering if somebody had stuck in a ringer. She looked at my hand, but she didn't touch it. Instead she said, "You are Chester Conway, aren't you?"

"Sure," I said. I pointed the gun at my identification on the right side of the dashboard. "There's my name and picture," I said. "You'll have to take my word that's my picture."

"And you are the one who found my brother dead."

"Sure."

"And you're the one who's been having an affair with Louise."

"Whoa, now," I said. "Not me, honey. Now you're thinking about somebody else. I didn't even know that woman's first name until yesterday."

"Do you expect me to believe that?" she said, but the scorn was mixed with doubt.

"To tell you the truth," I said, "I don't much care. And what I think I ought to do now is turn you over to the cops."

"You wouldn't dare," she said, still with that touch of doubt showing through.

"Why not?" I said. "You're the one pulled the gun on me."

"What if I tell them what I know?"

"Go ahead," I said. "They're liable to find out if it's true before they go running up six-dollar meters and sticking guns in my neck." I waggled the gun at her. "You get in the middle of the seat," I said, "where I can see you in the rear-view mirror."

"I don't—"

"Move," I said. I'd just heard a click, reminding me that the meter was still running. Another six bucks down the drain.

She licked her lips and began to look worried. "Maybe—" she said.

"Move now," I said. "I don't want to listen to any more. I'm supposed to be working now. Go on, move!"

She moved, being somewhat sulky about it, and when she got to the middle of the seat she sat up, folded her arms, gave me a defiant glare, and said, "All right. We'll see who's bluffing."

"Nobody's bluffing," I told her. "You just misread your hole card, that's all." I turned around, shut off the meter, flicked on the Off Duty sign, made sure the gun was safe on the seat beside me against my hip, made sure I could see her plainly in the mirror, and we took off.

10

"Maybe I was wrong," she said in a very small voice.

I was just making my left at Flatlands Avenue, the nearest police station I knew of being on Glenwood Road the other side of Rockaway Parkway. Since even after a snowstorm Brooklyn is full of elderly black Buicks being driven slowly but stupidly by short skinny women with their hair in rollers, I finished making the turn before looking in the rear-view mirror, where I saw my passenger looking very contrite. She met my eye in the mirror and said, "I'm sorry."

"You're sorry," I said. "You threatened me with a gun, you shot a hole in the roof, you accused me of all sorts of things, and now you're sorry. Sit back!" I shouted, because she'd started to lean forward, her hand reaching for my shoulder, and I didn't trust her an inch. That contrite look and little-girl voice could all be a gag.

She sat back. "It made sense," she said, "before I saw you. Before we had our talk. But now I believe you."

"Sure," I said.

"Because," she said, "if you *were* having an affair with Louise, and if you *did* help her kill Tommy, you wouldn't dare leave me alive now. You couldn't take a chance on having me running around loose."

"I *can't* take a chance on having you running around loose," I said. "That's why we're on our way to the cops."

She acted like she wanted to lean forward again, but controlled herself. "Please don't," she said. "I was desperate, and I did foolish things, but please don't turn me up."

Up? Most people would say "turn me *in*," given the situation; "turn me up" was a very insidey gangland way of saying the same thing. And come to think of it, that wasn't the first odd thing she'd said. Like quoting me twelve to one on my having helped kill her brother. Like talking about seeing who was bluffing when I said I'd take her to the cops.

It looked like she was really Tommy's sister.

And that might mean, it suddenly occurred to me, that she might know who Tommy's boss was. Maybe I wouldn't have to look for Tommy's wife at all any more.

This part of Flatlands Avenue is lined with junkyards with wobbly wooden fences. I pulled to the side of the road, next to one of these fences, and stopped the car. Then I turned around and said to her, "I tell you what. I'll make you a deal."

She got the instant wary look of the gambler in her eye. "What kind of a deal?"

"There's something *I* want to know," I told her. "You tell me and I'll forget the whole thing. I'll let you out of the cab and that'll be the end of it."

"What do you want to know?" She was still wary.

"I'll give you the background first," I said, and quickly sketched in the incident of Purple Pecunia. I left out the business about the hoods last night, seeing no purpose in opening *that* can of worms right now, and finished by saying, "So what I want to know is, who do I collect from now that I can't collect from your brother?"

"Oh," she said. "Is *that* why you've been hanging around the apartment?"

"I haven't exactly been hanging around," I said. "I've been over there a couple times is all."

"Three times yesterday and once today," she said. "I've been waiting in the apartment for Louise to show up so I could confront her—"

"With the gun?"

"With the fact that I know she's guilty," she said fiercely.

"Well, you're wrong," I told her. "Nobody on earth could do an acting job like that. When Tommy's wife saw him dead there, she had hysterics, and I mean hysterics."

"It could have been guilt," she said. "And nervousness."

"Sure," I said. "Only it wasn't."

"Then why did she disappear?"

"I don't know," I said. "Maybe she's staying with some relative, maybe she doesn't want to be around the apartment now."

She shook her head. "No. I called both her brothers and they don't know where she is either. And I had to make all the arrangements for the funeral and the wake myself."

"Wake? When?"

"It starts this evening," she said. "At six." She looked at her watch.

I said, "What time is it?"

She looked at her watch again. Did you ever notice how people do that? They look at their watch and a second later you ask them what time it is and they don't know. She said, "Twenty after four."

I said, "I'm losing a whole day's work because of you. Not to mention the six bucks you ran up on the meter."

"I'll pay you for that," she said. "Don't worry, I'm not a stiff."

"Never mind that," I said. "Just tell me who Tommy's boss was and where I find him."

"I can't," she said.

"Okay, sister," I said, turning around to the wheel again. "It's the hoosegow for you."

"No!"

I waited, both hands on the steering wheel. "Well?"

"I don't *know*," she said. "I'd tell you if I knew, honest I would."

"Tommy's sister would know," I said. "Especially if she was as close to him as you claim."

"I didn't claim to be close," she said. "I just came to town because he was killed."

"From where?"

"Vegas."

I turned around again. "You live in Las Vegas?"

"For a couple of years now," she said. "Can I show you something out of my purse?"

"If you move very slow," I said.

She moved very slow, and produced an airline ticket from her purse, which she handed over to me. It was TWA, it was the return half of a round-trip ticket between Las Vegas and New York, it showed she'd come in yesterday morning, and it gave her name as Abigail McKay.

I said, "Abigail?"

"Abbie," she said.

"That's very funny," I said. "Abigail. You don't look like an Abigail."

"I'm not an Abigail," she said. She was getting irritated. "Everybody calls me Abbie."

But I was enjoying needling her about it, maybe because of the trouble I have about Chester, maybe just
to get some of my own back with her. "Abigail," I said,
grinning. "It's hard to think of you as an Abigail."

"Well, you're a Chester, all right," she said. "You're a
Chester if there ever lived one."

"That's it," I said, twisted around, started the car, and
we moved out onto Flatlands Avenue again.

"I think you stink," she said.

"The feeling is mutual," I said. "In fact, the feeling is
paramutual."

In the mirror I could see her looking blank. "What?"

It had been a pun, on pari-mutuel, of course, the
betting system at race tracks. I'd meant "para" like *more
than* or *above,* like parapsychology or paratrooper. But
try explaining a pun. Explanations never get a laugh. So I
didn't say anything.

We were stopped by a traffic light at East 103rd Street.
We were into an area of brick projects and fake-brick row
houses now, the streets full of kids throwing snowballs at
each other. As we sat there waiting for the light to change,
kids flowing all around us, she said, "I'm sorry. I just hate
that business about Abigail."

"I hate that business about Chester," I said.

"What do people call you?"

"They call me Chester," I said. "I want them to call me
Chet, but nobody does."

"I will," she said. "If you don't call me Abigail I won't
call you Chester."

I looked at her in the mirror and I saw she was really

trying to be friends, and I realized that she did have the
same thing about her name that I had about mine, and it
had been kind of mean of me to make a thing about it.
"It's a deal," I said.

She said, "Would you please don't take me to the police, Chet? If you do, there won't be anybody to look for
Tommy's murderer, not anybody at all."

Watching her in the mirror, seeing that her chin was
trembling and she was on the verge of tears, I said, "What
about the cops? Let them find the murderer."

"Somebody who killed a bookie? Are you kidding?
How hard do you think they're going to work?"

"They're still working now," I said. "One of them came
out to see me just this morning. They don't suspect me of
anything, by the way."

"Neither do I," she said. "Not any more. And I'm not
saying the police won't do all the routine stuff. They'll do
all that, they'll do enough to be sure the record looks good
on paper, but they won't really *try*, not for a bookie, and
you know it as well as I do."

Somebody honked. I looked through the windshield
and the light was green. I went across the intersection
and found a hydrant to park next to in the middle of the
block. I stopped the cab again, turned around, and said,
"All right, maybe. The police aren't going to work as hard
as if it was the Governor, I'll grant you that. But what do
you know about any of it? You're running around with a
lot of dumb ideas in your head, leaping to conclusions,
waving a gun around, acting like a nut. You aren't going
to solve any murders, all you'll do is get yourself in
trouble."

"I was wrong about you," she said. "I admit that. I
admit I should have found out more before I made up my

mind. But now I've learned my lesson, and I'll be more careful from now on."

I shook my head. "You don't get the point. The point is, you don't know the first thing about detective work. You're like one of those people goes out to the track, doesn't know word one about handicapping, and picks the horses with the cute names."

"Sometimes those people pick a winner," she said.

"What's the odds?"

She frowned. "All right. But I'm not wrong about Louise! She's been having an affair with *somebody*. Tommy knew about it but he didn't know who it was. He wrote me months ago about it."

"Did she ask for a divorce? Did he say no?"

"She didn't bring anything out in the open," she said. "Tommy just knew about it, that's all."

I shook my head. "There's no reason for her to kill him," I said. "It isn't like she was going to inherit a million dollars. If she wanted to be through with Tommy, all she had to do was pack up and leave."

"There could be things we don't know about," she said.

"My point exactly," I said. "There could be all sorts of things you don't know about, and until you find out what they are you can't be sure about anything. And you certainly can't go around accusing somebody of murder."

"Then why did she disappear?" she demanded.

"How do I know? But I'm sure there's more than one possible explanation. She's liable to show up at this wake tonight, and you can ask her."

"I just bet she is."

"She might. How do you know?"

"If she shows up," she said, "I'll owe you an apology."

"You owe me an apology now," I said.

"I already said I'm sorry. And I did mean it." I had my forearm up resting on the top of the seat, and now she leaned forward and rested her hand on my arm, saying, "Will you help me? I'm all alone in the world now, I don't have anybody now that Tommy's dead."

I looked at her, and it just didn't sound right. This was a very good-looking girl, with big blue eyes and smooth skin and full blond hair, and she was dressed expensively and well, and it was hard to imagine her ever being all alone in the world. I said, "Don't you have anybody back in Las Vegas?"

She shrugged. "People I know," she said. "But nobody I'm really close to."

"I'm somebody you're really close to?"

She took her hand off my arm and sat back. "No, you're not," she said, and looked out the side window. "There isn't anybody, like I said."

"Frankly," I said, "I don't want to get mixed up in any murder situation, and I don't think you should either."

"I'm doing it for Tommy," she said, looking at me again. "Because somebody has to, and because he was the only brother I had. And because *I'm* the only one *he* has."

"Okay," I said. "I see your point. But you've got to handle things differently from now on."

"I will," she said. "Believe me, I will."

"I tell you what," I said. "I want to know where to collect my money, you want to know who killed your brother. We'll probably overlap a little anyway, so I'll help you for a little while. Until either you find out what you want to know or I find out what I want to know. Is it a deal?"

"Definitely," she said, and smiled a glowing smile, and stuck her hand out. I took it, and it was cool and smooth and very delicate. "Thank you," she said.

"I haven't done anything yet," I said. "Can I make a suggestion?"

"I wish you would."

"You go to this wake," I said. "Stay there from beginning to end. Check out everybody who comes in, find out who they are. If Tommy's wife shows up, ask her some questions about where she's been. If anybody that Tommy worked for shows up, ask them about where I can get my money. What time is the wake over?"

"Nine o'clock."

"Okay. There's a poker game I'm in on Wednesdays, I'll be there by then, I'll give you the number. You can—"

"Do they let girls sit in?"

Surprised, I said, "Well, we've had girls sit in a couple of times."

"I'm not like them," she said. "I promise I'm a good player."

"Not too good," I said, and grinned.

"We'll see," she said. "Do you think they'd mind if I sat in?"

"They won't mind," I said. "You come right along. It's in Manhattan, 38 East 81st Street. Between Park and Madison. The guy's name is Jerry Allen."

"All right. I'll be there around nine-thirty."

"Good. Where do you want to go now?"

"Back to Tommy's place," she said. "That's where I've been staying."

"Okay. I'm going to have to run the meter, you know, or a cop is liable to stop us."

"That's all right," she said. "I have money."

"Fine. You already owe me six forty-five for the trip down." I started the car and the meter and headed up to Rockaway Parkway and made my left to go back to the Belt.

"I'm glad you're going to help," she said.

"Only till I get my money," I reminded her. "I don't want to act unchivalrous or anything, but it really isn't my scene to go looking for murderers."

"It isn't mine either," she said. "But it has to be done. And I know you naturally don't have as strong feelings about it as I do, so I won't ask you to do any more than you want."

"Good," I said.

"Oh," she said, as though it had just occurred to her, "and could I have my gun back, please?"

"Ha ha," I said.

"What's wrong?"

"Nothing," I said.

"You mean I can't have the gun back?"

"Right."

"That's mean, Chet. I need that gun, for my own safety."

"You'll be a lot safer without it," I said. "And so will everybody else." And that was the end of that conversation.

11

What with one thing and another I didn't check the cab in till seven-thirty, and when I did I made no mention of the gunshot wound in the roof. It would have led to a very complicated conversation I didn't particularly want to get into, and if somebody did notice the hole eventually, who was to say when it happened or that I was the one driving the cab at the time?

The reason I worked till seven-thirty, even though the

game starts at seven, was because I was almost out of cash. I didn't know if my losing streak was over or if Purple Pecunia had been a fluke, and if I lost tonight at least I didn't want to have to write any markers in front of Abbie McKay. Don't ask me why I thought that was so important, because I don't know. But I did.

I'd already phoned my father a little after five that I wouldn't be home for dinner, so I went to a greasy spoon near the garage and had franks and beans before going across town to Jerry Allen's place. I kept being conscious of the weight of Abbie's gun in my coat pocket. I didn't particularly want to carry it around on me, but I couldn't think of what else to do with it.

I took the 79th Street crosstown bus and walked up to Jerry's apartment. And I do mean up. Jerry lives on the top floor of a five-story building with no elevator. People tend to arrive at his door out of breath.

As I did now. I rang the bell, and it was opened by Jerry himself. He's part owner of a florist shop over on Lexington Avenue, and it's possible he isn't entirely heterosexual, but he isn't obnoxious about it and none of us care what he does away from the card table, and besides that he's a fish. I think in losing to us and hosting the game he's sort of paying for the privilege of being accepted by a bunch of real guys, whether he realizes it or not. Anyway, he tends to laugh in an embarrassed way when he loses, and he loses a lot.

Jerry said hi, you're late, and I breathed hard and nodded. He went back to the game and I shut the door behind myself, took off my coat, and hung it in the hall closet. Then I went into the living room, where Jerry has a nice round oak table over near the front windows, at which five guys were currently sitting. There were two

empty chairs, and they were both between Jerry and Sid
Falco, Sid being the guy those hoods had mentioned last
night. Feeling suddenly very nervous about being in the
same room with Sid Falco, a guy I had known without
nervousness for about five years, I sat in the chair closer
to Jerry and forced my attention on what was happening
at the table.

There was a hand in progress, seven-card stud, which
on the fifth card was down to a two-man race, Fred Stehl
and Leo Morgentauser. Leo looked like a possible flush,
Fred a possible straight. Doug Hallman was dealing. I
looked at the hands and the faces and knew that Leo
either had it in five or was on his way to buying, and that
Fred was hanging in with a four-straight that wouldn't
ever fill, and even with Sid Falco over there to my right I
began to calm down and get into the swing of things.

This twice-weekly poker game had been a Wednesday-
and-Sunday institution with us for five or six years now,
with only minor changes in personnel all that time. There
were five regulars including me in the game these days,
plus half a dozen other guys who'd drop in from time
to time. Leo Morgentauser, the made flush currently betting up Fred Stehl's unmade straight, was one of the
irregulars, a teacher at a vocational high school in Queens,
teaching automobiles or sewing machines or something.
A tall skinny bushy-haired guy with a huge Adam's apple,
Leo was married and probably didn't make a very good
living, so he seldom came to the game, but when he did
he was usually a winner. He was a good poker psycholo-
gist and could run a very beautiful bluff when he felt like
it. His biggest failing was that he wouldn't push a streak,
so sometimes he'd go home with less of our money than
he should have had. Not that I'm complaining.

Everybody else at the table tonight was a regular. Fred Stehl, the guy currently head to head with Leo, was a gambling fool, and next to Jerry Allen, was the closest thing to a fish among the regulars. He was a fairly consistent loser, maybe four times out of five, but as he would begin to lose he would also begin to get more cautious, so he rarely lost heavily. The big joke with Fred was his wife, Cora, who was death on gambling and was always trying to track Fred down. Almost every time she'd call during the game, wanting to know if Fred was there, and Jerry always covered for him. A couple of times she'd actually showed up at the apartment, but Jerry hadn't let her in, and the last time, over a year ago, she punched him in the nose. It was really very funny, though Jerry, with a nosebleed, hadn't seen the humor in it very much. Fred ran a laundromat on Flatbush Avenue over in Brooklyn, and I guess he had to make a pretty good living at it because on the average he had to drop ten or twenty bucks a week at our two games. Also, he plays the horses a lot. In fact, it was through him I started placing my own bets with Tommy McKay.

Doug Hallman, currently dealing, was a huge hairy fat man who ran a gas station on Second Avenue not far from the Midtown Tunnel. He was a blustery sort of player, the kind who tries to look mean and menacing when he bluffs. Otherwise he was a pretty good poker player and won more often than he lost, and my only objection to him was the twelve-for-a-quarter cigars he smoked all the time.

And finally there was Sid Falco, thin, serious, narrow-headed, probably the youngest guy at the table. A deadly serious poker player, he was full of the math of the game, the only one at the table who could reel off the odds for making any hand given any situation and lie of the cards.

He played strictly by the book, which meant very conservative, no imagination, and he was a small but consistent winner. Two or three times a night he'd try a bluff, because the book says you should bluff every once in a while to keep the other players guessing, but his bluffs were always as transparent as wax paper. A bluff being so unnatural to him, he would start acting weird, like a robot going crazy in a science-fiction story. He'd light a cigarette with funny jerky movements, or start telling a joke in a high-pitched voice, or start comparing the time on his watch with the time on everybody else's watch. His bluffs tended to get called.

The current hand finally finished itself out, and when Fred Stehl bumped Leo Morgentauser's bet on the last card, everybody knew he'd bought the straight after all. Which was too bad, because everybody but Fred had known for a long time that Leo already had the flush.

Leo, naturally, went into his Actors' Studio number, frowning at his down cards, at Fred's up cards, at the chips in front of himself, at the pot, at the opposite wall, and then finally sighing and shaking his head and raising Fred back.

And Fred gave him another raise. Because he's a gambling fool, because his straight had come in and he couldn't believe it was a loser, and because it was early in the evening and he hadn't lost much yet.

And Leo cried, "Hah!" and with a great flourish and an evil grin of triumph he raised Fred back.

Fred's face was pitiful to see. He understood now he'd been suckered, but Leo's overacting had to keep him in because there was always that faint remote chance Leo was trying a double reverse bluff, which of course he wasn't. But Fred had to call.

Leo showed him the flush and pulled in the pot.

Fred didn't even bother to show the straight. He just folded his up cards and pushed them away.

Leo dealt next, seven-card stud again, the game he'd won at. I got a four and nine down and a Jack up, three different suits, and folded. I spent the rest of the hand watching Sid Falco, who was nursing a pair of showing Queens through a careful methodical hand in which his only competition was Jerry Allen, who looked to have Kings up with no pair showing.

So Sid Falco was a mobster. Or worked for a mobster. Or worked for somebody connected with mobsters. Or something. The point was, did he look any different now that I knew whatever it was I knew about him?

No. He looked like the exact same guy who'd always said he was a salesman for a wholesale liquor company.

Well, maybe that was true. There were still a lot of legitimate outfits that tended to have mob connections. Like bars, for instance, and soft-drink bottlers, and juke-box and vending-machine operators, and liquor whole-salers, and linen services, and real estate management companies, and God alone knows what all. So Sid Falco could have an apparently honest job and he could still be a mobster.

But why didn't he look different to me? Tougher, maybe, or more dangerous, or dirtier, or more mysterious. *Something.* But he didn't.

I wondered what would happen if I were to lean over close to him, as though interested in his hole cards (being out of the hand, so it was okay), and whisper in his ear, "Solomon Napoli." Just that. And sit back, and innocently look around at the other hands still in the game.

I wondered, and I looked at Sid's profile, and I decided

not to find out. In spite of his not looking any different, I decided not to find out. No, that isn't right, it was *because* he didn't look any different. His surface was still the same, there was no sign of whatever it was that lurked beneath, and that was more intimidating than any kind of blatant toughness. He showed nothing at all, and that meant the reality could be anything at all, and that meant I didn't want to know what it was. So I minded my own business, and did no whispering to Sid.

In the meantime Sid and his pair of Queens had pushed steadily but moderately through the hand, and at the finish there was no one left but Jerry with his probable Kings up. Sid made a limit bet, and Jerry had to stay in and make Sid show the trips, and Sid did. Jerry made that embarrassed unhappy laugh of his, and looked around the table to see if anybody had noticed his failure. We all know that move of his by now, so we were all looking some place else.

Fred dealt next. Seven-card stud again. Fred was the true gambling fool, he'd go back to the game that bit him time after time till he finally bit it back. This time I got a three and Jack down and a seven up, three suits again. I folded, naturally, and began to wonder if my luck with Purple Pecunia had been strictly a one-shot. These cards were costing me a quarter a hand.

Jerry took this one, with an eight-high straight that had obviously come in on the seventh card, against Doug Hallman's unimproved aces up. Doug puffed a lot of cigar smoke over that hand, but didn't say anything.

Sid was the next dealer. He switched to five-card stud and gave me a Jack in the hole, nine on top. I stayed, paired the Jack on the fourth card, and had only Fred to contend with at the end. Two other Jacks had been folded in other hands, which Fred had to be aware of. The highest card he had showing was a ten, so I had a lock, so naturally I bet the limit, which is two dollars, and when he bumped two dollars back to prove he had a pair of tens, I considered doing Leo's Actors' Studio bit, but then decided the hell with it and just threw in my two-buck raise. Fred called and I showed him my other Jack. "I didn't believe it," he said, and showed me his other ten. "I believed that," I said, which was maybe cruel.

Then, as I drew in my first pot of the evening, I said, "You guys hear what happened to Tommy McKay Monday?" Fred and Doug and Leo all knew Tommy, and Sid and Jerry had both heard us mention him at one time or another.

Doug said, "I been trying to call him."

"He's dead," I said.

None of them had heard. So I told them, and of course no more hands were dealt till I finished. When I told them Tommy had a beautiful sister from Las Vegas who was going to sit in a little later, though, all the other elements in the story suddenly grew very pale. At first the questions had been about Tommy, and then about the guy who'd given me the tip on the horse, but by the end there was nothing but questions about Abbie. "You'll see her," I kept saying. "She'll be here around nine-thirty."

Then Doug Hallman, who had a marker of mine, said something about me being rolling in dough now, and I told him not yet, with Tommy dead I hadn't been able to get my pay-off yet, I was going to have to see about that tomorrow. He nodded, and looked a little unhappy. Jerry, who also had a marker of mine, also looked unhappy.

Finally we got back to the game, and in the next two hours I did very well indeed. Doug Hallman was having a streak of cards almost as rotten as his cigars; Fred Stehl and Jerry were both chasing too much and staying in hands too long; and Sid was just about holding his own, which meant the money was all coming to Leo and me, and most of it was coming to me. By the time the doorbell rang at quarter to ten I was almost forty bucks to the good, which was fantastic for that game, particularly in only two hours.

The ring had come at one of the odd moments when I wasn't in a hand, so I pushed my chair back and said, "That'll be Abbie now." I left the living room and went to the door and threw it open and there was Abbie, still in her orange fur and black boots. "Hi, there," I said.

She came in and smiled and panted and waved at her mouth to let me know she couldn't talk yet.

"That's okay," I said. "I understand." I helped her out of the coat, and the boots continued on up under the miniskirt of her baby-blue wool dress. She was a very sexy-looking girl.

I hung up her coat and turned back to her, and she said, "Boy. Those are some stairs."

"You don't get used to them," I assured her.

"I believe it."

"You're going to have an unfair advantage, you know," I said. "None of us are going to be able to look at our cards."

She smiled. "What a nice thing to say."

"Did you find out anything at the wake?"

"Nothing important. I'll tell you later."

"Okay," I said, and led her into the living room to introduce her to the boys, all of whom acted very natural and nonchalant, except that Doug began puffing so much cigar smoke he looked like a low-pressure system, Leo knocked over all his little stacks of chips, Fred managed to kick over his chair when he blurted to his feet, Jerry began to giggle with the kind of unhappy laugh he makes when he loses, and Sid started to blink very rapidly as though he was trying a bluff.

Finally, though, everybody settled down. Abbie sat between Sid and me and got ten dollars' worth of chips from Jerry; we filled her in on the house rules; Leo dealt a hand of guts draw; and Abbie took a nice pot with Queens over treys. Welcome to the club.

Two hands later it was her deal. "My favorite game is stud," she said.

Doug, who wanted to make time with this beautiful girl but hadn't yet figured out how to go about it in the middle of a poker game, said, "Five-card or seven?"

"Five," she said. "Naturally." In the silence following that put-down she shuffled like a pro, slid Sid the deck to be cut, and fired the cards out like John Scarne. My ace up looked good, but it was the ten in the hole that paired with the fourth card that did the trick, and I raked in a small but pleasant pot. It was then my deal, and it just wasn't possible for me to deal anything but five-card stud.

Nor could anybody else switch, not after that announcement of Abbie's, so for the next hour or so we played nothing but five-card stud. Abbie did well, playing a fairly conservative game and winning small amounts. My streak slowed a bit, but didn't entirely turn off. Leo seemed to be holding his own, and Jerry just grew wilder and wilder, like a centrifuge going too fast and spinning all its money away. But the big surprises were Fred and Sid. Fred suddenly settled down and became a tight, sharp, wary, brilliant player, reading bluffs incredibly, betting his hands with the cunning of a tax lawyer, and all in all coming on like a graduate of Gardena. Sid, on the other hand, broke down totally. All math seemed to have left his head, and he played so erratically it was as though he was out of phase with the rest of us and was actually playing his hands five deals too late. Abbie was sitting at his left elbow, and the proximity was obviously more than he could handle. It was a great encouragement to know a gangster could also be human. If he'd been handy enough, I might even have whispered the magic name to him now, though come to think of it erratic people are more dangerous than any other kind, aren't they? Hmm.

Anyway, along about eleven o'clock, at a time when Abbie was just about to deal, Doug asked her what she did for a living in Las Vegas, was she a dancer or what, and she said, "I deal blackjack." And began to deal out the cards for stud.

Talk about a bombshell. Nobody looked at their cards at all, everybody just stared at Abbie.

It was Doug who asked the question in all our minds. Taking the cigar out of his face for once, he said, "Are you by any chance a mechanic?"

"We run strictly legitimate in Vegas," she said. "The house makes its money on the percentages."

"Yeah," Doug said, and pointed his cigar at the deck in her hand. "But *can* you do crooked dealing?"

She looked around at all of us, and reluctantly she nodded. "I know how to do some things," she said. "I wouldn't do them, I promise, but I do know how."

"Like what?" Doug asked her.

She shrugged. "I can deal seconds," she said. "Or bottoms. I can mark a deck at the table, all that sort of thing."

"Show us some stunts," Doug said. He pushed the

cards he'd been dealt over toward her. "Show us how it's done."

"But what about the hand?" she asked.

"The hell with the hand," he said, and the rest of us said yes, the hell with the hand. We all pushed our cards toward Abbie, and she shrugged and picked them up and began to show us things.

Fascinating. She spent half an hour going through her bag of tricks, and it was lovely to watch. She had long slender fingers with pale red polish on the nails, and it was really great to see those fingers do things with the cards. Ace of spades on top of the deck, the fingers would flick flick flick, cards would be dealt out to all of us, and there on top of the deck would still be the ace of spades. She palmed cards, she did fake cuts, she did one-handed cuts, she dealt out hands and then stacked the deck while pulling in the discards and then made the stack survive shuffling and cutting and everything else we could think of. She took an old deck Jerry had around and showed us how to mark it with thumbnail indentations on the edges of the cards while the deck was in play. She showed us how to crimp the deck to get it cut where you wanted.

That was the end of poker for that night. Jerry broke out beer and Scotch and we all sat around and talked about gambling and cheating and one thing and another, cutting up old jackpots as they say, and we had a great time. Even Sid relaxed after a while. Fred's wife Cora didn't call, amazingly enough, and that simply rounded out the perfection of the night.

We split up about twelve-thirty, everybody agreeing Abbie should come back Sunday if she was still in town, and then we all went our separate ways. It had been one of my finest moments. Not only was I the guy who knew this girl and had introduced her to the game, she and I were leaving together. Besides that, I'd won fifty-three bucks tonight, which was very healthy for that game. The losing streak was over, I could feel it.

12

Sid had gone downstairs ahead of us, and was waiting for us on the sidewalk. He said to me, "You going home, Chet? I'll give you a lift."

Before I could say anything, Abbie said, "I have a car."

"Oh," Sid said, and shrugged. "I'll see you, then," he said, and turned and walked away.

I looked after him. "That's funny," I said. "He never offered me a ride before. He knows I've got my own car."

"Is yours here, too?"

"No, not tonight. I came over straight from work."

"Then let's take mine," she said. "I just rented it today."

"I live out in Queens," I said.

"That's okay. We have to talk, anyway. Come on."

So I went on. Her car was a green Dodge Polara, the seats freezing cold. We got in and she started the engine and said she needed gas. Did I know of any place open now?

"There's a Sunoco station over on the West Side, but it's kind of out of the way."

"Is that the only place you know?"

Reluctantly I said, "Well, it's the only Sunoco station I know that's open now."

"Does it make a difference? Gas is gas."

"Well," I said, even more reluctantly, "the fact is, I'm playing Sunny Dollars."

She looked at me, and for a long time she didn't say anything, and then she grinned and said, "You're a nut, Chet."

"I suppose I am."

"Then it's Sunoco," she said.

"If it's okay with you."

"Why not? If you make out tonight I'll take twenty-five percent."

I grinned back at her. "You want to be in the action yourself."

"Always," she said, and pulled the car away from the curb. "Where to?"

"Through the park on 84th."

We went around the block and headed west, and she said, "There's other gasoline games, you know. Why not spread your play around a little?"

"You just worsen the odds against yourself that way," I said. "There's only a certain number of times you're going to stop in at a gas station. You split that number into two games, you cut your odds back fantastically."

"You double them," she said.

"No, it's a lot worse than that. I'm no mathematician, but I think you get multiples in there that kill you. My father could probably work it out."

So then naturally she had to know about my father. I told her about him and the insurance thing, and then she told me something about her childhood, hers and Tommy's. Their father had been in real estate in Florida, a real boom-or-bust business, and they had plenty of both extremes throughout their childhood. The booms were made shorter and the busts longer by the fact that the father was a real bangtail chaser, a horseplayer with an abiding faith in hunch bets and horses with funny names. Purple Pecunia would have been a natural for him, but he was dead now, having expired during the sixth race at Hialeah one afternoon seven years before when his thirty-seven-to-one shot, a horse called Mickey Moose, while five lengths ahead of the field had stumbled and fallen two strides from the finish line. The mother thereafter became a religious fanatic, moved to Nutley, New Jersey, and didn't miss a church bingo game for the next four years, until the night the hit-and-run driver got her.

"They never did get him," she finished. "There was nothing I could do about Dad's death, and I didn't do anything about Mom's, but I'm going to do something about Tommy if it's the last thing I do on earth!"

I looked at her, and she was glaring grimly through the windshield, and for just a moment my own grail—nine hundred thirty bucks—seemed trivial in comparison. I found myself tempted to offer my services, like a knight protecting some helpless damsel in distress, but fortunately the realities of the situation forced themselves back into my mind and I kept my mouth shut. In the first place, in the world in which Tommy McKay's probable murderer moved I would be much more of a hindrance than a help, getting underfoot at all the wrong times, and so on. And in the second place, Abbie McKay was no helpless damsel in distress. She could take care of herself, that girl, I was sure of it.

So instead of volunteering, I switched the subject of conversation altogether, and we discussed the poker game for a while. She had some interesting things to say about the personalities and playing styles of the other players, and also suggested to me one of my own flaws in the game, being a too-great respect for aces. An ace visible in somebody else's hand would tend to chase me at times that I had a perfectly respectable stay, and an ace in my own hand would keep me in at times when I had nothing but a clear-cut fold. I had to agree with that, and filed everything she said away in the back of my mind, to be used next week.

At the gas station we got two Sunny fives and a Dollars ten. "Anything good?" Abbie asked.

"No. These are the easy halves."

After the gas station we went back across town and through the Midtown Tunnel and up onto the Expressway, and Abbie said, "We're being followed, Chet."

I turned around and looked and there were four pairs of headlights spaced out behind us. I couldn't see any of the cars behind the lights at all. "Which one?" I said.

"Second car back in the left lane."

"How do you know he's following us?"

"He was behind us when we stopped for the light at Fifth Avenue on the way to the gas station. Then I saw him behind us again in the tunnel."

"You sure it's the same car?"

"I noticed the hood ornament," she said. "It's very sexy."

I looked at her, abruptly more aware of the man-woman thing than of any car following us around the nighttime city, and she glanced at me, grinned, and said, "I'm putting you on, Chet." She looked front again. "But it is the same car, I know it."

I looked back again. The car was maintaining its distance back there. I said, "There's something I didn't tell you about. Maybe this would be a good time to." And I told her about the hoods grabbing me last night.

She was very interested but didn't interrupt at all, and when I was done, she nodded and said, "I didn't think the mob had done it. It just didn't look like their kind of thing. If they're going around trying to solve it, too, that proves it."

"They think this guy Solomon Napoli did it," I said. "The cop that came to see me mentioned the same name, too."

"We'll have to find out who he is," she said. "But in the meantime let's get away from those people back there." And she stood on the accelerator.

Dodges have more pep than they used to. We took off like the roadrunner in the movie cartoons, shooting down the Expressway like a bullet down the barrel of a rifle.

"Hey!" I said. "We have cops in New York!"

"Are they staying with us?"

I looked back, and one pair of headlights was rushing along in our wake, farther back now but not losing any more ground. Fortunately, there was very little traffic on the road, and our two cars wriggled through what there was like a snake in a hurry.

I said, "They're still there."

"Hold on," she said. I looked at her, and she was leaning over the wheel in tense concentration. I couldn't believe she meant to take that exit rushing toward us on the right, but she did, at the last minute swerving the car to the right, slicing down the ramp without slackening speed.

There was a traffic light ahead, and it was red. There was no traffic anywhere in sight. Abbie got off the accelerator at last and stood on the brake instead. Bracing myself with both hands against the dashboard, I stared in helpless astonishment as we slewed into the intersection. I believe to this day that Abbie made a right turn then simply because that was the way the car happened to be pointing when she got it back under control.

Anyway, we leaped another long block down a street absolutely empty of traffic, which was lucky for them and lucky for us, and then we squealed through another right turn. We were on a block of scruffy-looking storefronts now, dark and silent and dismal. About mid-block there was a driveway between two buildings on the right side, and Abbie made an impossible turn, shoved the Dodge in there, screamed to a stop inches from a set of crumbling old garage doors, and cut the engine and the lights.

We both looked out back, and a minute later we saw a flash of light go by, white in front and red in back. "There," Abbie said in satisfaction, and twisted around to sit normally again.

I sat sideways, facing her, my back against the door. "Abbie," I said, "you have achieved a rare distinction. You have driven an automobile in such a way as to terrify a New York City cabdriver."

It was very dark back there, but I could see her grinning at me. "We got away, didn't we?" she said, and I could hear the smugness in her voice.

"We got away," I agreed. "I'd almost rather I was caught."

"No, you wouldn't," she said.

Something in her voice gave me pause. I said, "I wouldn't? What do you mean?"

"Who could that have been," she said, "but the same people who were after you last night? And if they want you again, it can only mean one thing."

"What one thing?"

"They've decided you are guilty after all," she said.

"The heck," I said. "That doesn't make any sense at all."

"*I* thought you were guilty for a while," she said. "And

why would they come back after you again? Why follow you around?"

"Maybe they want to ask me more questions. There's nothing to worry about."

"Nothing to worry about. The next thing you'll say," she said, "is that you want to go home, just as though nothing had happened."

"Well, naturally," I said. "Where else would I go?"

"They'll be waiting for you," she said. "If you go home, they'll kill you."

"Kill me? Abbie, at the very worst they've thought of something else they want to ask me. In fact, I've got questions I want to ask *them*, like where I go to get paid. Unless you found out tonight at the wake."

"I didn't find out anything at the wake," she said. "Chet, if you show yourself to those people, they'll shoot you dead."

"Don't be silly," I said. "Did Tommy's wife show up at the wake?"

"No," she said. "I'm not being silly. I'm trying to save you from being killed."

"I'm not going to be killed," I said. "Will you stop talking about that? Wasn't there anybody interesting at the wake at all?"

"Some of Louise's relatives," she said, "but none of them knew where she was. And some other people came, some of them looked pretty tough, but none of them would admit he worked for the same people as Tommy, so I couldn't ask any questions. And *you* better not ask any questions, because you'll get your head blown off for the answer."

"This is the same kind of jumping to conclusions you did when you first got into my cab," I said. "Then you were convinced I was a killer, and now you're convinced I'm a killee."

"A what?"

"Marked to be killed," I said.

"Because you are," she said. "Won't you even consider it as a possibility?"

"No. Because it isn't."

"Chet, I don't want to take you home. They'll be watching your place."

"Say," I said. "*There's* a flaw in your theory. Those people last night knew where I lived, they were waiting for me there, so they wouldn't have to follow me anywhere. That had to be somebody else just now."

"Who?"

"I don't know."

"What do they want with you?"

I shook my head. "I don't know," I admitted.

"But you don't think it's possible, whoever they are, that they might want to kill you."

"There's no reason," I said, "for *anybody* to want to kill me. Will you get off my back about that? You're too goddam melodramatic by half."

"Chet, don't be nasty. I'm just trying to tell you—"

"You're just trying to get me caught up in your paranoia," I said, being maybe sharper than necessary because the idea she was suggesting was very nervous-making. "Now," I said, "I've had enough of it. It's late at night, I've got to work tomorrow. If you've got nothing else to tell me about the wake, let's just get going."

I could see her controlling her temper. "You don't want to listen, is that it?"

"That's it," I said.

"That's fine by me," she said, and faced front. She

started the car, backed us out the driveway to the street, and headed back for the Expressway.

She drove the rest of the way maybe a little too fast and hard, because she was angry, but nothing outlandish. I spoke to her in monosyllables from time to time, giving her directions to my house, but other than that we didn't talk at all.

When she pulled to a stop in front of my house, I said coldly, "Thanks for the lift." If she could be hard-nosed, so could I.

"Any time," she said coldly. So could she.

I opened the door, the interior light went on, I leaned toward the opening, and somewhere there was a backfire. Almost simultaneously, something in the car went *koot* and something fluffed the hair on the back of my head.

I looked around, bewildered, and saw a starred round hole in the windshield. "Hey," I said.

Abbie yelled, "Shut the door! The light, the light, shut the door!"

I wasn't thinking fast enough. I looked at her, confused, meaning to ask her what was going on, and then something very hard hit me all around the head and all the lights everywhere clicked out.

13

I thought: *I've been drinking.* It was the only explanation I could think of for the head I had. I thought it was morning, and I was waking up in the usual way, but with the kind of splitting headache I get from drinking Scotch or bourbon. I knew the cure was two aspirins and a quart of orange juice followed by another thirty minutes in the sack, but getting out of bed long enough to start the cure was going to be difficult. In fact, impossible, and as you recall, the impossible takes a little longer.

I knew one of the worst moments of the morning would be when I opened my eyes. Brightness was already beating against my eyelids, wanting to slice through my eyes and directly into my brain. Even with my eyes closed I was squinting, my face wrinkled up like a chipmunk. Tentatively I inched up one eyelid, testing my capacity to withstand torture, and what I saw made me snap both eyes open wide and lunge upward to a sitting position on the bed.

I was in a strange bed in a strange bedroom in the middle of the night, the ceiling light was on, and a girl in bra and panties, her back to me, was getting something out of a dresser drawer.

"Detective Golderman!" I shouted.

The girl turned around, and it was Abbie. "I'm sorry," she said. "Did I wake you? I thought you were out for the night." Without haste she walked over to the closet and slipped on a robe.

I had too many things to be confused about at once. I said, "What did I say *that* for?"

Tying the robe's belt, Abbie said, "What did you call me, anyway?"

"Detective Golderman," I said, still bewildered.

So was she. She looked down at herself and said, "Detective Golderman?"

Then I got it. "The room," I said. "This is Tommy's bedroom."

"That's right," she said.

"The only other time I was ever in here," I explained, "was when Detective Golderman questioned me after— This is Tommy's *bed!*"

"Sure," she said.

I leaped out of bed.

"You're naked, Chet," she said.

I leaped back into bed. "What—what—"

"The doctor and I undressed you," she said. "He helped me carry you up here."

"Doctor?" My confusion getting worse and worse, I lifted a hand to my head, meaning to lean my head against it for a minute, and felt cloth. I felt around on my head, and it was covered with cloth and what felt like adhesive tape. I said, "What the heck?"

"You were shot," she said.

Then it all came back to me. The car stopping, me opening the door, the light coming on, the backfire, the starred hole in the windshield, the fluttering of my hair, Abbie screaming at me, and then the abrupt darkness, as though I was a television set that had been switched off.

I was awed, I was absolutely reverent in my presence. I said, "I was shot?"

"In the head," she said.

That struck me as impossible. "That's impossible," I said. "If I was shot in the head I'd be dead. Or anyway in the hospital."

Abbie said, "The bullet just skinned you."

"Skinned?" What an awful image *that* conjured.

"It didn't go *into* your head," she said, explaining patiently. "It just sort of side-swiped you. On the side of the head there, above your left ear."

I touched the side of my head above my left ear, and it hurt. Very badly. Underneath the bandages, my head reacted to the touch of my fingers by going *twwaaannngg*. "Ow," I said, and left my head alone after that.

Abbie said, "The doctor said it removed some skin and put a little teeny crease in your skull, but you'll be all—"

"Crease?" It seemed as though my part of the conversation was limited to astonished repetitions of individual words from Abbie's sentences, but there were so many different things to be baffled about that I hardly knew where to begin, and in the interim I was reduced to recoiling from everything she said.

"Just a little crease," she said, and held up two fingers very close together. "Hardly anything," she said. "The doctor said you should stay in bed for a day or two, and after that you should take it easy for a while, that's all."

"I shouldn't be in the hospital?"

"You don't have to be," she said. "Honest, Chet, it isn't really a bad wound at all. The doctor said the heat from the friction of the bullet going by sort of cauterized it right away, and besides that, it bled a lot, which helped to clean it, so there's—"

"I don't want to hear about it," I said. I put my hand to my head—the front, not the part that twanged—and said, "My head hurts."

"The doctor gave me some pills to give you," she said, and went away.

While she was gone I had leisure at last to do some sorting out in the jumble of my mind, and when she came back I was more or less clear on the situation and had a few questions I wanted to ask. I waited till I swallowed the two small green pills with some water, then gave the glass back, thanked her, and said, "What about the police?"

"What about them?" she said. She put the glass down on the dresser and sat down on the edge of the bed.

"Didn't you call them?"

"Good Lord, no," she said.

"Good Lord, no? Good Lord, why not?"

"Because," she said, "the mob tried to kill you."

I was getting confused again. "Excuse me," I said, "but it seems to me that would be a hell of a good reason *for* calling the cops. To get police protection, if nothing else."

She shook her head, saddened a bit by my ignorance. "Chet," she said, "don't you know what happens when the mob is after somebody and he goes to the police for police protection?"

"He gets police protection," I said.

"He does not. More often than not he gets thrown out a window. Haven't you ever heard of bribery? Pay-offs? Crooked policemen? Do you think Tommy managed to run a book in plain sight here in his apartment in the middle of Manhattan without the police being paid off somewhere along the line? Don't you think Tommy's bosses have a lot of cops on their payroll, too?"

"Oh, come on," I said. "You're getting paranoid again. You keep—"

"The last time you said that," she reminded me, "you got shot in the head."

I felt myself duck, which was ridiculous. Like the old superstition about three on a match. On the other hand, how many people do you see either light the third cigarette with a new match or go ahead with the original match but then look vaguely nervous for a few minutes afterward? Hundreds. And I'm one of them.

Still, it struck me there was something wrong somewhere. I'd been shot. In the head. How could I be even contemplating not calling the police?

I said, "What do I do instead? For Pete's sake, they'll

take another shot at me the next time they see me. I can't go home, I can't go to work, I can't even walk down the street."

"You're not supposed to, anyway," she said. "The doctor said you're supposed to stay in bed for a couple of days, so you stay right here and you'll be perfectly safe. Nobody knows you're here. Nobody even knows *I'm* here."

"That's wonderful," I said. "I lie around here for two days, and *then* I go out and get shot."

"No, you won't, Chet," she said. "They won't be after you any more by then."

"That's good news," I said, "but I believe I have a doubt or two."

"Well, you shouldn't," she said. "Just think about it for a minute."

"I'd rather not."

"Chet, don't be silly. Ask yourself, why did they try to kill you?"

"I don't want to ask questions like that. I don't want to think about it."

"Well, the answer," she persisted, "is that they still think you had something to do with Tommy's death. They think you work for that man Napoli or somebody, and you killed Tommy, and so they're paying Napoli back by killing you."

"They're paying *Napoli* back!"

"That's the way they'd think," she said. "An eye for an eye."

"Yeah, but it's my eye."

"But what if they find out," she said, "that you *didn't* have anything to do with killing Tommy? Then they won't be after you any more."

"Praise be," I said. "Only, how are they going to find out this good news?"

"From me," she said.

"From you?"

"I'm going to find out who the murderer is. I still think Louise had something to do with it—"

"She didn't."

"Whether she did or not," Abbie said, "I'm sure she wasn't working alone. There's a man in the case somewhere, the man who actually pulled the trigger. He's the one I'm going to find."

"You are?"

"Yes. Then the mob will know it wasn't you after all, and they'll leave you alone."

I shook my head. "I'm not hearing right," I said. "Everything's okay because sometime in the next two days you're going to find Tommy's murderer and prove he's the murderer and turn him over to the police and then the mob won't try to kill me any more."

"That's right," she said.

"Abbie," I said. I reached out to where her hand was resting on the blanket near my knee. I put my hand over hers and said, "Abbie, I don't want to suggest I don't have perfect faith in you or anything, but face it. You aren't a detective, you're a blackjack dealer."

"Don't you worry, Chet," she said. "I'll find him." She slipped her hand from under mine, patted mine, and got to her feet. "You go to sleep now," she said. "We'll talk some more in the morning."

"I don't want to go to sleep," I said. "I'm not tired."

"The doctor said those pills would make you drowsy."

The fact was, the pills had made me drowsy, but I was fighting it. "I'm not drowsy," I said, "and I don't want to talk in the morning, I want to talk now. I want to talk about what—"

"Chet," she said. "I'm sorry, maybe *you* aren't drowsy, but I am. I was going to take a shower when you woke up, and I really need one. I'm exhausted, I'm sore all over from helping carry you up here, and I'm still sticky." She made still-sticky wiggles with her fingers.

I said, "Still sticky?"

"Well, you bled all over the place, Chet," she said. "You should see the car. I don't know what the Avis people are going to say."

"Oh," I said. I suddenly felt very faint, and twice as drowsy as before. I began to blink, blinking because my eyes wanted to be closed and I wanted them to be open.

"I'll look in on you after I shower," Abbie said. "And we'll talk in the morning. Whatever we decide, Chet, it can wait till morning."

"All right," I said. I couldn't struggle against it any more, I was drowsy. I lay back on the bed, tiredly pulling the covers up to my chin. "See you later," I murmured.

"See you later," she said, and through my blinking I saw her in the doorway, pausing to grin at me. "You are cute bare-ass," she said, and left.

That almost woke me up again. I stared at the doorway for a few seconds until my eyelids grew too heavy to maintain the posture, and then subsided. What a way to talk. Well, a girl who dealt blackjack in Las Vegas for a living, you wouldn't expect her to be exactly a sheltered maiden. No, neither sheltered nor a maiden.

As my eyes slowly shut, I found myself counting the months. How long had it been since I'd been in bed with a member of the opposition? Six months? Seven months. Not since that girl Rita had last refused to come out to the track with me.

That's a long time, seven months. I lay there thinking

about that, listening to the far-off shush of the shower running, imagining the flesh that water was pouring over, thinking about pouring over that flesh myself sometime maybe, and in an oddly good frame of mind for somebody who had just recently been shot at with bullets I drifted very gradually and pleasantly into a soft and dreamless sleep, not waking till Abbie screamed.

14

I sat up, and the room was full of a man with a gun. He was standing one pace in from the doorway. The light was off now, but gray daylight ebbed in the airshaft window, and unfortunately I could see him. He was wearing a hat and an overcoat and a gun, and the gun was pointed at me, and his eyes were looking at me, and his eyes appeared to be made of slate.

Abbie screamed again, and something crashed. She was in some other room in the apartment, and she was in trouble, but I was convinced I was as good as dead, so I didn't move.

In that other room something else crashed, and a male voice roared in what sounded like a triplicate combination of anger and surprise and pain. The man with the gun glanced back at the doorway in irritation, then glared at me again and waggled the gun. "Don't move," he said, in a voice that was forty percent gravel and sixty percent inert materials.

Move? Wasn't he going to shoot me anyway? Wasn't he the one who shot me last night? If not, what was he doing here? What was his gun doing here? What was his friend doing to Abbie?

Crash. The male voice roared again.

What was Abbie doing to his friend?

The man with the gun wanted to know that, too. He backed up a step, looking very irritated, and was about to bend backward and stick his head through the doorway when a table lamp sailed by from the direction of the living room. We both heard it crash, and then we both heard something else crash in or near the living room, and Abbie and the male voice hollered at once, and the man with the gun growled at me, "You don't go nowhere, see? Not if you don't want nothing to happen to you."

"I don't want nothing to happen to me," I said, hoping his double negative had been bad grammar.

"Then just stay where you are," he told me. "Don't move outa that bed."

"You can count on it," I assured him, but I don't think he heard me. He had already backed up through the doorway and was standing in the hall. With one last glare and gun-waggle at me, he took off toward the living room.

Nothing changed for a minute, the ruckus continued unabated, and then all of a sudden it went absolutely insane. The crashing doubled, it tripled, it sounded like St. Patrick's Day on Third Avenue.

And then, abruptly, silence.

I squinted, as though to hear better. Silence? Silence.

What had happened? What was happening now? Was Abbie all right?

I should have gone out there, I told myself. Regardless of whether or not I could have gotten out of bed, regardless of the fact that I was naked and weaponless and too weak to move, I should have gone out there and done what I could to help. If anything had happened to Abbie—

Abbie came hurtling into the room, brought up against the dresser, spun around, and shouted at the guy who'd shoved her, "You stink, you bastard!" She was dressed but disheveled, hair awry, makeup smeared, clothing wrinkled and all twisted around. She was the most insanely beautiful thing I'd ever seen in my life.

My old comrade with the gun came through the doorway, pointed the gun at Abbie as though he was pointing a finger at her, and said, "You ain't no lady."

"And you're a gentleman," she snapped. She turned away from him and came over to me. "How are you, Chet?" she said. "Did they do anything to you?"

I was lying flat on my back, sheet and blanket tucked up around my neck. I blinked up at her, and I felt like an absolute lummox. "How are *you*?" I said. "Did they do anything—"

"Them," she said with total disdain.

The man with the gun said, "Lady, you're outa your mind. My partner would of been dead within his rights to let you have it. You know that? You know what you done to him, if I'd been in his place I'd of shot you down like some kind of wild beast. I think you're nuts or something."

"You force your way in here—" she shouted, blazing at him, all set to start brawling again, and I could see by his face that what she was going to get this time was at the very least a hit on the head from the gun-butt, and I reached out and grabbed her hand and said, "Abbie, cool it."

She tugged, trying to get her hand free. "These people think they can—"

"They can, Abbie," I said. "They've got guns. Don't try their patience."

"That's right," the man with the gun said. "You just listen to him, lady, he's got sense. You been trying our patience, and you shouldn't ought to do that. You should ought to soak your head in some brains for a while and think about things. Like we don't want to give you two any more trouble than we have to, so why make us make things tough on you?"

"That's right," I said. "That's exactly right." I tugged on Abbie's hand, like pulling a bell rope to get the butler, and said, "Abbie, they don't want to kill us or they'd have done it already. Sit down, why don't you, and let's see what they want."

"That's a good thought, pal," the man with the gun said. "You just sit down on the bed there, lady, and let's conduct this like civilized people and not like a bunch of crazy nuts."

Abbie, her attention finally caught by my bell-rope pulling, turned to me and said, "Those two *forced* their way into this apartment, absolutely *forced* their way in. Am I going to stand for that?"

"When they have guns in their hands," I said, "yes. Yes, you are going to stand for it. At least until we know what's what."

Movement attracted my attention to the doorway. I blinked.

There was a guy standing there. He was wearing a white shirt, the left sleeve of which was torn off and absolutely gone. Also, several buttons were missing and the pocket was ripped half-off and was dangling there. He was wearing black trousers, and the right leg was ripped from knee down to cuff. He had an angry-looking bruise just above his left eye, and he was holding a wet wash-cloth to his right cheek. He had long black hair in wild disorder on top of his head, like Stan Laurel, and he overall had the stunned look of somebody who's just been in a train wreck.

"Good God," I said.

In a weak and disbelieving voice this apparition said to Abbie, "You chipped my cap."

"Serves you right," Abbie said.

"I don't believe it," he said. He turned to his partner, the man with the gun, and said, "Ralph, she chipped my cap. Right in the front of my mouth." He opened his mouth and pointed at one of his teeth with the hand that wasn't holding the washcloth to his cheek. Trying to talk with his mouth open he said, "Do you know how nuch that cat cost ne? Do you hathe any idea at *aw*?"

"You forced your way in here," Abbie told him, "and you deserve whatever you get."

"Ralth," the walking wounded said, still holding his mouth open and pointing to the crippled tooth, "I'n gonna kill er. I'n gonna nurder her. I'n gonna *dlast!*"

"Get hold of yourself, Benny," Ralph said. "You know what Sol said. He wants to talk to these two."

I said, "Sol? Solomon Napoli?"

Ralph turned and looked at me. "That's the one, pal," he said. He crooked a finger at me. "Time for you to get up outa there," he said. "Sol's waiting."

I let go of Abbie's hand, preparatory to rising, but she grabbed it again, sat on the bed beside me, put her other arm on the pillow around my head, leaned protectively over me so that I was peeking at everybody over her right breast, and turned to Ralph to say, "He's not supposed to move. The doctor said he isn't supposed to move for a week. He was *shot* last night."

"We know," Ralph said. "We saw it happen. That's one of the things Sol wants to talk to him about."

I said, "You saw it happen?" But I was drowned out by Abbie, saying, "I don't care who wants to see Chet, he can't be moved."

"Shut up, lady," Ralph said. "I've had all of you I'm going to take."

"It's okay, Abbie," I said, struggling to get out from her protective circle. "I feel pretty good now, I could get up. Just so I don't have to move fast or anything, I'll be fine, I know I will." And I sat up.

Abbie touched my bare shoulder. She looked worried. She said, "Are you sure, Chet? The doctor said—"

"Let him alone, lady," Ralph said. "He knows what he's doing."

She glared at him, but for once she didn't say anything.

I said, "What about my clothes?"

"They were all bloody," she said. "I ran out and took them to the cleaner's this morning."

Ralph went over to the closet, opened it, and pulled out some clothing. "How about this stuff?" he said, and tossed it beside me on the bed.

"That's not mine," I said. "That was Tommy's."

"You can wear it," he said. "Be my guest."

Did I want to wear a murdered man's clothing? I didn't think so. I looked at Ralph, feeling very helpless, and didn't say anything. In the meantime he was going to the dresser and opening drawers. He tossed me underwear and socks and said, "There. Now get dressed."

I said, "Tommy was shorter than me."

"So don't button all the buttons," he said.

I looked at the clothing, at Ralph, at the clothing, at Abbie, at the clothing. There didn't seem to be any choice.

Abbie said, "Chet, are you sure you're up to this?"

I wasn't, but I said, "Sure I'm sure. I feel fine."

"Get up from there, lady," Ralph said. "Let him up."

Abbie reluctantly got to her feet. She looked at me worriedly and said, "I'll turn my back." She did so, and folded her arms, and said coldly to Ralph, "If anything happens to him because of this, I'll hold you responsible."

"Sure, lady," said Ralph.

I pushed the covers back, surprised at how much they weighed. I put my legs over the side of the bed, stood up, and fell down. I had no balance at all, no equilibrium, no control. I just went on over, like a duck in a shooting gallery.

Abbie, of course, heard me hit the floor. She spun around and yelled my name, but what I heard more than that was Benny's exasperated "He's faking, Ralph. Let's just bump him now."

"I'm all right," I said. "I can do it." I pushed with my hands, my head and torso came up, and then my arms failed and I flopped onto my nose like a fish.

"God damn it," said Ralph.

"He can't *help* it!" Abbie cried. "He's wounded, can't you see that? Do you *like* seeing him fall on the floor?"

"I do," Benny said. "I'd like to see him fall out a window."

Ralph said, "Shut up, Benny. Okay, lady, we'll leave him here. He can talk, can't he?"

"I can talk," I told the floor.

"That's good. Come on, Benny."

Hands gripped me. I was lifted, the floor receding,

and dumped on the bed like a bag of laundry. I bounced, and just lay there. It must have been Abbie who covered me up.

Ralph said, "Watch them, Benny, but don't do nothing."

Benny growled.

I was rolling over, a slow and painful process. I got over in time to see Ralph leaving and Benny glowering at me.

Abbie said, "Are you hungry?"

"Yes," I said. "I am very hungry."

"I'll get you something," she said, and got up from the bed and started for the door.

Benny blocked the way, saying, "Where do you think you're goin?"

"To the kitchen," she said coldly.

I said, "Don't worry, I'm not going anywhere."

He glared at me. "You better not," he said. Then, to Abbie, he said, "And I got my eye on you."

She disdained to answer. She left the room, and Benny went after her.

I sat there alone a minute, thinking my gloomy thoughts, and then I noticed a telephone on the bedside table.

Call the police? I remembered what Abbie had said about the cops, the chance of getting a crook on the same payroll as Tommy, but thinking about it I decided the chance of a crooked cop was still better than the certainty of a couple of crooks, which was what I had now.

I reached out and picked up the phone.

I heard, "—could tell us— Hold on a second, boss."

"Right."

I heard the small thud of a receiver being put down on a table. Very gently I put my own receiver back in its cradle. I lay down in bed, covered myself to the chin, folded my arms over my chest, looked at the ceiling, and tried to look absolutely innocent.

Ralph walked in. He looked disgusted. Without glancing at me at all he walked around the bed, reached down to the baseboard beside the bedside table, and yanked the phone wire out of the box. He then straightened, gave me a look, and said, "You got no brains at all."

I looked sheepish.

He shook his head, turned away, and left the room.

Nothing happened for about five minutes, and then Abbie came, carrying a tray and followed by Benny. Benny took the chair in the far corner and Abbie put the tray down on the foot of the bed. She helped me sit up, adjusted the pillows behind me, and put the tray on my lap, its little feet straddling my legs.

Clear chicken broth. Buttered toast, two slices. Tea with lemon. A dish of vanilla ice cream.

I ate everything in sight, while Abbie sat on the edge of the bed and watched me in approval.

At one point, taking a break from eating, I said, "How long was I out? This is Thursday, isn't it?"

"Yes. You practically slept the day away. I was afraid you were dying there for a while, you just lay in one place and didn't move at all."

"My father must be worried," I said. "I always call him when—"

"I called him," she said. "I told him you were all right. I couldn't tell him where you were, in case somebody put pressure on him, so I sort of let him get the idea you were shacked up with me. So he wouldn't be worried."

Benny didn't seem to be listening to our conversation. I looked at her and said, "Shacked up, huh?"

She slapped my blanketed knee. "You're too weak to

be thinking about things like that," she said, and smiled
at me.

"I'll get well soon," I said, and Ralph came in.

Abbie turned to him. "What now?"

"We wait," he said.

"For what?"

"For Sol," he said.

I said, "He's coming here? Solomon Napoli?"

"Yeah," said Ralph. "He wants to talk to you."

15

By the time the doorbell sounded nearly an hour later I
was about ready to come apart like a broken kaleidoscope.
Abbie was sitting beside me on the bed, and I reached out
and grabbed her hand, and we gave each other nervous
smiles that were supposed to be encouraging, and I began
to blink a lot.

There were voices in the hall, and then Ralph came in,
and behind him three other guys.

Solomon Napoli?

Even in my astonishment there was no question which
of the three was Napoli. The two on either side were just
hoods, Benny and Ralph all over again, just better-dressed.
It was the one in the middle who was Solomon Napoli.

I couldn't help staring at him. He was barely five feet
tall, for one thing, the top of his head just about reaching
the shoulders of the two guys flanking him. He was
dressed very formally, as though on his way to an opera
first night. But the most amazing thing was his head,
which was too big for his body. Not enough to look de-

formed, just enough to make him look imposing, commanding, impressive. Leonine, a leonine head, and with the thick mane of hair that goes with it. A square jaw, magnificent white capped teeth, strong level eyes, a healthy hint of tan. He was about forty, with the smooth weathered look of a man who keeps himself in shape with handball and self-esteem.

And he was smiling! He came in smiling like a politician opening a campaign headquarters, his teeth sparkling, his eyes showing bright interest in everything they saw, his stride youthful and determined-without-crabbiness. He came in, and his flankers stopped just inside the door, and he came over to the bed, hand held out, saying to Abbie in a resonant voice, "Miss McKay! How do you do? I thought very highly of your brother. A shame, a shame."

Through my own paralysis I could see that Abbie, too, was mesmerized. Her hand left mine, she rose uncertainly to her feet, she took his outstretched hand, in a vague and uncertain voice she said, "Uh, thank you. Thank you."

He turned her off, turned me on. You could see him do it. He kept her hand, but he looked past her at me, his eyes and smile full of candle power, saying, "And how's our patient?"

"Okay, I guess," I mumbled.

"Good. Good." He turned me off, turned Abbie on. "My dear, if you'll go into the living room for just a few minutes, Chester and I have one or two things we want to discuss. We won't be long. Ralph."

"Here, boss," said Ralph, and in his saying that the spell was broken. I had been totally hypnotized by Napoli up till now, his magnetism, his aura, the massive presence with which he filled the room. It wasn't until Ralph said,

"Here, boss," that I remembered who this man really was. Solomon Napoli. Gangster.

I had to remember that. For my own good I had to remember it.

Suddenly I was twice as frightened as before. A cigar-chewing tough-talking obvious hood would have terrified me, but I would have understood him, I would at least have felt I knew what I was dealing with. But this man? I remembered how Sid Falco's very ordinariness had been the most frightening thing about him, and this was Sid's boss. A super-Sid.

I pulled the covers up around my chin and waited to see what would happen next.

Ralph led Abbie out of the room, she glancing back at me with a worried look just before going out of sight, and then I was alone with the crocodiles. One of the new hoods brought a chair up beside the bed, Solomon Napoli sat down in it, and we were off.

He had turned me on again. "I guess you had a close call, Chester," he said. His smile showed sympathy, but I didn't count on it.

"I guess I did," I said warily.

"Who would take a shot at you, Chester?" he asked, and now his smile implied an urge to be helpful, but I wasn't about to count on that one either.

"I guess the people Tommy worked for," I said.

"Why would they do that?" His smile was as delicate an instrument as a theremin, and now it projected polite curiosity.

I shook my head. "I don't know. I suppose they think I had something to do with killing Tommy."

Can a smile be threatening? Can it glint as though it would bite? Napoli sat back in the chair and his smile changed again and he said, "Chester, I'm a very busy man. I'm due at the Modern Museum in"—he looked at his watch—"forty minutes for a meeting of the board of trustees. Please just take it for granted we already know your involvement, we already know Frank's involvement, a lot of wide-eyed innocent lying isn't going to get you anywhere. There are a few things I want you to tell me, after which I promise you you will not find me an unreasonable man. You know Droble's people are after you now, it shouldn't take too much intelligence to realize that under my wing is the safest place for you right now."

I closed my eyes. "Oh, go ahead and shoot," I said. "I really can't take any more." And at that moment I think I really meant it.

Nothing at all happened. I lay on my back, head against the pillow, eyes closed, hands folded over my breast, already laid out you might say, and absolutely nothing happened.

Well, it wasn't up to *me* to make the next move. I was done. I went on lying there.

Napoli said, "Chester, you don't impress me."

I continued to lie there. My eyes continued to be closed. But my despair, if that's what it was, had already been diluted by my unsinkable liking for life, and I could feel myself beginning to tense up again. I had shut down like this out of conviction, but I was staying shut down as a kind of technique, mostly because I couldn't think of anything else to do.

Napoli, with irritation finally creeping into his voice, said, "This is ridiculous. I have thirty-five minutes to get— Chester, I don't *have* to give you a break."

"A break?" I said. I didn't open my eyes, because I

knew if I was looking at him I wouldn't be able to talk. Keeping my eyes shut and my body still, it was almost like talking on the phone, and I can talk to *anybody* on the phone. So my eyes were shut as I said, "You call that giving me a break? Getting a lot of wrong ideas into your head about who I am and what I've done, calling me a liar when I just so much as *hint* at the truth, sending people around to threaten me with guns, you threaten me with your *teeth* for God's sake, you think—"

"Now just a—"

"No!" I was thrashing around in the bed by now, waving my arms to make my points, but my eyes stayed squeezed shut. "Ever since Tommy was killed," I yelled, "one God damn fool after another comes after me with guns. Nobody asks *me* what I'm doing, oh, no, everybody knows too God damn much to ask *me* anything, everybody's so God damn *smart*. Those clowns in the garage, and then Abbie, and then whoever shot at me, and now you. You people don't know what you're *doing!* You're so God damn *smug*, you know—"

"Keep your voice down!"

"The hell I will! I've been pushed around long enough! I've got a—"

I stopped because a hand was clamped over my mouth and I could no longer talk. The hand was also over my nose and I could no longer breathe. My eyes opened.

One of the new hoods was standing over me, his arm a straight line from his shoulder to my face. He was leaning a little, pushing my head deeper into the pillow. I blinked, and looked past his knuckles at Napoli.

Napoli at last had stopped smiling. He was looking thoughtful now, studying me with his arms folded and the side of one finger idly stroking the line of his jaw. He seemed to be thinking things over.

I needed to breathe. I said, "Mmmm, mmm."

"Shut up," he said carelessly, and went back to thinking.

"Mm *mmm* mmmm," I said.

"Maybe," he said. "Maybe there *is* a different explanation."

Things were turning a darkish red. There was a roaring deep inside my skull. I began to thrash around like a fish in the bottom of a boat.

Napoli pointed at me the finger with which he'd been stroking himself. "*That* won't do you any good," he said. "You just be quiet and let me think."

"Mm mmm *mmmmmmm!*" I said.

"We saw you with Frank Tarbok," he said. "We followed you and the other two from your place. Now you talk about the clowns in the garage as though you don't know Frank, as though you don't work for him, don't know anything about him. Is that possible?"

I scratched feebly at the hand between me and air. Far away, up through the red haze, the hood looked uncaring down the length of his arm at me. I tugged at his pinkie, to no avail.

Napoli was still talking, slowly, thoughtfully, considering all sides of the matter. I could no longer make out the words, the roaring in my head was too loud, it blotted out all other sounds. But through the darkening haze I could still see him, see his mouth moving, his brow furrowed in thought, his eyes gazing into the middle distance. How civilized he looked, but the red haze was closing in and I could no longer make him out clearly.

My head was a balloon, a red balloon, being filled up and up, filled up and up, the pressure increasing on the inside, the pressure increasing too much, the pressure increasing.

The last thing I heard was the balloon exploding.

16

How had I gotten so tiny? Swimming upside down in a cup of tea, warm orange-red tea, rolling around, needing air, wanting to get to the surface but sinking instead to the bottom of the cup. White china cup. Looking up through all the tea at the light in the world up there, knowing I had to get out of this cup before I drowned. Before somebody drank me. Holding my breath, orange-red in the face, the weight of the tea too much for me, pressing me down. Straining upward, pushing against the bottom of the cup, and then everything confused. Had the cup broken? I was falling out the side, tea splashing all around me, white cup fragments, falling out, falling down, landing hard on elbow and shoulder and cheek.

I was on the floor surrounded by legs, feet, and even though I was awake now I cowered as though I was still tiny and the feet would crush me. My left arm was pinned under me, but I managed to get the right arm up over my head.

Then hands were holding me, lifting me, voices were jabbering, and the confusions of the dream faded away, leaving the confusions of reality in their wake. When last I'd heard from the real world, somebody was strangling me.

I was placed on the bed and the covers drawn up over me. People were speaking, but I kept my arm up over my head and didn't look at anything or listen to anything until Abbie touched my shoulder and spoke my name and asked me how I was. Then I came out slowly, warily, like a turtle in a French kitchen, to see Abbie sitting on the bed and leaning over me, with a lot of people I didn't like in the background.

Abbie asked me again how I was, and I muttered something, and the leader of the pack came forward to say, "I want you to know that wasn't intentional, Chester. I don't do business that way."

I looked at him.

"I hope there's no hard feelings," he said, and the expression his face wore now was concerned. Not that I believed there was ever any relationship between what he was thinking and what his face showed.

I looked at Abbie, and she gave me a look that said, "Be circumspect." So I looked back at Solomon Napoli and said, "No damage done." My throat was a little hoarse, so that my voice rasped a little, slightly undercutting the meaning of my words, but not so much that he couldn't ignore the discrepancy, if he chose.

He chose. "That's good," he said. He glanced at his watch, gave me a smile that I guess was supposed to be friendly, and said, "I missed my meeting to be sure you were all right."

"I'm all right," I said.

"Good. Then we can get back to what we were talking about. Miss McKay?"

So Abbie squeezed my hand and went away, leaving me once again with Napoli and his two elves. Napoli seated himself in his bedside chair once again and said, "I've been thinking over what you said, and it's entirely possible you're telling the truth. It could be you're just an innocent bystander in all this, you don't work for Droble at all."

Droble. Was that one of the names Detective Golderman had asked me about? It seemed to me it might have been, but I was in no condition to pursue the question. I didn't really care one way or the other.

Napoli went on, "But if that's true, if you are an innocent bystander, how is it you're underfoot all the time? You found the body, you had a meeting with Frank Tarbok, you kept hanging around this apartment, you're traveling with McKay's sister, you got yourself shot at. An awful lot of activity for an innocent bystander."

"I've been trying to collect my money," I said.

He raised an eyebrow. "Money?"

"I had a bet on a horse and he came in. That's why I came here the time I found Tommy dead. I was coming to get my money."

Napoli frowned. "And all of your activity since then has been concerned with collecting it?"

"Right. With Tommy dead I didn't know who should pay me. I wanted to ask Tommy's wife, but she's disappeared some place."

"And the meeting with Tarbok? Didn't you collect your money then?"

"I didn't ask," I said. "I didn't think to ask till it was all over."

The frown deepened, grew frankly skeptical. "Then what *did* you talk about, you and Frank?"

I said, "Frank Tarbok is the man in the garage, right? The one I was taken to see Tuesday night."

"Of course," he said.

"You say of course, but I didn't know his name till just now. He wanted to see me because he wanted to know if I worked for you."

That surprised him, and he actually showed it. "For me?"

"He thought maybe I killed Tommy for you," I said. "So he had those other two guys grab me and take me to him, and he asked me questions. The same as you."

Napoli grew thoughtful again. "So he thought I might have had Tommy taken care of, eh? Mmmm. I wonder why."

"He didn't say," I said.

"But you convinced him," he said. "Convinced him you didn't work for me."

"Sure."

"Then why did he try to kill you last night?"

"I don't know," I said. "Maybe he changed his mind. I don't know."

He sat back, smiling reminiscently. "It's a good thing for you he did," he said.

I wasn't sure I understood. I said, "A good thing he tried to kill me?"

He nodded, still with the reminiscent smile. "If he hadn't," he said, "you'd be dead now."

That didn't make any sense at all. I said, "Why?"

"Because," he said, "I'd ordered you shot. What do you think my people were doing outside your house? They were there to kill you."

I stared at him. A man had just calmly told me to my face that he'd ordered me murdered. What was the correct social response to a thing like that? I just lay there and stared at him. He was unconcerned. The whole thing struck *him* as no more than amusing. Mildly amusing.

"And the funny part of it is," he said, incredibly enough, "*I* was going to have you killed for the same reason as Walt Droble. I figured you'd killed McKay, you were working under Frank Tarbok."

I shook my head. "No," I said. "No."

He held a hand up. "I'll accept that," he said. "I'll accept it now. Naturally, I'll have to check it. My men did the right thing. They were about to contract you out when somebody else took a shot at you. So they did nothing. They followed you here, and phoned me to tell me the situation, and I told them to get you, if you were still alive, and bring you to me to explain yourself. To explain why *other* people are trying to kill you when *I* want you killed." His smile turned chummy, pals together, confidential buddies. "I found it confusing," he confided.

I nodded, vaguely. I was still stuck on a phrase he'd used, a euphemism that was new to me but which I found as grisly as anything I'd ever heard. "They were about to contract you out," he'd said. "Contract you out."

For Pete's sake. Contract me out? Is that any way to talk about something as brutal and final as murdering me in front of my own house? It sounds like a magazine subscription lapsing. "Sorry we didn't get your reorder, we'll just have to contract you out."

Napoli looked at me. "What's the matter?"

"I don't know what's going on," I said faintly.

"You mean, why should I think you were responsible for killing Tommy McKay?"

"That. And why should you care? And who are all the people you mention all the time? Droble, and Frank Tarbok."

"Frank Tarbok," he said, "works for Walter Droble. Walt is what you might call a competitor of mine. There are territories he has, there are territories I have. For some time there've been a few territories in dispute between us."

"And Tommy was in the middle?"

"Not exactly. McKay worked for Droble, but was also in my employ. I am nearly ready to make a move I'd been planning for some time, and McKay was a part of that move. You'll forgive me if I don't get more specific."

"That's all right," I said quickly. "I don't want to know too much."

"That's wise," he agreed, smiling at me, pleased with me. He looked at his watch and said, "I must be off. You take it easy now."

"I will," I said.

He got to his feet. "Get well soon," he said, and smiled, and left.

17

I had two or three minutes to be alone with my thoughts after Napoli and his bodyguards left, and then Ralph and Abbie came into the room. Ralph said to me, "The boss says, as long as you're good I leave you alone. Got the idea?"

"Yes," I said.

He turned to Abbie. "You, too?"

"Me, too," she said.

"Good," he said, and went out and shut the door. We both heard the key turn in the lock.

Abbie immediately came over and sat on the edge of

the bed. Looking concerned, she put a hand on my fore-head, saying, "Are you all right?"

"I'm fine," I said.

"You've been through so much," she said.

I said, "What about you? Did they give you a bad time?"

She shrugged the whole crew of them away with one shoulder. "They don't bother me," she said. "They just talk tough."

"I'm not so sure about that," I said, and went on to tell her Napoli's amusing anecdote about how my being shot in the head had saved my life.

She was amazed. "You mean he actually sat here and *said* that?"

"He thought it was funny."

"That's the most insulting thing I ever heard in my life," she said. "What did you say to him?"

"Nothing."

"Well, *I* would have—"

I took her hand. "I know you would," I said. "You've got no more self-preservation instinct than a lemming. But I'm twenty-nine years old, and I don't think that's enough. I'm supposed to get forty-one more, and I want them."

She said, "What's going on now? They wouldn't tell me anything."

"Napoli is going to check my story," I said. "When he finds out I really don't work for Frank Tarbok and Walter Droble, he'll leave me alone. He'll call Ralph and tell him everything's okay, and Ralph will leave."

She spread her hands, saying, "Then we're all right, aren't we?"

"*You* are," I said. "I still have Tarbok and Droble after me."

"Who are they?"

I'd forgotten she wasn't up to date on all that. "Droble was Tommy's boss," I said. "Tarbok works for Droble. Tarbok is the one I was taken to see Tuesday night."

"Ah. Why can't Napoli tell Droble you're all right?"

"Because Napoli and Droble are enemies," I told her, and went on to explain as much as I knew of the gambling barons' feudal wars, including Tommy's part in it all.

When I was done, she said, "That would be Tommy, all right. Play both sides against the middle every time. He always had to copper his bets."

"Well, he left *me* in a mess."

Sitting back, frowning, gazing at the opposite wall, Abbie said, "If both sides were after you for killing Tommy, that means neither of them is the murderer. It isn't a gang killing at all."

"No," I said. "*I'm* the gang killing. Tommy was extra-curricular."

"Yes," she said. "And Louise is still missing. I knew it was her."

"You don't know it," I said. "You think it, and you could be right, but you don't *know* it."

"Who else is there?" she demanded.

I didn't know. "I don't know," I said.

"I'm hardly jumping to conclusions," she said, "when I pick the last one left."

Since I didn't have any answer to that one, I stopped thinking about it, and instead my mind went back to something that had struck me a long time ago. I'd been meaning to ask Abbie about it, but then things started to happen, and I forgot. So I asked now. "What about the doctor?" I said.

She stared at me. "The doctor? Tommy's doctor? Why would *he* kill him?"

"No, no. The doctor that took care of my head. The one you called, that helped you carry me up here."

"He didn't even know Tommy," she said. "He never even knew me before last night. What makes you think *he's* the killer?"

Confusion was setting in again. "I don't," I said. "I'm not talking about the killing at all. I'm talking about something else now."

"I was talking about the killing," she said, "and who could have done it, and there's nobody left but Louise."

"All right," I said, not wanting to go around that barn again. "You're probably right."

"So what's all this about the doctor?"

"I was shot in the head," I said. "Aren't doctors supposed to report gunshot wounds to the police?"

"They're supposed to," she agreed.

"Then shouldn't we be getting cops here sooner or later, asking questions?"

She shook her head. "He won't report it. I told him you were my boyfriend, and my husband shot you, and we couldn't stand the scandal and notoriety, and I promised him his name would never come up if there was a police investigation."

"And he agreed?"

"I also bribed him a hundred dollars." She winked. "You have to know what neighborhood to get your doctor in."

"You bribed him?"

"It was the only thing to do," she said, and shrugged.

That girl just kept amazing me. I had known capable competent take-charge women before, but none of them came within a mile of Abbie McKay. I shook my head and said, "You're a wonder. How about taking care of Tarbok and Droble for me?"

"Sure thing," she said. "First thing in the morning." Then she looked at her watch and said, "Which will be coming along any minute. I've got to go to the funeral tomorrow, too. At ten o'clock." She looked around and said, "It looks like we spend the night co-ed."

"I'd offer you the bed," I said, "but I'm not sure I can get out of it."

"That's okay," she said. "We can share."

"Share?"

"In your condition," she said, "what virtue I have left is probably safe. Just move over to the side a little bit. No, the inside, I don't want to have to crawl over you all the time."

"Yeah, we wouldn't want that," I said, and hunched myself over against the wall. What's that old image about a sick person, when they're about to die, they turn their face to the wall? That's what ran through my head when I got over by the wall, of course. My mind isn't always so full of morbid notions, but even Mary Poppins would have had a grim thought or two if she'd had my last four days.

Meanwhile Abbie was stripping to her underwear again, the second night in a row I'd seen her like that. I said, "Hey."

She glanced at me. "What?"

"I may be wounded," I said, "but I'm not a eunuch. I was shot up at this end, up at the head."

She grinned and said, "Oh, don't be silly, Chet. You've seen girls before."

"That's perfectly true," I said. "But."

She looked at me. "But what?"

"Nothing," I said. "That was the whole sentence."

"Oh, you'll be all right," she said, and went over and switched off the light.

I heard her moving around in the dark, and then the bed sagged, and then a knee touched my near leg. It moved around a little, the covers shifted this way and that, the knee left, a hip touched my hip, the hip left, the covers settled down, she sighed in contentment, and there was silence.

I said, "This is ridiculous."

"What's the matter?"

"I'm in bed with you."

"Haven't you ever been in bed with a girl before?"

"Not like this, Abbie."

"It's kind of a nice change of pace," she said.

"Change of pace," I said.

"Sure," she said.

"Sure," I said.

She went to sleep before I did.

18

My arms were around somebody. Somebody warm. Somebody soft. Somebody who smelled musky and nice. Somebody female.

Female? My eyes popped open, and I was looking at a lot of tangled blond hair. I blinked at the hair, felt the warm female body snuggled against mine, and for just a second I was afraid I was in terrible trouble. Then I remembered. I *was* in terrible trouble, but not that kind.

I must have moved or something, because all at once the mass of hair lifted, like a drawbridge going up, and two wide-open blue eyes were three inches from my face, staring at me. I blinked. They blinked.

I said, "Good morning."

She jumped a mile, or at least out of my arms, and sat beside me, holding the covers up against herself and staring down at me.

I said, "Abbie, this was your idea. You were very cool about the whole thing last night, so don't fly off the handle now."

Comprehension flowed into her eyes as though poured in from above, and she said, "Chet?" As though to be sure what she was seeing was right.

"It's me," I said.

She shook her head, fluffed her hair, scrubbed her face with her palms. "Whoof!" she said. "Boy, did I sleep!"

"Me, too," I said.

She smiled at me. "That was kind of nice. Together like that."

"We'll have to do it again sometime," I said. "When I'm stronger."

Her smile turned a touch lewd. "It might be fun," she said.

I reached out and touched the bare skin of her side, between panties and bra. "It might be."

She pushed my hand away and got out of bed. "You shouldn't excite yourself," she said. "You're still sick."

"*I'm* not exciting me."

"I'll get dressed. You look away or something. How are you this morning, anyway?"

"All cured."

"Oh foo." She put on her robe. "Now. How do you feel?"

It was a peculiarly uninteresting robe, a pale blue terrycloth with a pale blue terrycloth sash. I turned my attention inward instead, and said, "I'm starving."

"That's a good sign." She picked up her watch, wound it, put it on, looked at it. "I've got to hurry. How do you like your eggs?"

"Over easy. And coffee regular."

"Tea," she said.

"For breakfast?"

"Make believe you're English." She went over and knocked on the door, and after a minute Ralph let her out. He glanced in at me and decided to leave the door open.

Abbie came back a while later with a tray for me, and dressed while I ate. Surprisingly, I did not stab myself in the cheek with my fork. When she was dressed she took the tray away again and came back in her orange fur coat and said, "I'm off to the funeral. Isn't this an awful thing to be wearing? But it's all I have."

"You look great," I said.

"Do I? Thank you." She smiled and frowned at once. "But you're not supposed to look great at funerals."

"Don't worry about it," I told her. "Nobody will complain."

"You say very nice things," she said. "See you."

"See you."

She left, and Ralph came in to help me to the bathroom. He was morose and bored, and when he had me back in bed he asked me if I played gin rummy, asking in a fatalistic way as though sure I was going to say no. He perked right up when I said yes, went and got a deck of cards and a pencil and a score pad, and we settled down to business.

An hour and a quarter later, at a tenth of a cent a point, I was thirteen dollars to the good and Ralph was looking morose again. Not bored, just morose. Then we heard the unmistakable sound of a key turning in a lock, and Ralph was suddenly on his feet and a gun had appeared magically from within his clothing and leaped into his hand.

I said, "That's Ab—"

He waved the gun urgently at me to shut up, and whispered, "I told her to ring so's I'd know it was her."

Oh, good. Fine.

We heard the door open. Ralph pointed at the closet, at himself. He put his finger to his lips. I nodded. He drifted away into the closet, pulling the door not quite shut behind him.

The cards were laid out for a gin hand. I heard the hall door close. I grabbed the cards up and held them in my left hand as I stared at the doorway, holding the cards like the hero holding a crucifix in a vampire movie.

Someone was walking. The bandage around my head began to itch.

Detective Golderman appeared in the doorway, looking toward the living room. He glanced in at me, as though at an empty room, and did a double-take. He took his hands out of his pockets, stepped to the doorway, pushed his hat back from his forehead, and said, "You."

"Hello," I said. I waved the deck of cards in greeting.

19

"You do get around, don't you?" He came into the room, glanced this way and that. He didn't pay any special attention to the closet.

"I guess I do," I said. And I was probably more nervous now than when I thought it might be somebody coming to kill me. At least a murderer wouldn't be asking me a lot of difficult questions, and I had the feeling that's exactly what Golderman was going to start doing.

Which he did, right off the bat. He came over to the bed, looked down at it, and said, "Playing solitaire for money?"

I looked down. Crumpled bills, coppered quarters, loose change all on the blanket. "Uh," I said.

He sat down, in the chair Ralph had just left. He watched me, waiting for an answer.

Ralph. Would he know who this was? He might think it was one of Droble's men, and come out and shoot him. I said, "Well, Detective Golderman, the fact is, I was playing gin rummy with Abbie before she left."

"Abbie?"

"Abbie McKay. Tommy's sister."

He nodded. "She's at the funeral?"

"She'll be back afterwards," I said. "Is she the one you wanted to see?"

"Just looking around, Chester. What happened to your head?"

I'd been waiting for that question, I'd known it was

coming, it had to be coming, and I was fascinated to know what I would say in response to it. So here it was, and what did I say? I said, "My head?" As though I hadn't realized I had one. And touched the bandage.

"Your head," he agreed, and nodded at it.

"I fell down," I said. "I slipped on the ice outside and fell down."

"That's too bad. Did you see a doctor?"

"Yes. Abbie called one. He came and he put this bandage on. He said I shouldn't move for a while, that's why I'm still here."

"It didn't happen today?"

"No. Wednesday night."

"Must have been a bad fall."

Why did I always feel as though Detective Golderman was disbelieving me? Maybe because I was always telling him lies. "It was," I said. "I got like a cut on the side of my head." I made vague motions with the hand holding the cards.

"You're lucky you didn't have to go to the hospital," he said.

"Yeah, I guess I was."

"Lucky you weren't killed," he said. "You an old friend of Abbie McKay's?"

"No, uh. I just met her a little while ago."

"When was that?"

"Uh, Wednesday."

He smiled faintly. "You might say you fell for her on first sight, eh?"

"Heh heh," I said.

"Nice of her to go out of her way to take care of you," he said. "After just meeting and all."

"Yeah, well…Yeah, it was."

He looked around the room again. "I take it Mrs. McKay isn't staying here these days. Tommy McKay's wife."

"No. No, she isn't."

He glanced at me, with that casualness I distrusted. "Where is she staying, do you know?"

"No, I don't," I said. "I haven't seen her since Monday. Since Tommy was killed."

"That isn't her in the closet, in other words," he said.

I said, "Uh. In the closet?"

"In the closet," he agreed. "If Tommy's sister is at the funeral and you haven't seen his wife since Monday, that can't be either one of them in the closet, can it?"

"Uh...Well..."

"So it has to be somebody else," he said. "Doesn't it, Chester?"

"I..." I made a helpless gesture with the deck of cards, and Ralph came out of the closet. He looked morose again.

Detective Golderman casually turned his head and looked at Ralph. "Do I know you?"

"No," Ralph told him.

"You waiting for a bus in there?"

"Developing pictures," Ralph said.

"Ah," said Detective Golderman. "Would you have some sort of identification on you?"

"Yeah," said Ralph. He dragged his wallet out and extracted a driver's license from it, which he handed over to Detective Golderman.

Detective Golderman reached into an inner pocket for notebook and pencil and copied some information into it from Ralph's license, then handed the license back and put the notebook away. Finally he got to his feet and said, "Ralph, you wouldn't mind if I frisked you, would you?"

Ralph's face showed that the thought didn't make him happy, but all he said was, "If you got to." And lifted his arms up at his sides.

"Thank you, Ralph," Detective Golderman said, and patted him thoroughly all over without finding the gun I knew Ralph possessed. When he was done, he glanced at the closet and said, "I wonder if I should go over the closet, too."

Ralph made an after-you-Alphonse gesture and said, "Be my guest." But his tone was still morose and not at all sarcastic.

"Not worth the aggravation," Detective Golderman decided, and looked back at me again. I'd known he would get back to me again sooner or later, and I hadn't been looking forward to it. "Chester," he said, "you haven't told me the entire truth, have you?"

"Uh," I said. That seemed to be my favorite word with him. "About what?" I said.

"Well, Ralph, for instance," he said. "You hadn't planned on introducing me at all, had you?"

"Well," I said. "I felt it was up to him. Whether he wanted to come out or not."

"Still and all, Chester," he said, "you did hold out on me."

"Yes, sir," I admitted. "I guess I did."

"It would have been a very simple thing, Chester," he said. "When I came in, all you had to do was say, 'I'd like you to meet my friend Ralph Corvaccio in the closet.' Then I would have gone on believing you were somebody I could trust. Somebody whose word I could take on various things." There was nothing for me to say. That's what I said. Detective Golderman stood there looking at me. He seemed to be thinking about things, considering various ways of dealing with me, none pleasant. At last he said, "Do you remember when I came to see you at your house Wednesday?"

"Yes. Sure."

"Do you remember I mentioned some names to you, and asked you if you knew any of those men, or had ever heard of any of them?"

I nodded.

"Do you remember those names?"

"I think so," I said.

"Let's try your memory," he said.

"Frank Tarbok," I said. "Walter Droble. Bugs Bender. Uh, and Solomon Napoli."

"Very good," he said. "And do you remember what you told me?"

"That I didn't know them."

"Didn't know a thing about them." He jabbed a thumb over his shoulder at Ralph. "Is Ralph an old friend of yours, Chester? Or do you just know him since Wednesday, too?"

"Thursday," I said. "Yesterday."

"Yesterday. In that brief time, Chester, has Ralph mentioned to you who he works for?"

"Well—"

"Do you know who Ralph works for, Chester?"

I looked at Ralph, but he was moodily studying the back of Detective Golderman's head and was of no help to me. In a low voice, not looking at anybody at all, I said, "I think he works for Solomon Napoli."

"Solomon Napoli. That's one of the four men I asked you about, isn't it?"

"Detective Golderman, until I got mixed up in all this stuff, I didn't know any of those people, I swear I didn't. And I don't *want* to know them now, take my word for it."

"Mixed up in all what stuff, Chester?"

"All these people," I said, and limped to a halt. Even if I wanted to tell him what was going on, there was nowhere to begin. I waved my hands vaguely and said, "Ever since Tommy got killed. I got caught up in all this because I'm the guy that found him."

"Is that all, Chester?"

"Yes. That's the worst of it, I'm an innocent bystander and nobody believes me."

"You're very convincing, Chester," he said, "except that I have trouble squaring your innocence with the fact that you seem to be keeping known gangsters in your closet."

"I am *not* keeping anybody in my closet! That was *his* idea!"

"Still, Chester, you—"

The phone rang. Quickly Ralph said, "That's for me. That's the call I been expecting." He started for the door.

Detective Golderman pointed to the phone beside the bed. "Why not answer it there?"

"That one don't work," Ralph said, and left the room.

Detective Golderman looked at the phone. He came over, picked up the receiver, put it to his ear, cradled it again. He bent, looked at the wire under the table, picked it up, fingered the frayed end, glanced at me. I looked at him with my poker face.

He said, "Chester, while we're alone for a minute, is there anything you want to say to me?"

"No," I said. "I've said it all. I'm not hiding anything from anybody."

"I find that hard to believe, Chester," he said.

"Everybody does," I told him.

He dropped the phone wire, walked to the doorway, and stood there a minute, listening to Ralph talking on the phone in the living room: I could hear his voice, too, though I couldn't make out the words, and it sounded as though the major part of the conversation was happening at the other end, with Ralph's part limited mostly to monosyllables.

Detective Golderman looked back at me. He said, "Do you have an explanation for him being here?"

"His boss wouldn't believe me either," I said.

He came back into the room. "Wouldn't believe what?"

"That I wasn't involved in something somehow."

"Involved in what?"

"How do I know? I'm not involved in it, so how would I know what it is?"

"I suppose that makes sense," he said. "So Napoli thinks you're involved in something, and that's why Ralph is here."

"Yes."

"That doesn't explain why Ralph is here," he pointed out.

"He's here," I said, "to wait for a phone call from his boss telling him I'm not involved in anything after all. Then he'll go away."

"What if the phone call says you are involved?"

"It won't, because I'm not."

"But what if it did? What would happen then?"

"I suppose I'd get shot at," I said, stopping myself just barely in time. I'd been about to say *again*, a word Detective Golderman would have leaped on with both feet.

As it was, he had sentence enough to intrigue him. He

said, "Doesn't that worry you? Isn't there a possibility they'll make a mistake?"

"Not this time," I said.

"You wouldn't like to go into the details, would you, Chester?"

I shook my head. "The details are beyond me," I said. "I'm not trying to be a smart aleck or evade the question or anything, the details are just absolutely beyond me and that's all there is to it. There are too many details, and they don't make any sense."

"Try me," he said.

"I wouldn't know where to begin."

"At the beginning."

"I found Tommy McKay dead, and all hell broke loose."

Ralph appeared in the doorway. "That was our friend," he told me. "He says to tell you everything's okay."

"Good," I said. I looked at Detective Golderman. "See?"

"I see," he said. He was looking at Ralph.

Ralph returned the look and said, "You mind if I go away now?"

"I'm not sure," Detective Golderman told him. "I might want to take you along to the station with me and ask some questions."

"You'd waste your time," Ralph told him.

"You're probably right," Detective Golderman said. "All right, Ralph, you can go."

"Thanks," Ralph said. It was impossible to tell whether that was sarcastic or not.

"I'll see you around, more than likely," Detective Golderman told him.

"Yeah, maybe," Ralph said. He looked at me. "You're lucky," he said. "With the cards."

"Uh huh," I said, and he left.

Neither of us said a word till we heard the door close behind Ralph. Then Detective Golderman said, "Well, Chester? Anything you'd like to say now?"

I considered it, I trembled on the brink of telling him the whole thing, but I didn't quite do it. In the first place, when you've told the same lie to a policeman long enough you tend to shy away from admitting the truth. In the second place, the truth by now really was too complicated for a wounded man with a headache to try to explain. And in the third place, I shouldn't talk to anybody without checking with Abbie first, it wouldn't be fair to her.

I believe that third place might have been just an excuse, but any excuse in a storm. I said, "Nothing. Not a thing."

"Very well, Chester," he said. "I'll probably see you around."

"You probably will," I said gloomily, and he left.

20

I was napping over an insoluble hand of solitaire when the doorbell rang. I roused sufficiently to wiggle my knees and knock half the deck off onto the floor, which woke me the rest of the way. My first thought was that my mouth tasted like the inside of a metal garbage can behind a Chinese restaurant, and my second thought was that somebody had rung the bell.

Well, I wasn't going to do anything about it. If it was Abbie, giving the departed Ralph the signal he'd wanted, she'd let herself in eventually. If it wasn't Abbie, I didn't want to have anything to do with them. So I sat there, moving my tongue unhappily over the fur on my teeth, thinking about the fact that my back ached and my head felt fuzzy, and when I heard the hall door open I was surprised to discover that I was scared. I lay there and watched the door.

Abbie. She came in all red-faced and sparkly from the cold air, the orange fur coat making her look like a sexy gift-wrapped present from Olympus, sent me to make up for all the bad stuff that had been happening, and she said, "Hi. You look like death warmed over."

"Thanks," I said. "You look great."

"Thank you. Where's Smilin Jack?"

"He got his phone call and left," I said. "Napoli found me innocent."

"Good. Are you hungry?" She shrugged out of the coat, tossed it on a chair.

"Not till I brush my teeth. Then I'm famished." I threw the covers back. "Was Louise at the funeral?"

"Of course not. Just me, a couple of Tommy's old customers, a business associate or two, and a couple of anonymous old ladies. Not even any detectives around to take notes. Do you need help walking?"

"All I need is a robe," I said.

"Coming up." She went to the closet, got an old brown robe of Tommy's, and carried it over to the bed. "Heavy," she said, frowning, and held the robe up to pat its pockets, from one of which she drew a tough-looking gun. "For Pete's sake," she said. "Is this Tommy's? What a place to keep it."

I laughed, saying, "No, it's Ralph's. He must have forgotten it. I forgot all about it myself."

"Ralph? Ralph was wearing this robe?"

"Let me brush my teeth first," I said. "Then I'll tell you the story."

"I can hardly wait," she said.

With her help I got out of bed and into the robe, and found myself only a little weaker and dizzier than usual. I was somewhat short of breath, and my legs were a trifle unsteady when I tried to walk, but compared to yesterday I was now a giant among men, a force to be reckoned with.

By the time I emerged from the bathroom I felt even better. I went down the hall to the kitchen and found Abbie sitting at the table there, making liverwurst sandwiches. I sat across from her and said, "A policeman came to call. A detective named Golderman. So Ralph hid in the closet. Is it all right for me to have coffee, or am I still limited to tea?"

She looked at me. "A detective?"

"Named Golderman. May I have coffee?"

"How do you feel?"

"Strong like an ox."

She grinned. "Okay. Coffee. But tell me about Ralph and the detective."

So I did, and in the course of the telling she made a pot of coffee. She found certain parts of my story funny, and so did I now that it was all over. Much funnier in the telling than in the living. When I was done, she said, "I think I'd like to meet this Detective Golderman. He sounds interesting."

"A dull man," I said. "With warts. Besides, I think he's married."

She looked askance. "You're jealous and I've never even met the man."

"No, but you want to."

"I think you're getting healthy too fast," she said.

"Growf," I told her.

21

We spent a quiet weekend, with me doing a lot of sleeping, a full eight or nine hours at night plus a couple of naps during the day. Every time I woke up I was a little stronger, and Abbie kept telling me I was getting color back in my cheeks.

She changed the bandage Friday to a smaller one, and Saturday to a still smaller one, and Sunday she took the bandage off and washed the wound and decided not to put a bandage on at all. "We'll let it air," she said.

It looked odd. Not horrible, the way I'd thought, just odd. There was a line along the side of my head above my left ear, about half an inch wide, in which there wasn't any hair, just pink flesh, with some dark red scar showing. It was still very sensitive, not in a stinging way like a cut, but with a deep massive head-pounding thump of a pain if I made the mistake of touching the wound or the area around it. I always had to grit my teeth and hold on tight to the rim of the sink when Abbie was cleaning it, and each time I had a bad headache for about half an hour afterward.

We spent most of the weekend with a deck of cards in our hands. We played gin, and ah hell, and after we found the cribbage board we played cribbage. All for money, of course, but it was seesaw, neither of us ever more than a few bucks ahead.

Abbie also taught me a few stunts with the deck. It took me a while to get used to the mechanic's grip, a funny way of holding the deck from underneath with the left hand so that the right hand can burrow into it like a mouse into a sack of grain without anybody being the wiser. It would take me years to learn to be as smooth with a deck as Abbie, but I did pretty well, and by Sunday night I was even faking her out every once in a while.

Our sleeping arrangements were less satisfactory. She insisted on me keeping the bed, since I was the wounded one, but she switched to the living-room couch. I told her I saw no reason to change the policy we'd established Thursday night, and she said I didn't have to see any reasons, she could see them for both of us. "You trusted me then," I said, and she said, "You were weaker then."

Well, that was true enough. By Sunday afternoon I was just about my old self again, and beginning to get bored. I'd been here since Wednesday night, and I'd really had about all of this apartment I wanted. On the other hand, the outside world was potentially full of people who didn't wish me well, so I didn't chafe very much about having to hang around here. In between the card-playing I watched television or ate snacks or just sat around bored.

And I napped, whether I wanted to or not. Abbie insisted, and I believe her main concern wasn't my health at all. She just wanted me out from underfoot for a while. Still, every time she hounded me into the bedroom for a nap I did actually go off to sleep for an hour or two.

I was asleep, in fact, late Sunday afternoon when the visitors arrived. What woke me was a scream. I popped awake, sat up, and saw Frank Tarbok, the blue-jawed questioner from the garage, standing in the hallway with his velvet-collared overcoat on, staring at me. The voice that had screamed was still echoing in my head, recognizable as Abbie's, but I had already fallen flat again and thrown the covers over my head before it occurred to me the scream hadn't been a mere and simple scream, it had been a word. A name. Abbie had screamed a name.

Why had Abbie screamed *Louise?*

22

When nothing happened for several days, I peeked up over the top of the covers, blinking and wincing already from the bullet I was sure was coming.

Nobody was there.

What? I pushed the covers down completely off my face and stared at the doorway, and it was absolutely empty. Nobody standing there at all. Not Frank Tarbok, not Louise McKay, not anybody.

Had it been a dream? Had the scream been real and all the rest a dream, or had the scream also been part of the dream? A dream scream. Was I going loony?

I sat up, looked around the room, looked at the empty doorway again, and heard voices. They seemed to be real voices, and they were coming from the direction of the living room. Male and female both.

I got out of bed. My shirt and pants—back from the cleaner's—were draped carefully on a chair; shoes were on the floor beside the bed. I dressed hurriedly, left the bedroom, and walked down the hall to the living room, where Frank Tarbok was standing and talking, Louise McKay was standing and talking, and Abbie was standing and talking.

Maybe I was still asleep. Maybe this was part of the dream, too. I said, "Hey," and several other things, trying to attract everybody's attention, and then I realized I was standing and talking like everybody else, so I said, "Oh, the hell with it," and went away again. If the world wanted to be crazy, I could be crazy, too. With Frank Tarbok and Louise McKay actually standing and talking in the living room, I went out to the kitchen and made myself a liver-wurst sandwich. I also heated the coffee, a pot of which we kept permanently on the stove since both Abbie and I were endless coffee drinkers.

The yammering in the living room gradually settled down, but I could not have cared less. Here I'd spent five days terrified that Frank Tarbok or one of his minions would find me and shoot me, and when Frank Tarbok finally did show up he didn't even pay any attention to me. Stared at me through a doorway for a second, and that was that.

As for Louise McKay, her husband had died a week ago, she'd disappeared without a trace, and all of a sudden there she is in her own living room, standing and talking as though she'd been there all along. No, it was all too crazy to be contended with, particularly when I'd just come out of a nap. Particularly when I'd just been thrust out of a nap by a scream.

I was sitting at the kitchen table, eating liverwurst, drinking coffee, and reading the *News*, when they came looking for me. Abbie came in first, the other two behind her. She said, "Chet? Are you out of your mind?"

"Murmf," I said, with a mouthful of liverwurst. I also shook my head, meaning *no*.

"Don't you see who's here?" she demanded, and actually pointed at Frank Tarbok as though she thought I couldn't see him for myself, standing there as big and ugly as life.

I nodded, and pointed at my mouth, and held my hand up to ask for a minute's grace. Then I chewed rapidly, swallowed, helped the food along with a swig of coffee, swallowed again, burped slightly, and said, "Yes. I see him. I see the two of them."

"I don't understand you," she said. "You're just sitting there."

"When your scream woke me up," I told her, "and I saw Frank Tarbok there in the bedroom doorway, I did some of the most beautiful terror reactions you ever saw. I carried on like the heroine of a silent movie. And what did he do? He turned around and walked away. So what did I do? I got up and got dressed and went into the living room to find out what was going on, and nobody would pay any attention to me. Everybody was talking at once, nobody was listening, it was like a clambake out at Jones Beach, so I decided the hell with everybody, and I came in here and made myself a sandwich. If you're all willing to pay attention now, I am prepared to fall on the floor, or scream, or beg for mercy, or try babbling explanations, or whatever you think the circumstances call for. But I'll be damned if I'll perform without an audience." And I took another bite of liverwurst sandwich.

Abbie just stared at me, open-mouthed. It was Tarbok who spoke next, saying in that heavy voice of his, "Conway, for somebody who don't know nothing about nothing, you do keep turning up."

I pushed liverwurst into one cheek. I said, "Up until now I thought it was you. Or somebody working for you. But here you are, and you aren't doing anything, so now I don't know. Unless maybe you've changed your mind since Wednesday."

"Wednesday?" His face was too square and blocky and white and blue-jawed and heavy to manage very much expressiveness, but he did use it now to convey a sort of exasperated bewilderment. "What do you mean, Wednesday?"

I pointed the sandwich at him. "Did you," I asked him, "or any other employee of Walter Droble, or any friend of yours or Walter Droble's, or Walter Droble himself, or an ally of the same, take a shot at me Wednesday night?"

He squinted, as though there was suddenly a lot of cigarette smoke between us. "Take a what?"

"A shot," I said. I used the sandwich for a gun. "Bang bang," I said, and pointed with my other hand at the healing scar on the side of my head.

He put his head to one side and squinted at the scar. "Is that what that is? You was grazed?"

"I was grazed. Did you do it?"

The heavy face made a heavy smile. "Conway," he said, "if I'd took a shot at you, it would have got you a little bit to the right of that."

"It wasn't anybody working for you, or Walter Droble, or et cetera."

He shook his head. "We don't kill people just for practice," he said. "A guy has to really call attention to himself in some outstanding way before we go to a lot of trouble."

"All right," I said. "It wasn't Napoli or any of his people, and it wasn't—"

"Who says it wasn't Napoli?"

"Napoli says it wasn't Napoli."

His head leaned forward, as though to hear me better. In a soft voice he said, "*Solomon* Napoli?"

"Of course."

"He told you it wasn't him? Personally he said so?"

"Yes. Right in that bedroom down there, Thursday night."

"How come he happened to tell you?"

"It's a long story," I said. "I don't want to go into it now."

"I'll tell you the reason I'm asking," he said. "When we had our talk last week, you said you didn't know Sol Napoli. And I believed you. And now you say he come to visit you Thursday and tell you personally he didn't order you rubbed out."

"That was the first time I ever met him," I said. "I'm beginning to feel like Nero Wolfe. I don't have to leave the apartment ever, sooner or later everybody involved in this damn thing comes calling on me."

"That was the first time you ever saw Sol Napoli?" Tarbok persisted. He was running his own conversation, and my part of it hardly mattered at all. "And he come here expressly to tell you he didn't have nothing to do—"

"Oh, really, Frank!" Louise McKay suddenly said, her voice dripping with scorn. "Who are you trying to kid? Why go on with it? Leave these people alone."

Immediately he turned on her. "I'm done telling you, Louise," he said. "You got one hundred percent the wrong idea. Now lay off."

"Is that why you've been keeping me under wraps? Because I've got the *wrong* idea? Is that why I've been a prisoner for a week, I couldn't even go to Tommy's wake, his funeral, I couldn't—"

"Yeah," he said, his heavy voice crushing hers beneath

the one word. "Yeah, that's just why. Because you got the wrong idea, but wrong ideas have got guys strapped in up at Sing Sing before this. You go around yapping to the cops, that's all they'd need. No questions asked, brother, they could mark the McKay homicide solved and pat each other on the backs and not lose a minute's sleep."

"If you were innocent?" she demanded.

"You're damn right! Come off it, Louise, you know it as well as I do. I'm guilty of anything the law can pin on me, it don't matter whether it's a railroad or not. They figure if they get me for something I didn't do, it still works out because I'm paying for something I did do."

"You killed my husband," she said, very bitterly and Abbie and I exchanged quick glances.

"I didn't," he said, his heavy voice almost a physical weight in the room. "Any more than I shot at this shlemozzle here."

"You did."

Abbie said to him, "Did you?"

He looked at her with a kind of sullen surprise, like a lion who's just been poked with a stick through the bars of the cage. Don't people realize he's the king of the jungle and has big teeth? He said, "You, too?"

"I'm Tommy's sister," she said. "I want to know who killed him."

Louise McKay said, "Well, there he is, honey, take a look at him." And pointed at Tarbok.

Tarbok made a fist and showed it to her. "Once more," he said, "and I smash you right in the head."

"Sure," she said. "Why not kill me, too? Why not rub me out the way you rubbed out Tommy."

Tarbok rose up on his toes, as though to recapture his temper, which he was about to lose out through the top of his head. It looked as though maybe he *would* rub her out, or anyway smash her right in the head, if something didn't happen to break the tension, so I said, as calmly and nonchalantly as I could, "Women are like that, Tarbok. Abbie thought I did it for a while."

He settled down again, coming off his toes, his fist slightly uncurling. Turning as slowly as Burt Lancaster about to make a plot point, he said, "She did? How come?"

"Everybody did, at one time or another," I said. "*You* thought I maybe had something to do with it, Napoli thought so, Abbie thought so. For all I know the cops thought so."

Tarbok leaned forward, the hand that had been a fist now supporting his weight on the table. "Why is that, Conway?" he said. "How come everybody thinks you did for McKay?"

"Everybody had different reasons," I said. "You remember yours. Abbie thought I was having an affair with Mrs. McKay and killed Tommy so we could be together."

"That's what *this* moron did," Louise McKay shouted, glaring at Abbie and me as though to defy us to question her.

Tarbok turned his head and looked at her. "Shut up, sweetheart," he said, slowly and distinctly. "I'm talking to the shlemozzle."

"I'm not a shlemozzle," I said.

He gave me a pitying look. "See how wrong people can be? How come Sol Napoli thought it was you?"

"He thought you people found out Tommy had secretly gone over to his side, and you hired me to kill him."

Tarbok stared at me. The silence suddenly bulged. Tarbok said, "Who did what?"

"Tommy was secretly on Napoli's side. Napoli told me so him—"

"That's a lie!"

I looked at Louise McKay. "I'm sorry, Mrs. McKay," I said. "All I know is what I was told." I looked back at Tarbok. "And why would Napoli be involved if it wasn't true?"

Tarbok said, "Don't nobody go nowhere." He pushed past the two women as though they were strangers on a subway platform, and left the kitchen, heading in the direction of the rest of the apartment.

We all looked at one another, and I was the first to speak, saying to Mrs. McKay, "Abbie thinks it's you, you know."

She looked at me, and I was an annoyance that had just forced itself onto her attention. "What was that?"

Abbie, embarrassed, said, "Chet, stop."

I didn't. I said, "Mrs. McKay, your sister-in-law there is convinced that you're the one who killed Tommy."

She was a very bad-tempered woman. Her eyebrows came threateningly down and she glared at the two of us. "What the hell is that supposed to mean?"

Abbie said to me, "Chet, I've changed my mind."

I didn't much care. I said to Mrs. McKay, "Tommy wrote her about your running around with somebody, so naturally—"

"He never did!"

Abbie said softly, "Yes, he did, Louise, I still have the letter, if you want to see it. I tried showing it to the police, but they didn't seem to much care."

Mrs. McKay's glare began to crumple at the edges. She tried to keep it alive, beetling her brows more and more, but when her chin began to tremble, it was all over.

Abbie got a sympathetic look on her face and moved forward with a consoling hand out, and Mrs. McKay let go. She dropped into the chair across the table from me, flopped her head down onto her folded arms, and began to catch up on a week of weeping. Abbie stood next to her, one hand on her shoulder, and looked at me with a what-can-we-do? expression on her face. I shook my head, meaning all-we-can-do-is-wait-it-out, and Frank Tarbok bulled back into the room, saying, "What the hell's the matter with the phone in the bedroom?"

I said, "One of Napoli's men pulled it out when I tried to call the police."

He gave me an irritated frown, gave Mrs. McKay a more irritated frown, and pounded away again.

We had about thirty seconds of silence, except for Mrs. McKay's muffled sobbing, and then somebody pounded on the front door.

I said, "I'll get it."

"Be careful," Abbie said.

"Naturally," I said. I left the kitchen, went to the front door, and looked through the peephole at Ralph, who was looking both impatient and disgusted.

Oh. I opened the door and he pushed in without a word and thumped on down the hall toward the bedroom. I shut the door again and went bck to the kitchen. At Abbie's raised eyebrow, I said, "It was Ralph. He came back for his gun." I went around the table and sat down again.

Abbie said, "Come to think of it, what did you do with my gun?"

"It's in my overcoat pocket," I said. "You know, I'd forgotten all about that?"

"No, it isn't," she said.

"What?"

"It isn't in your overcoat pocket. I looked."

"Well, that's where I put it," I said, and Ralph appeared in the doorway. I looked at him.

He said, "Okay, where is it?"

"Oh, I'm sorry," I said. "It's on the dresser."

"On the dresser?"

"Yes," I said. "On the dresser."

He went away again, and Abbie said, "Believe me, Chet, I looked through all your clothing for that gun. I thought it might come in handy."

"Somebody swiped it," I said.

"That's fine," she said. "I give you the thing to hold for me, and you lose it."

"In the first place," I said, and Frank Tarbok came back. "Later," I said to Abbie, and looked at Tarbok.

"Walt Droble is coming over," he said.

"I *am* Nero Wolfe," I said.

He said, "Hah?" and Ralph appeared in the doorway behind him, waving the gun in the air so we could see it, saying, "I got it."

Tarbok turned, not having known till now that Ralph was in the apartment. He saw the gun, saw Ralph's face, yelled, and hit the dirt. That is, he hit the linoleum, rolled under the table and into a lot of chair legs, and was pawing around inside his clothing down there when I stooped and said, "It's okay. He isn't going to shoot anybody, it's okay."

Ralph, meanwhile, suddenly looking wary, was saying, "Was that Frank Tarbok?"

"Just wait there," I told Tarbok, and got to my feet. To

Ralph, I said, "Come on now. Let's not make things any more confusing than they already are."

"*Is that Frank Tarbok?*"

"Yes," I said. "It's Frank Tarbok."

Ralph's gun was suddenly pointing at me. "Against the wall, mother," he said.

23

Tarbok came out from under the table with his hands up, the way Ralph ordered, and stood next to me at the refrigerator. "I won't forget this, Conway," he told me.

"Shut up," Ralph said. He waggled the gun at Abbie and Mrs. McKay. "You two over there with them."

"No," Abbie said.

He looked at her. "What?"

"Go away, Ralph," she said. "We have trouble enough already, so just go away."

"Oh, yeah? Maybe you don't think Napoli's going to be interested about this? How Chester Conway here, who doesn't know nothing about nothing, is having a nice private chat with Frank Tarbok."

"Oh, don't be stupid," I said.

"Watch it, you," he told me.

I said, "Think about it, Ralph. If anything was going on here, would I have let you into the apartment?"

Tarbok said, out of the corner of his mouth, "You and me are gonna talk about *that*, Conway, believe me."

"Oh, you shut up, too," I said. "You people are the shlemozzles, not me. I never in my life saw so many people jump to so many wrong conclusions. You're all either paranoid or stupid, and I'm beginning to think you're both."

Abbie said, dangerously, "I hope you're not including *me* in that, Chet."

"Now don't you start," I said. I walked away from the refrigerator toward Ralph, who put a menacing expression on his face. "Ralph," I said, "Frank Tarbok is not here to make any plans with me to do anything mean to Solomon Napoli. Frank Tarbok is here as a private citizen, escorting the widow of Tommy McKay, who is that tear-stained lady sitting at the kitchen table."

"So you say," said Ralph.

"So I say," I agreed. "And so it is. You came back for your gun, Ralph, and you have your gun, and now it seems to me you've got your choice of either using that gun or going away. Which is it?"

Abbie said, "Chet, be careful."

I turned to her and said, "No. I've had it, Abbie. Every time things quiet down a little, some other lamebrain comes running in with a lot of stupid ideas in his head and starts—"

"Hey," Ralph said.

"Yes," I said, turning back to him, "I do mean you. If you weren't a lamebrain I wouldn't have taken thirteen bucks from you at gin in an hour."

"You had the cards," he said. "I can't do nothing when you keep getting the cards."

"Sure," I said. "And if you weren't a lamebrain you wouldn't have walked out of here without your gun."

"That was that cop." Ralph was becoming very defensive now. "He screwed things up, made me—"

"Sure, the cop," I said. "And if you weren't a lamebrain you wouldn't be carrying on like a nut just because

Frank Tarbok is in Tommy McKay's apartment. Tommy *worked* for Frank Tarbok, what's so surprising that Tommy's widow is *with* Frank Tarbok?"

"I'm not with that bastard!" Louise McKay suddenly shouted, leaping to her feet in order to throw a monkey-wrench into the works just as I was beginning to make Ralph see a glimmer of light. She shouted at Ralph, "Go ahead and shoot him! He's the one killed my Tommy!"

"Oh, for God's sake," I said. "He did not. Mrs. McKay, you're carrying on worse than Ralph."

"Just a second there," Ralph said. "Let the lady talk."

"The lady runs off at the mouth," I told him. "She doesn't have the brains of a chipmunk."

"Chet!" Abbie said, shocked. "Louise has been through a lot!"

"Well, it hasn't smartened her up any," I said. "She's had a week to get used to being a widow, and frankly I'm not impressed by how broken up she is, seeing she was running around behind Tommy's back when he was alive. If you ask me, she's just making all this fuss because she feels guilty now about what she did to Tommy herself."

"You've got a dirty mind, Chester Conway," Mrs. McKay told me, "and a dirty mouth to go with it. But it doesn't change the fact of the matter, and the fact of the matter is, Frank Tarbok killed my Tommy."

"Why?" I said.

"Because he thought he could get me that way," she said.

"Don't be silly," I said. "He already had you, as often as he wanted."

She went white. "You're a filthy little bastard," she said.

"Yeah, and you're a nun." I turned to Ralph, saying, "Ralph, think about it. Is Frank Tarbok the kind of man who would kill somebody for a woman? Particularly for a woman he was already shacked up with."

Ralph was looking from face to face. The whole thing was miles over his head, but he had just enough brains to know it. "I don't know nothing about nothing," he said. "All I know is, Sol is going to be very interested in all this."

"Then you better hurry and tell him about it," I said. "Maybe he'll give you a merit badge."

"Watch that," he said.

I opened my mouth to say one or two things, but then I changed my mind and instead I said, "Ralph, you weren't bad to me while I was your prisoner. You were a pretty nice guy, in fact, and believe me I am doing my best right now to remember that. And please, you try and remember me. I haven't done anything to Sol Napoli or anybody else, and what's more I'm not in a *position* to do anything to Sol Napoli or anybody else. I am not a threat to you, Ralph, honest to God. Think about it."

He thought about it. I could see him struggling with the problem, and his eyes kept straying to Frank Tarbok, standing in front of the refrigerator with his hands up. I could see what he had to surmount. Frank Tarbok was the enemy, and I was with the enemy, and that had to mean something was going on. On the other hand, what could be going on? It was a problem.

He finally gave up on it. "All right," he said. "Okay. I'll just go talk to Sol. Maybe he'll want to see you again."

"I will more than likely be right here," I said. "Drop in any time. Join the crowd."

"Sol can find you if he wants you," Ralph said darkly.

"I know," I said.

Ralph glared around at everybody, wanting to be sure his reputation as a tough guy was still unflawed, and then he hefted his gun one last time, backed out of the kitchen like the evil foreman leaving a western saloon, and disappeared to the right. A second later we heard the door open and shut.

Tarbok lowered his arms. "Conway," he said, "just why in holy hell did you let that guy in here?"

"He left his gun behind," I said, "and he came back for it. To be honest, I completely forgot about you being here. About the implications, I mean."

"He left his gun behind." Tarbok picked up an overturned chair and heavily sat down on it. Shaking his head he said, "Every time I have a conversation with you, Conway, things go crazy."

"I thought it was the other way around," I said, and walked around the table and sat down again in front of my liverwurst sandwich. Picking it up I said, "What time do we expect Walter Droble?"

"Half an hour."

"Shall we make some onion dip? Does he play bridge?"

Louise McKay suddenly said, "Abbie, it's perfectly all right for you to stay here while you're in New York, but I'd rather you didn't bring other people in with you. Particularly a foul-mouthed individual like that one."

I said, "Mrs. McKay, I'm sorry if I offended you."

"Huh!" she said.

"But," I said, "you're going around being very shrill and emotional and you're not thinking sensibly. We could *all* have gotten killed if Ralph had decided to start shooting. Do you think he'd have shot Tarbok here and left three witnesses alive to tell about it? Just exactly at the moment when I was about to get him quietly out of here you start yelling all this stuff about Tarbok killing your husband, when you know perfectly well he didn't."

She stared at me. "I know no such thing."

"Maybe you didn't," I said. "You probably did think he'd done it at first, but now you know he didn't and you're just going on momentum. You're mad at him and maybe you should be, but that's why you're going on saying he killed Tommy."

"He did."

"No. You know the motive isn't right, you know he wouldn't have killed Tommy in order to marry you. And besides that," I said, pointing at the wound on my head, "somebody shot at me Wednesday night."

She sat there waiting for me to go on, but I'd said all I wanted to say, so finally she said, "Well? What difference does that make?"

I said, "The Droble gang didn't do it, and the Napoli gang didn't do it. So who did it?"

"I don't know," she said coldly. "Who else have you insulted recently?"

"Come on," I said. "Be serious. Nobody's ever shot at me before, and nobody's going to be shooting at me now except in connection some way with the murder of Tommy McKay. It would be too much of a coincidence if the shootings weren't related."

"I don't see what point you think you're making," she said.

I said, "The point I think I'm making is that the only person who would take a shot at me has to be the same person who killed Tommy. And Frank Tarbok didn't do it. He didn't shoot at me Wednesday night."

Tarbok said, "What time?"

"Around one-thirty," Abbie told him.

Tarbok looked at Mrs. McKay. "You know where I was at one-thirty Wednesday night."

"That doesn't prove anything," she said. "All we have is your word for it," she told me, "that you were shot at one-thirty Wednesday night."

"Well," I said, "there is also this healing wound on the side of my head, which ought to count for something."

She glanced at the side of my head, but her expression didn't change. It remained locked up, cold, unreachable. "It doesn't say one-thirty Wednesday night on it," she said.

"I say one-thirty Wednesday night," Abbie said. "I was with Chet when it happened."

She faltered for a second at that, but then she said, irritably, "What difference does it make anyway? The shooting doesn't prove anything, it doesn't have to be connected to all this at all. If you associate with underworld figures, you shouldn't be surprised if sooner or later you get yourself shot at."

"The only underworld figure I ever associated with up till now," I told her, "was your husband."

She stiffened even more, and got to her feet. "Nothing you say is going to change the facts," she said. "And the fact is that Frank Tarbok killed my husband. He's held me incommunicado for a week to keep me from telling the police what I know, and that's proof enough for me."

"What if he hadn't held you for a week?" I said. "What would have been proof enough then?"

But she was done with listening. No, she'd never listened, she was done now with answering. She turned and walked toward the kitchen door, very haughty.

Tarbok said heavily, "Don't try making any phone calls."

She left the room without deigning to answer.

Abbie looked at the doorway, frowning. "Maybe I ought to go talk to her," she said.

"Forget it," I said. "She's got a closed mind."

"I didn't mean to convince her of anything. Just to comfort her a little." She got to her feet. "In fact, I will." She also left the room.

I said to Frank Tarbok, "Care for some liverwurst?"

"No, thanks," he said. "My stomach's been acting up the last few days."

"I wouldn't wonder. Can you take coffee?"

"No, nothing for me." He looked at me. "You got any idea who it is?"

"The killer?"

"Who else?"

"No, I don't. I wish I did. Abbie thought it was Louise, but I never did think so and I still don't."

He shook his head. "Naw, she didn't do it. She ran around on him, but she liked him okay. Just like I like my wife. Louise and me, we both knew it was just for kicks, neither of us was looking for no permanent change."

"Right," I said. "So it wasn't her, and it wasn't you—"

"You're damn right."

"Right. And it wasn't Napoli or any of his people, because Tommy was working with them, and it wasn't Droble or any of his people, because he didn't know Tommy was double-crossing him. So who's left? I don't know."

"We oughta find out," Tarbok said. "It'd help us both if whoever he is he got found out."

"Yes, it would," I said. "You'd have Mrs. McKay off your back, and I'd have the killer off mine."

"Maybe we oughta work together," Tarbok said. "Maybe the two of us could maybe find out something."

I stared at him. "You mean, play detective? You and me?"

"Why not? The cops ain't playing detective, and somebody ought to."

"The cops are still working on the case," I said. "They were as of Friday, anyway."

"Well, they're off now," Tarbok told me. "I get information, I can guarantee it."

"Oh," I said. "That makes for a problem, doesn't it?"

"We're both of us in big trouble if the guy ain't found," Tarbok said.

"You're right."

"So why don't we join up and take a look for him?"

"Abbie's looking, too," I said. "You know, to avenge her brother."

"She can come aboard," he said. "Plenty of room. What do you say?"

I grinned at him. "You want to team up with a shlemozzle?"

He grinned back, and it was amazing how the change of expression lifted his face. He almost looked human now. "You're a kind of a super shlemozzle," he said. "You do dumb things, but you always got smart reasons."

"Hmmm," I said, because it was a description I couldn't find myself disagreeing with, though I would have liked to. He stuck his hand out. "Is it a deal?"

I shrugged, shook my head, and took his hand. "It's a deal," I said. We shook hands, the unlikeliest team since the lion and the mouse, and once again the doorbell rang.

24

Walter Droble.

Now, Walter Droble was more like it. A stocky fiftyish man of medium height, with a heavy jowly face, graying hair brushed straight back, wearing a slightly rumpled brown suit, he looked like the owner of a chain of dry cleaners. No, he looked like what he was, the kind of mobster executive who shows up on televised Congressional hearings into organized crime.

He smoked a cigar, of course, and he viewed me with unconcealed suspicion and distaste. His attitude made it plain he was used to dealing at a higher level.

He said, "What's this about McKay?"

The three of·us were sitting at the kitchen table, Droble's bodyguards having joined the ladies in the living room. I'd cleared away the coffee cup and the remains of the liverwurst sandwich—except for a few crumbs—and except for the refrigerator turning itself on and off every few minutes you could sort of squint and make believe you were in an actual conference room somewhere in Rockefeller Center.

So I told Walter Droble about Tommy McKay. Midway through, Frank Tarbok got to his feet and I faltered in my story, but he was only getting a white saucer for Droble to flick his cigar ash in, so I went on with it. Droble sat there and listened without once interrupting me, his eyes on my eyes at all times, his face impassive. He was a man who knew how to concentrate.

When I was done he looked away from me at last and frowned down instead at his cigar. He stayed that way for a hundred years or so, and then looked back at me again and said, "You know why I believe you?"

"No," I said.

"Because I don't see your percentage," he said. "I don't see where it makes you a nickel to convince me McKay had sold me out. That's why I believe you."

"That's good," I said.

"Now," he said, "do you know why I *don't* believe you?"

I blinked. "Uh," I said.

"Because," he said, "it don't make any sense. What did McKay *do* for Sol? What did Sol want with him?"

"I don't know."

"You don't know. I don't know either. I also don't know where's McKay's percentage. What's in it for him to sell me out?"

"Insurance," I said. "That one's easy. Apparently the trouble between you and Napoli is coming to a head. If you win, he's always been one of your people. If Napoli wins, his true loyalty was to Napoli all the time."

He worked on his cigar, which did not smell like elevators in the garment district, so I assumed it was very expensive. "Maybe," he said, conceding the point. "Just maybe." He glanced at Tarbok. "Get his wife in here," he said.

Tarbok said, "Walt, she didn't know a thing about it. It was as big a surprise to her as anybody."

"Maybe so," Droble said. "Let's ask her."

I said, "I think you can take Mr. Tarbok's word for it, Mr. Droble. He knows Mrs. McKay pretty well."

Tarbok gave me a dirty look, and Droble said, "What's that supposed to mean? Frank?"

Tarbok hemmed and hawed.

Droble frowned at him. "Frank, you been playin around with the woman? Are you the reason she's been hiding out for a week?"

Tarbok sighed, gave me another look, and said, "Yeah. She and me had a thing going."

"Well, that's fine," Droble said. "Whose idea was it she should cop a sneak?"

I was sorry I'd gotten Tarbok into this, but I'd learned in the last week that the only way to keep confusion from spreading like crab grass was to tell the truth every chance you got. Sometimes the truth made for an initial increase in confusion, but sooner or later it always had a calming effect.

So now I sat back and kept out of the conversation while reluctantly Tarbok explained things to his boss. Droble had to keep asking questions, but at least Tarbok didn't try telling any lies, so when they were done Droble had a clear understanding of the situation.

And it didn't make him happy. He said, "Frank, you should have put more trust in our lawyers. Let the woman go bitch to the cops. So it makes for a little unpleasantness, we would of got it straightened out in jigtime. McKay was killed when was it, last Monday, in the normal course of things the cops should have wrapped it up and put it in the pending file by Wednesday morning, but with the wife all of a sudden out of sight they kept being underfoot till Thursday night. We finally got our boys to convince the rest of them the wife took off only because she was afraid to get mixed up in the middle of a gang war, but the other way would have been a hell of a lot simpler. The wife goes in Monday night and makes her squawk, you spend Monday night in a cell, Tuesday morning we get it all straightened out, Tuesday they do their regular paperwork and routine, Wednesday morning the case is filed on schedule. You cost us a day and a half of irritation, Frank."

Tarbok hung his head. "I'm sorry, Walt," he said. "I just got panicky, I guess."

"You should of come talk to me, Frank. You know my office door is always open."

"I didn't want to disturb you."

"That's what I'm here for, Frank. You know I want the organization to run smooth, and it can't run smooth if everybody's private life gets in the way on the job. That's why I'm always ready to help, Frank. You should of come to me."

"You're right," Tarbok said. "I should of thought."

"Okay," Droble said. He reached out the hand without the cigar and patted Tarbok's hand. "Now we forget it, Frank," he said. "What's over is over. Now we think about tomorrow."

Tarbok's head came up. "That's what I wanted to talk to you about, Walt," he said. "The question is, who did for McKay if it wasn't Napoli?"

Droble frowned. "I don't get you."

"We been taking it for granted it was Napoli," Tarbok said. "Paying us back for that Corona incident."

Droble gave me a quick look and said to Tarbok, "Easy. Not in front of civilians."

"I wasn't going into any details, Walt. Anyway, the point is, if McKay was working for Napoli, Napoli didn't rub him."

"If," Droble said. "We never did get that straightened out." He looked at me again. "I already told you I'm of two minds on this one," he said. "You think you can convince me one way or the other?"

I'd been waiting for the chance. I quickly told him about my having been shot Wednesday night, and the presence of Napoli's men, and the fact that they'd been planning to kill me themselves to avenge Tommy, and their presence in this apartment for the next twenty-four hours, and Napoli's visit—Droble had me describe Napoli, which I did—and the inescapable conclusion that Napoli's presence and interest meant Tommy really had been working for him.

When I finished, Droble looked very sour. He said, "Okay. I don't get it, but okay."

Tarbok said, "So that's what raises the question, who did for McKay if it wasn't Napoli?"

Droble said, "What do we care?"

I knew why Tarbok cared, but I doubted it was a motivation Droble would find much sympathy with. It mattered to Tarbok whether or not his sweetie believed he'd killed her husband, but it was unlikely to have the same urgency for Droble. So I wondered how Tarbok was going to handle it.

With a mask on. Leaning forward he said, "Walt, we got to know. It happened inside our organization, we can't remain ignorant about it. Whoever he is, the guy's caused us trouble. He almost made us move against Napoli before we were ready, he—"

"Shut up, Frank."

Tarbok glanced at me, remembering my presence, and leaned closer to Droble to say, "Okay. You know the situation, Walt, I don't have to spell it out."

"You better not spell it out."

I said, "I could wait in the living room if you want."

Tarbok said, "No. You stay here, you're a part of this."

"That's right," said Droble. "You just sit right where you are."

Tarbok said to Droble, "Okay, I'm not spelling it out. But you know and I know we can't have no wild card in the deck. There's somebody out there doing something we don't know anything about. He killed McKay, he took a shot at Conway here, who knows where he'll crop up again? So we don't have the balance screwed up we need to know who he is. Whether we turn him over to the cops is another question. What we got to know is who he is and what he's up to."

Droble nodded, reluctantly but judiciously. "You're right," he said. "And you want to handle it, is that right?"

Tarbok, being a lot more deft than I would have given him credit for, said, "Right. After all, I got a private stake in this, too. I don't like Louise McKay thinking it was me killed her husband."

"The question is," Droble said, "what's the situation with this guy?" Meaning me.

"I'll keep him with me," Tarbok said. "He's been in the middle of it all along, while I been holed up with Louise."

Droble looked at me. "There's another question," he said. "How come you been in the middle of it all along?"

I said, "I've been meaning to talk to you about that," and I then proceeded to tell him about my nine hundred thirty dollars, finishing, "So you're the one I should talk to about it, I guess."

"About what?"

"My nine hundred thirty dollars."

Droble frowned. "What about it?"

"I want to collect it. You still owe it to me."

He shook his head. "Not on your life," he said. "That money was turned over to McKay. As far as the organization is concerned, you've been paid."

"Hey, wait a second," I said. "Maybe *Tommy* got the money, but *I* never did."

"That's not our problem," he said. "You want to take it up with his widow, you go right ahead."

I looked at Tarbok, but he was no help. I said, "What happened to the money?"

Tarbok shook his head, and Droble shrugged. They couldn't care less.

I said, "Wait a second, this might be important. Are you sure he got it? Are you sure the money was actually paid to him?"

"Our courier got here at five thirty-five," Droble told me. "We already checked that out."

I said, "Are you sure? What about this courier?"

"He's my son-in-law," Droble said drily. "He's being groomed for the top, and he knows it. He didn't bump McKay for your nine hundred thirty dollars."

"Hmm," I said. "And he got here at five thirty-five? Tommy was alive then, and he was dead when I got here at six-ten. That's thirty-five minutes."

"He was alive at five-fifty," Droble said. "We've done some checking out, and somebody in our organization talked to him on the phone at ten minutes to six."

Tarbok said, "So it's down to twenty minutes."

I said, "It's a good thing I didn't get here much earlier. What happened to the money afterwards?"

"Gone," Droble said. "Our cop on the scene told us the bundle wasn't here."

"How much can you trust *him*?" I asked.

"He picks up no percentage in lying on that one,"

Droble said. "If the money was here the cops would have picked it up and divided it, and our cop would of told us so. There wouldn't be any question about us getting it back or anything."

"So the murderer took it with him."

"Right," Droble said. "So there's your answer. Go find the killer, and collect your nine hundred from him."

"I don't think that's fair," I said. "I made my bet in good faith, and just because you have an administrative problem inside your organization is no reason I should—"

"Administrative problem!"

"What else do you call it? I didn't get my money because somebody in your organization lost it in transit. It should be up to you to make it good."

"You want to take us to court?" he asked me.

"Oh, come on," I said. "That money's important to me."

"It isn't the money," he said, "it's the precedent. We don't pay off twice, and that's all there is to it. Look, the other big winner that day didn't come squawking, *he* understood the situation. Why don't you?"

"Another big winner?" I said.

"Yeah. Another guy had the same horse as you, only he had a hundred on it. That's almost three grand."

"Who was he?"

"What difference does it make?" Droble said.

"I don't know, I'm just asking. Who was he?"

Droble shrugged in irritation. "I wouldn't know. McKay would have the name, it might be in his records around here some—"

He stopped. He looked wide-eyed. He glanced at Tarbok, who looked back in bewilderment and said, "Walt?"

"I'll be a son of a bitch," Droble said. "*That's* what

the bastard was doing for Napoli! He was robbing me blind!"

I was happy to see Tarbok didn't get it any more than I did. He said, "How do you figure that, Walt?"

"I remember," Droble said, "Higgins in Accounting said it to me a couple months ago, how McKay had a couple of consistent winners, guys who'd pick two, three horses a week, long shots. Cleaning up. McKay was actually running at a loss because of those guys, but it disappeared in the overall accounting picture. Don't you see it, Frank? The bastard was past-posting us!"

I grinned. How lovely. Napoli, in other words, had been feeding Tommy the names of one or two good money winners a day, getting the information to Tommy right after the race, before the news would be on the wires. Then Tommy would make those bets for non-existent players, and probably he and Napoli split the proceeds. A nice way for Napoli to hit his competition in the cash register and build up his own funds for when the open warfare started. Particularly if Napoli had more than one of Droble's bookies doing the same thing.

I said, "Mr. Droble, if it wasn't for me you would never have found out about this. Napoli was suborning your organization from the bottom, and financing it with your own money. Now you know about it and you can do something about it, and if it wasn't for me you'd have gone under. Now, if *that* isn't worth nine hundred thirty dollars, I don't know what—"

"Will you shut up about that lousy nine hundred?" Droble was angry and worried, and in no mood to be fair about things.

But Tarbok, surprisingly, was. He said, "Walt, I think Conway's right. I think we owe him a debt. And I also think he could go on being helpful to us for some time to come. We could afford to—"

"With that bastard Napoli sucking my blood? Not on your life. Don't either of you say another word about that nine—"

The doorbell rang.

I said, "I'll get it," and got to my feet. As I left the room, Droble started to say something to Tarbok about having the Accounting Department check all the other retail bookies.

I was really angry, and there wasn't a thing I could do about it. To be too cheap to pay me my money, when in reality he owed me a heck of a lot more than that. Boy, some people are really pigs.

I looked through the peephole in the front door, and there was Solomon Napoli himself, with several tough-looking types behind him, that snitch Ralph among them.

What did I owe any of these clowns? The debts were all the other way, it seemed to me. I opened the door and bowed them in with a flourish. "Come on in, fellas," I said. "You're just in time for the punch."

25

Did you ever see two cats meet unexpectedly coming around a corner or through a doorway? Then I don't have to describe the meeting between Walter Droble and Solomon Napoli. Or how full the hall became of assorted henchmen, with Napoli's commandos crowding in from outside and Droble's irregulars hurrying down from the living room.

I slithered back into the kitchen—not bad for somebody who can't stay on a diet—and over to the far side of the refrigerator, wanting to be out of the line of fire in case there was a line of fire, from where I watched the opening stages of the drama.

Droble had leaped to his feet, of course, the minute Napoli had appeared in the kitchen doorway, and for what seemed several years they just stood glaring at each other, both in a half-crouch, hackles rising everywhere, like the opening of the gun duel scene in a western movie. There was noise and commotion out in the hall from the rival gangs of extras, but that all seemed to be happening in a different world, as though a thick pane of glass separated this room from the planet Earth as we know it. Frank Tarbok had stayed exactly where he was, seated at the table, hands in plain view on the table top.

Droble spoke first: "You've been past-posting me, you son of a bitch."

Napoli, small and dapper and vicious, said, "But you were a real boy scout in that East New York business, weren't you?"

"If you hadn't pulled that stunt with Griffin, nothing would have happened in East New York."

Napoli was about to reply, but Tarbok said, "Walt. Remember the civilian."

Droble looked angrily around, irritated at the interruption, and when he met Tarbok's eye, Tarbok nodded in my direction. Then everybody looked at me.

I never felt so present in my life. I was right there, right out in the open, plain as the sweat on my face. I resisted the impulse to say, "Uh."

But I was going to have to say something, because I could sense the mood changing all of a sudden. The room was full of tension looking for an outlet, and I was the stranger, the foreigner, the civilian, the one who didn't belong. It would relieve everybody's feelings if they all got together and stomped me into the linoleum.

I said, "Well," and put a horrible smile on my face. "Here's a chance for all you people to settle your differences. All you do is make trouble for each other when you argue like this, and New York ought to be big enough for everybody. And here's a perfect opportunity to sit down and discuss things and work everything out so everybody's satisfied. Mr. Napoli, why don't you take my chair, that one there, and I'll just go wait in the living room. I know you won't want any outsider listening in. So I'll just, uh, go on into, uh, the living room now, and if you want to talk to me later on," as I started moving, slowly but with a great show of the confidence I didn't feel, toward the doorway, "I'll be right in there, on tap, ready to help out any way I can," as I edged around Napoli, talking all the time through the ghastly smile painted on my face, "and looking forward to hearing that you two have ironed out your differences, buried the, uh, settled everything to your mutual…" and through the doorway, and out of their sight.

Successfully. So far. I inched my way through all the hard-noses in the hall, all standing around like a Mafia wake, filling the hallway with the dark awareness of all the guns tucked just out of sight inside all those suit coats, and though all of them gave me the evil eye none of them made a move to stop me. They wouldn't without orders from the kitchen.

Which didn't come. Neither Napoli nor Droble shouted out, "Stop that guy!" or, "Kill him!" or, "Bring that bum back here!" or any other fatal commands. I got past the

last of the heavies and continued on to the living room,
where Abbie and Mrs. McKay were sitting now alone at
opposite ends of the room, and fell in nervous paralysis
into the nearest empty chair. "Uhhhhhh," I said, and let
my arms hang over the sides.

Abbie hurried to me and whispered, "What's going
on?"

"Summit meeting," I said. I took a deep breath and sat
up and wiped my brow. "Napoli and Droble are talking
things over in the kitchen."

"Napoli and Droble? Both of them?"

I nodded. "You don't know how it felt to be in there
with them," I said.

"I can imagine," she said.

I wasn't sure she could. I said, "You know, years ago
somebody put an ad in a couple of papers in New York
for a guaranteed bug killer, to be delivered with complete
instructions. It cost a dollar or two, I don't know how
much. So a lot of people sent in their money, and they got
a package back, and in the package there were two ordi-
nary bricks, one lettered A and the other one lettered B.
And a sheet of paper with instructions: 'Place bug on
brick A. Hit with brick B.' In that kitchen just now, I
finally understood what the bug felt like."

Abbie, hunkered down in front of me, elbows on my
knees, took my hand in hers and squeezed. "I know," she
said. "It must have been terrible."

"I only hope," I said, "that when it's over they don't
decide we're a couple of loose ends that ought to be tied
off. Like Captain Kidd taking care of the diggers after
burying treasure. I wish we still had that gun of yours."

"We're better off without it," she said. "It was just
about useless anyway. It shot way off to the left all the

time, you had to aim *there* if you wanted to hit over *there*, and it was so light even if you did hit somebody you wouldn't do him much damage. And if we *did* have it and you showed it to that bunch in the hall, they'd fill you up with so much lead we'd have to paint you yellow and use you for a pencil."

"You don't have to paint me yellow," I said.

She smiled and shook her head. "You're braver than you pretend," she said.

"Not me. You've got it wrong which is the pretense."

Somebody shouted, angrily.

We looked at one another. We looked at the hallway.

Somebody else shouted, also angrily. Two voices shouted angrily at the same time.

I said, "The foolish thing is, I let them all in. I can't remember why."

Abbie said, "Do you think we're in any danger?"

"Oh, no," I said. "We're in a cage full of irritated crocodiles. There's nothing for *us* to worry about."

"Maybe we ought to get out of here," she whispered.

"Have you seen lately what's between us and the door?"

She leaned closer to me. "Fire escape."

"What?"

She gestured with her head at the window beside which Mrs. McKay was sitting. She'd continued to sit there since I'd come into the room, ignoring the two of us, ignoring the shouts which had subsided now, ignoring everything. Her arms were folded, her back was straight and her jaw was set. She glared into the middle distance as though seeing an apparition there of which she disapproved.

I put my head next to Abbie's and whispered in her ear, "There's a fire escape there?"

"Yes," she whispered.

"Where does it go?" I whispered.

"Away from the apartment," she whispered.

"That's a good place," I whispered. "Come on."

I got to my feet and hoisted Abbie up, and the two of us tippy-toed across the room. The only person in sight was Louise McKay, who continued to ignore us until we were almost on top of her, at which point she focused on me with a glare intended to rout me in case I had it in mind to start a conversation.

I didn't. "Excuse me," I said, and edged around between the chair she was in and the floor lamp next to it. I raised the window shade.

Mrs. McKay said, "What are you doing?"

I didn't answer her, I was too busy unlocking the window, but Abbie said, low-voiced, "We're getting out of here. Do you want to come along?"

"I *live* here!" she said, very loudly.

I raised the window, and an icy blast rushed in. I'd completely forgotten it was winter outside and here I was in shirt sleeves. Not to mention Abbie in a miniskirt.

Mrs. McKay shouted, "Close that window! What do you think you're doing?"

"Oh, you're a pain," I said, exasperated beyond endurance, and threw a leg over the windowsill. "Come on, Abbie, before this nut rouses the crocodiles."

Abbie tried, low-voiced, to talk sweet reason to Mrs. McKay, who interrupted with another shouted question or demand or order or something. In the meantime I slid through the open window and out onto the fire escape. I turned around and stuck my head back in and whispered shrilly, "Abbie, come on!"

Mrs. McKay was really yelling now. For some damn reason she was tipping off the heavies. Abbie finally gave

up her missionary work on the idiot woman, came hurrying around the chair to my frantically waving hands,
and as I helped her over the windowsill I saw past her
shoulder the other end of the living room filling up with
mean-looking guys with guns in their hands.

"Stop!" somebody shouted.

Was he out of his mind?

26

Five P.M. of a freezing windy Sunday in late January,
the sky a solid mass of gray clouds seven miles thick, the
thin vague daylight already fading toward twilight, the
temperature somewhere in the teens, and where am I?
Standing on a fire escape four stories up in my shirt sleeves
with gunmen shouting *Stop* at me. Not to mention the
crease in the side of my head where I've already been
laid low by one bullet.

The thing is, we'd been more or less safe up till now
because nobody had really known what was going on,
everybody had been confused and had wanted to find out
which end was up before doing anything irreversible like
bumping off witnesses. But now Napoli and Droble were
working it all out in the kitchen, and whether they succeeded in reaching an entente or not was unimportant,
because either way Abbie and I were about to become
extraneous. We knew too much to be let go and too little
to be kept around, and that left only one choice. Ergo,
the fire escape.

This was the rear of the building, and looking down it
seemed to me there was nothing down there but a cul de

sac, concrete all the way around, high walls on three sides and this building on the fourth with what you know and I know was a well-locked door. I looked up, looked down again, looked up again, looked through the window at all those big-shouldered gun-toting gorillas pounding across the living room toward me, and when Abbie started to go down the fire escape I grabbed her arm and shouted, "No! Up!"

"Come *on!*" she cried, either not hearing me or not understanding me. She kept wanting to go down.

There was no time to explain things. I just clamped a hand around her wrist and took off.

She fought me for a while, yelling my name and other things, but a certain feeling of urgency gave me strength, and as I lunged up the metal stairs Abbie came bouncing and ricocheting and complaining along behind me. That is, she complained until the sound of the first shot.

That was a very strange sound, actually. It went BANG-*dingdingdingding,* the first part being the sound of the gun being fired and the rest being the sounds of the bullet ricocheting around the fire escape. So far as I know, it came nowhere near us, but it sure stopped Abbie from hanging back.

The building was six stories high. We went tramping and clanging up the steps, the railings ice-cold to our touch, the wind blowing all around us, and a half a dozen or so shots were fired, none of them doing any good at all. The fire escape served as a kind of screen, through which bullets couldn't seem to find their way.

Then we were on the roof. I looked back down and saw two of them climbing out the window down there, in a hurry and in each other's way. As I watched I saw them squabbling and pushing at each other, neither able to get out the window with the other one in the way. One from each gang, no doubt.

Well, they wouldn't be able to hold each other up forever. I turned back to Abbie, who was standing there rubbing her wrist and glaring at me. Shouting to be heard above the wind, she yelled, "What did you come up *here* for? Now we're trapped!"

"Cul de sac!" I shouted, pointing down. "No way out down there!"

"Well, there's certainly no way out up *here!*"

"Come!"

I grabbed her other wrist this time, and started running. She might have wanted to argue, but you can't argue and run at the same time, so there wasn't any more discussion for a while.

We were in the middle of the block, on one of a row of similar buildings with identical roof heights. Knee-high brick walls separated the roof areas of each building, and on each roof there was a brick structure containing the staircase and elevator housing, a chimney, a few narrow air shafts surmounted by shielded fans and a number of teetering television aerials. We ran around all the structures and jumped over all the walls, and when we'd gone three buildings I paused to try a staircase door. Locked. I grabbed Abbie's wrist again and ran on.

The fourth building's door was locked. The fifth building's door was locked. Somebody took a shot at us, and a television antenna near us said *ping*. I looked back, and here came half a dozen of them, all piling out onto the roof back there where we'd started.

"Oh, God damn it," I said, and went on running. There were more bangs from behind us, more *pings* all around us. I initiated a dodging sort of run, back and forth, angling this way and that.

The sixth building's door was locked.

"Hell!" I said. "If only we had that blasted gun of yours! It would get us through a door anyway."

"Don't talk," Abbie advised me, gasping. "Run."

I ran. Without my holding her wrist, Abbie ran alongside me. I don't know about her, but I didn't feel the cold at all.

Seventh building. I slammed into the door, it fell open, I fell downstairs.

27

Abbie was shaking my shoulder and saying, "Chet?"

"Boy," I said. I struggled to sit up. "Wow," I said.

"Are you all right?"

"I think my chassis's out of alignment." With the help of Abbie and a handy wall I dragged myself to my feet.

"You ought to be more careful," she said. "You scared me half to death."

"Thoughtless of me," I said. I moved all my limbs and turned my head back and forth. Everything seemed to work all right.

"Can you run?" she asked me.

"Yes," I said, and staggered up the stairs.

"Not *that* way!" she shouted. "That's the way we came from!"

"I know it. Buzz for the elevator."

I tottered to the top of the stairs and slammed the

door. There was a bolt, which I threw home, and then I blundered back down again, this time managing to stay on my feet.

The elevator wasn't there yet. "It was on one," Abbie said. She squinted at the little dial by the call button. "Just passing four."

Somebody thudded on the door up there.

"I wonder if they'll shoot the lock off," I said, looking up, and a gun went bang and the door went *ngngngngngn* but didn't open.

The elevator oozed into view. We jumped in, I pushed the first-floor button, and the roof door took another bullet. We began to drift leisurely down the elevator shaft.

I said, "Where's your car?"

"In a lot on 48th Street. But I don't have the ticket. I don't have my purse. I don't have anything."

I patted my behind. Yes, I had my wallet. I was wearing my own clothes, the only problem being that I wasn't wearing enough of them. I said, "We'll just have to hope they remember you."

"It was a huge lot," she said, "with a hundred guys working there. They won't remember me, and I don't have any identification."

The elevator inched past three. I said, "We have to have a car. We can't run around the streets. If *they* don't get us, the cold will."

"I know," she said. "Do you suppose they all ran out? Maybe we could sneak back into the apartment and get our things."

"Abbie," I said, "you aren't thinking."

"I guess that was kind of fantasizing, wasn't it?" she said.

The second floor went by, lingeringly.

I stared at the elevator door. "We've got to have a car," I said. I knew it was up to me. Time to start being the resourceful hero.

The elevator door opened. First floor, everybody out.

Abbie said, "What are we going to do, Chet?"

She was counting on me. I looked at her and said, "We're going to run. Think later."

"Listen!"

I heard it. Feet pounding down the stairwell. I grabbed Abbie's hand and we ran.

Standing in the elevator we'd had a chance to cool off a bit, and when we hit the outside air with our clothing damp from perspiration we both staggered at the impact of the cold. "Oh, *boy!*" I shouted.

"*H-h-h-h-h,*" Abbie said.

I looked down to the right, just as three guys on the sidewalk in front of Tommy's building saw us and started frantically pointing us out to each other. Any minute now they were going to stop pointing and start running. I turned and ran the other way, Abbie's hand still clutched in mine, Abbie herself trailing along somewhere in my wake like a water skier.

I got to Ninth Avenue, and took a second to look back. The three on the sidewalk were just passing the building we'd come out of, and the rest of them were boiling out that building now. Hail, hail, the gang's all here.

I turned left, for two carefully-thought-out reasons. First, it didn't involve crossing any streets. Second, it got me out of their sight faster. Which is to say I was running blind.

People in New York never pay any attention to anything. The middle of January, two coatless, hatless people go running pellmell up Ninth Avenue at five o'clock in the afternoon, the sidewalk full of kids walking around and fat women talking to each other and guys in cloth hats waiting for buses, and I doubt any one of them gave us more than a passing glance. Maybe some kid, more impressionable than most, said to some other kid, "Hey, look at them nuts," but that would have been about the extent of the excitement we caused.

I was running in a straight line now, so when I got to the corner of 47th Street, I ignored my carefully-thought-out reasons from before and just went straight ahead across the street. I also ignored whether the traffic light was red or green, and was therefore nearly run down by an off-duty cab. He slammed on his brakes, I slammed on his hood, and Abbie piled on me from behind.

The cabby rolled his window down and stuck his head out and said, "Whatsa matter witchoo? Wyncha watch where you're goin?"

I'd been in the wrong, of course, but I knew better than to admit it. I was about to go into my automatic offensive response when I looked again and realized I recognized the cab. Not the driver, the cab. It was one I'd driven, it belonged to the V. S. Goth Service Corporation.

Of course! A cab!

I said, "Take us to—"

"Don'tcha see the sign, dummy?" He leaned out farther to stick an arm up and point at it.

"You're going to Eleventh Avenue and 65th Street, dummy," I told him, "and so are we." I ran around his head and pulled open the rear door. Half a dozen slightly overweight hoods were puffing away at full steam in the middle of the block, a sight that even some New Yorkers couldn't resist looking at.

Abbie jumped into the cab and I jumped in after her. The cabby said, "Them guys friends of yours?"

"We're eloping," I said. "Those are her brothers. Let's go."

He looked at the track team again, made a how-about-that? face, and we finally got moving.

It took him half a block to start talking, and then he said, "Don't do it."

I looked at the back of his head. "Don't do what?"

"Don't get married," he said. "I got married, and what did it get me?"

"You got to be careful who you marry," I said.

He glared at me in the rear-view mirror.

"You making cracks about my wife?"

That's the kind of conversation you can't win. I said, "No," and looked out the window.

We were stopped by the light at Tenth Avenue, of course. It has been my experience in my six years as a cabdriver that I would say I have spent four and a half of those years sitting in front of red lights. I looked out the back window, and here they came, just turning the corner way back at the other end of the block, running full tilt, arms pumping, ties whipping out behind them, jackets open. Most of them were just in suits, only two wearing overcoats, and if they ever slowed down they were going to be mighty cold.

The light turned green and we crossed Tenth Avenue and went to Eleventh Avenue, where the light was red. "You folks left without your coats," the cabby pointed out. He'd apparently decided to forgive my slur against his wife.

"We were in a hurry," I said.

"You must be elopin' to Miami."

"That's right," Abbie said, and grinned at me, and reached over to squeeze my hand.

"Don't I wish I was there right now," the cabby said, and the light turned green. We made our right and went one block to 48th Street, where the light was red. "You folks flyin?"

"You bet we are," Abbie said.

"That's the only way to go," he said. "Right? Right?"

"Right," Abbie said.

The light turned green. We made eight blocks, and at 56th Street got stopped by another light. All in all it took us three greens to get to 65th Street, and it turned out we had us a talkative driver. By the time we got where we were going he'd told us about his two airplane rides, about Miami, and about his brother-in-law's car-wash operation in Long Island City which he could have had a half interest in only it had been during New York's water crisis and he'd figured it was too dangerous to invest in something that used water and now he could kick himself.

I could have kicked him, too. My own feeling when driving a cab is that the customer should decide if he wants to hold a conversation or not. If somebody says something to me, I respond. But I don't push conversations on people who don't want conversations.

Anyway, we finally got to the garage, at which point it occurred to him to ask, "Why come here? Don't you want the West Side terminal?"

"We've got to get married first," I said.

"Oh," he said. At the rate his mind turned over, it should be three or four days before it occurred to him there weren't any churches or anything around here.

I paid him, and gave him a good tip because I want

people to give me good tips—but no more horses, please
—and we got out into the cold. He drove on into the
garage, and I said to Abbie, "See that gas station down
there? Wait in the office in there. I'll pick you up in a
couple minutes."

"What are you going to do?" Her teeth were chattering.

"Get a car," I said.

"You're going to steal a cab?"

"What steal? I'm an employee here, I'm going to sign
one out."

"Oh," she said, and smiled in wonderment. "Of course.
How easy."

"Go get indoors," I said. "You're turning blue."

"Thank God I'm wearing my boots," she said, and
turned and hurried away. I watched her go, and I hoped
for her sake the boots went up to her waist, because the
skirt was barely long enough to reach her legs.

I went on into the garage and talked to the dispatcher.
He had a couple of remarks about my not having called
in the last three or four days, but there's a lot of guys less
dependable than me and he knew it, so I didn't say anything and he didn't keep it up. I signed out a car and
while I was walking across the floor to get it, here came
the cabby we'd just ridden with, bringing his time sheet
into the office.

He stared at me. "Where's your girl?"

"The hell with her," I said. "I don't like her family."

I felt him staring at me as I walked on.

28

At the gas station, the guy who came out to service me gave me a dirty look when Abbie hopped into the cab and I immediately drove away. She'd started to get in front, but I'd waved her to get in the back instead, and as we started up I threw the meter flag. I didn't want to get stopped by a cop at this stage of the game.

Abbie said, "You didn't need gas?"

"That wasn't a Sunoco station," I said, and looked at the gas gauge. "And I don't need gas."

"It's freezing in here."

"It'll warm up in a couple minutes."

"Where are we going now?"

"I have no idea," I said. "None at all. There's a diner I'm partial to down here a ways, let's go in there and have a cup of coffee and think things over."

"Fine," she said.

So that's what we did, and in the warmth of the diner we both began to relax a little. I ordered two Danish with our coffee, and when they arrived Abbie said, "That's what puts the pounds on, Chet."

"When people are chasing me with guns," I said, "I think dieting is a little irrelevant." I chomped into my Danish, and found it good.

"All right," she said. "But when this is over, you go on a diet."

"By the time this is over," I said, "if I'm still around, I expect to be very very thin. Let's not talk about dieting any more. Let's talk about what we're going to do."

She sipped at her coffee. "I don't know," she said. "I can't think any more."

"What if we found the killer?" I asked. "What if we did solve things, and then let the gangs know we weren't going to tell anybody about any of the stuff we overheard, we were—"

"*I* didn't overhear anything," she said.

"Do you want to go back to that apartment and tell them so?"

"No," she said.

"The only reason we managed to stay alive as long as we did," I said, "was pure dumb luck. Both gangs were too confused, they wanted to know what was going on before they did anything drastic. But it was in the cards all along that we were going to be nuisances they'd feel happier without."

"What I don't understand," she said, "is why you let that second bunch in the apartment. Napoli and his people. With Droble and all the others already there."

"I didn't know exactly what would happen if I let them in," I said, "but I did know what would happen if I didn't let them in. They'd break their way through the door, they'd probably come in shooting. Droble's people would have been shooting at the people forcing their way in, and we would have had an immediate war on our hands, with us in the middle. The other way, there was a chance the confusion could be maintained for a while. Besides, I didn't see anything else I could do."

"All right," she said. "What about for now? Any ideas at all?"

"One," I said. "And I'm not sure how much I like it."

"What is it?"

"Detective Golderman."

She looked at me, uncomprehending.

I said, "I think I can trust him. He's had me alone a couple of times and he hasn't tried any mayhem on me. And I know he's working on the case. Maybe if we talk to him, tell him everything we know, he can put it together with what the police have and come up with something. And in the meantime he can hide us out somewhere. You and I are amateurs, Abbie, and it's about time we turned our business over to a professional."

I didn't know if I'd talked her into it, but in the process of talking to her I'd convinced me. It had been an idea in the back of my head, and I hadn't been sure whether it was a good one or not, but now that I'd heard it spoken out loud I thought it was a great idea, so I said, "Unless you have some very strong objection, I'm going to phone him right now and see if I can arrange a meeting in some neutral territory. Like this booth, for instance."

"I'm not sure," she said. Her brow was furrowed. "I hate to trust anybody," she said.

"So do I. But we've come to the point where we've got to trust somebody, and like I say, Golderman has already had a couple of chances at me and hasn't taken them. I think we can be sure he isn't the guy who killed Tommy or took that shot at me, and if he isn't we should be able to trust him."

"I suppose you're right," she said. "All right, go ahead and try it. But listen very carefully to how he sounds on the phone."

"Don't worry," I told her. "In the last week I've grown as paranoid as you are."

"Good," she said. "You might last a few years that way."

"Mm," I said. I took another mouthful of Danish,

slurped some coffee, and left the table. The phones were at the rear, and I went back there, dug out a dime, stepped into the booth and called Information, from whom I got the number for the police precinct covering West 46th Street. Then I called that number, asked for the Detective Squad, and when I got them I asked for Detective Golderman.

"Not here today."

"Not at all? Not all day?"

"Won't be in till tomorrow morning. Can I do anything for you?"

"No, I need Detective Golderman. Do you have any idea where I could get in touch with him?"

"Hold on."

I held on. The phone booth grew stuffy, and I opened the door a little, and the light went out. I shut the door enough for the light to come on, and the booth got stuffy again. I had my choice of light or air, it seemed, and I opted for air, opening the door all the way.

Then he came back and I shut the door again, opting for privacy. He said, "He's at home. I can give you the number."

"Good. Thanks."

"Do you have a pencil?"

"No, I'll have to remember it. I'm in a phone booth."

"Okay. He lives out on Long Island, in Westbury. It's area code 516."

"Yeah, I know that."

"Right. The number is ED3-3899."

"ED3-3899." I looked at the phone dial, and E and D were both 3, so the number was 333-3899. "I've got it," I said. "Thank you."

"Don't mention it."

So I called the Westbury number. The operator wanted twenty cents and I had to give her a quarter. Then the phone rang six times before it was answered, by a woman. I asked for Detective Golderman, and she said, "He's taking a nap right now. Is it important?"

I said, "I could call when he wakes up, I suppose. When would be a good time?"

"I'll be waking him at six," she said.

"That's fine," I said. "I'll call a little after six."

"Who shall I say called?"

"I'm sorry," I said, "but I'd rather tell him myself." And I broke the connection, not liking to be rude but also not wanting to give my name ahead of time. Just in case, just in case.

I went back to the table and told Abbie my adventures on the phone, and she said, "So what are we going to do now? Sit here till six o'clock?"

"Not a bit of it. We'll drive out to Westbury and go straight to his house."

"You got his address?"

"I got his phone number."

"What good does that do you?"

"How many Goldermans do you suppose are going to be in the phone book," I asked her, "with the same telephone number?"

"Oh," she said. "Sorry, I wasn't thinking."

"You're not drinking either. Let's finish up and get going."

She looked out the window. "Out in that cold again. Brrrr."

I couldn't have agreed more.

29

Detective Golderman's house was a nice white clapboard Cape Cod on a quiet side street in Westbury. We got there at twenty-five minutes to seven and parked out front. A Volkswagen and a Pontiac stood side by side on the cleared driveway in front of the attached garage. In the city there was practically no sign left of last week's snowstorm, but out here in the suburbs there was still plenty of it, on lawns and vacant lots and piled up beside driveways.

It was fully night by now of course, but a light was shining beside the front door. We got out of the warm cab and hurried shivering through the needle-cold air up the walk to the door. I rang the bell and we stood there flapping our arms until at last it opened.

A pleasant-looking woman in her late thirties, wearing a wool sweater, stretch slacks, and a frilly apron, looked through the storm door at us, astonished, and then opened it and said, "You must be freezing. Come in."

"We are," I said, and Abbie said, "Thank you," and we went in.

She shut the door, and I said, "I'm the one who called about an hour ago."

"And wouldn't leave his name," she said. "Arnie and I have been wondering about that."

"I'll give it now," I said. "Chester Conway. And this is Miss Abbie McKay."

She frowned at us. "Should I have heard of you? Abbie and Chet, like Bonnie and Clyde?"

"No," I said. "We're more victims."

"Well, that's cryptic," she said. "Come in and sit down, I'll call Arnie."

"Thank you."

The living room was spacious, modern, and very very neat. I wouldn't have lit a cigarette in that room for a thousand dollars. The two of us sat on the edge of the sofa while Mrs. Golderman went away to get her Arnie.

Abbie said, under her breath, "It does make you feel safe, doesn't it?"

I looked at her. "What does?"

She waved her hand, indicating the room in general. "All this. Neat, respectable, middle-class. Germ-free, stable, dependable. You know."

"I see what you mean," I said. "Yes, you're right."

"You should see my place," she said. "In Vegas."

"Not like this?"

She rolled her eyes heavenward. "Ooh. It looks like the day the riot broke out in the whorehouse."

"My father keeps our place pretty neat," I said. "Not as neat as a woman would, of course."

"Depends on the woman," she said.

I looked at her. "You mean if I took you home you wouldn't clean the place up?"

"Depends what you took me home for," she said, and looked past me to say, "Hello, there."

I turned my head, and Detective Golderman had joined us. He was in tan slacks and green polo shirt and white sneakers and he looked very summery and relaxed and not at all like the wintry sardonic detective I was used to meeting in the snow around New York.

"So it is you," he said.

"Yes, sir." I got to my feet. "I came to tell you a long story," I said.

"Then you'll want a drink," he said. "Come along." And he turned away.

Abbie and I looked at each other, shrugged, and followed him. We went through a dining room that looked like a department-store display, and entered a hallway with duck-shooting prints on the walls. "Hold on," he said, and went to the end of the hall to stick his head into what looked like a yellow-and-white spick-and-span kitchen and say, "We'll be downstairs, Mary." Then he came back and opened a door and gestured for us to precede him down the stairs.

"This is my pride and joy," he said, coming after us and shutting the door again. "Just got it finished last fall."

A basement game room. Would you believe it? Knotty-pine walls, acoustical tile ceiling, green indoor-outdoor rug on the floor. A dart board. A Ping-Pong table. A television-radio-record-player console next to a recessed shelf containing about a hundred records. And, of course of course of course, a bar.

You know the kind of bar I mean, I hope. The kind of bar I mean is the kind of bar that has all those things all over it. A little lamppost with a drunk leaning against it. Electrified beer signs bouncing and bubbling and generally carrying on. Napkins with cartoons on them. Funny stirrers in a container shaped like a keg. Mugs shaped like dwarfs.

I could go on, but I'd rather not. The mottoes on the walls, and the glasses and objects on the back bar, the ashtrays— No, I'd rather not catalogue it all. Suffice it to say that Abbie and I looked at one another in a moment of deep interpersonal communion. Our two brains beat as one.

"Sit down," Detective Golderman said, going around behind the bar. "What's your pleasure?"

The bar stools were light wood with purple seats. We sat on two, and I said, "I'll take Scotch and soda, if you've got it."

"Of course I've got it. What's yours, Miss McKay?"

"A sidecar, please," she said sweetly, and smiled at him in all innocence.

A hell of a thing to do. I considered kicking her ankle, but I was more interested in seeing how he'd handle it.

Very well. "One sidecar," he said, hardly blanching at all, and when he turned around he opened the drawer in the back bar with no fuss at all. We should have chatted with one another now, if we'd done so we probably never would have noticed him leafing through the little book in that drawer, or adjusting the drawer partway open so the book would stay open to the page he wanted.

Of course, the end result was that he made the sidecar first and I didn't get my simple Scotch and soda forever.

But he did have the ingredients. Out of a little refrigerator under the bar he took a bottle of lime juice and set it down on his work area. He looked around and then said, "Be back in one minute," and hurried away upstairs.

I whispered, "What a nasty thing to do."

"I know," she said. "I just couldn't help it."

"You didn't even try."

"Oh, Chet, let me have my fun. Don't be a wet blanket."

"Nasty woman," I said, and back came Detective Golderman. Would you believe he was carrying a little bowl containing the white of an egg? Well, he was.

What was eventually set down in front of Abbie looked

like a perfect sidecar, and when she tasted it I could see the biter had been bit. "Beautiful," she said. "This is really great."

Opening my bottle of soda, he basked in the praise. "I have to use my little recipe book sometimes," he said, "but I pride myself on having the real touch. Say when, Chester."

"When."

He handed over my drink, put the soda and lime juice away, put all the bottles back where they belonged, put the bowl in the bar sink and ran water in it, poured himself a short brandy, took a sip, made a face, leaned his elbows on the bar, and said to me, "Well, now. I believe you're here to tell me something, Chester."

"I'm here to tell you everything," I said, and I did.

He listened quietly, interrupting only once, when I suggested that I'd been shot by the same person who shot Tommy, and added, "Using the same gun." Then he said, "No, not the same gun. We found that one the same day McKay was killed."

"You did?"

"Yes, in a litter basket just down on the corner. No fingerprints, naturally."

"Naturally."

"And it's a lucky thing for you it wasn't the same gun," he said. He gestured at my wound and said, "It would have made a lot more of a mess than that. It was a .45 automatic. All it would have had to do was brush your head like that and you'd still be looking for the top of your skull."

"Don't talk like that," I said, and put my hand on the top of my skull, glad I knew where it was.

"Anyway," he said. "Go on with it."

So I went on with it, and when I was done, he said, "Chester, why didn't you simply come to me in the first place and tell me the truth? You could have saved yourself an awful lot of trouble."

"I suppose so," I said.

"Now you've not only got two complete gangs of racketeers after you," he said, "you've got a pretty violent amateur killer after you as well."

I said, "Amateur?"

"Definitely," he said. "Bears all the earmarks. Undoubtedly fired in anger when he killed McKay."

"But what about the dum-dum bullets?"

"Exactly," he said. "Professionals don't have to do that, their aim is too good. And they prefer to avoid excess mess. Anger again. Some sorehead sitting at his kitchen table, muttering to himself while scoring those bullets, not really sure whether he'd ever use them on anybody or not."

"But how would he know about doing it?"

"How do you know about it?" he asked me.

I shrugged. "I don't know. Movies or television, I suppose."

"Exactly," he said.

"The question is," Abbie said, "can you help us at all?"

"You want the murderer found," he said. "And you want both gangs off your necks."

"Please," I said.

"I'll see what I can do. The investigation into McKay's death isn't active any more, you know."

"We know," I said. "Not since Thursday night. They didn't spend much time on it, did they?"

"The force is short-handed," he said. "If a thing doesn't start to break fast, and if it isn't something really special and out of the way, the only place for it is the inactive file." To Abbie he said, "I'm sorry, Miss McKay, I understand your brother *is* something special to you, but to us he's only one more homicide. And nothing broke fast. On the other hand, we didn't know all the things you two have just told us, so that might make a difference. Let me make a phone call or two. I'll be right back."

Abbie said, "You aren't going to tell your superiors where we are, are you? We don't want police protection, not regular police protection."

He smiled at her. "Worried that somebody could be bought off? You might be right. Don't worry, I'll take care of you myself."

"Thank you," she said.

"Not at all." Coming out from behind the bar he said, "If you want refills, help yourself. I'll try not to be long."

I said, "One last question before you go."

"Certainly, Chester."

"When you came out to my house," I said, "you mentioned four names. Since then I've met three of them, but not the fourth."

He nodded. "Bugs Bender."

"That's the one," I said. "Who is he?"

"It doesn't matter any more," he said. "We think he was a free-lance assassin, he worked for both Napoli and Droble at one time or another. He'd disappeared a couple of months ago, and we were wondering what had happened, but he turned up late last week."

"Oh," I said.

"In the bottom of a garbage scow," he said. "He'd been there for quite a while."

"Oh," I said.

"So it's just as well you didn't meet him," he said, and smiled at me, and went away.

"What a lovely story," Abbie said.

"I'm glad I didn't miss it."

"Oh, well." She swung around on her stool to look at the length of the basement. "Can you believe this room?" she said.

"I bet you," I said, "if you were to burrow through that wall over there and keep going in a straight line across Long Island, you'd go through a good three hundred basement rooms just exactly like this one before you reached the ocean."

"No bet," she said. "But where do they get the money? Golderman must have put his salary for the next twenty years into this place."

"Fourth mortgage," I said.

"I suppose so."

"Aside from his house, what do you think of him?"

She turned back to her drink. "All right, I guess," she said. "He does those facial expressions like he's very sharp, very hip, but I think really he isn't at all. It's all front."

"That's because you are seeing him in his basement," I said. "If you want to see the ultimate in cool, you should have been there Friday morning, when he caught Ralph in the closet."

She grinned. "Yes, I can see how he'd have handled that."

I squinted at the back bar. "That's weird," I said.

She looked where I was looking. "What's weird? The Gay Nineties lamp that says 'Bar?' "

"No," I said. "If Tommy's murder was put on the inactive list by the police Thursday night, how come Detective Golderman came around Friday morning?"

"I don't know," she said. "Maybe he had one or two last questions he wanted to ask."

"Ask who?"

"Me, I guess. Or Louise."

"How come he didn't ask them? And, honey, he had to know when the funeral was, and he had to know if he was going to find any of Tommy's relatives it would be at the funeral. He came there then, at that time, because he thought the place was empty."

She looked at me. "Meaning what?"

"Meaning it seems to me I remember Walter Droble saying something about one of the cops on the case being his man on the scene."

"You mean—Golderman?"

"Maybe he didn't have to take out a fourth mortgage after all," I said.

"But—what was he doing at the apartment?"

"I'm not sure. Maybe he thought there might be something there to connect him with Droble's mob. A pay-off record or something like that. Maybe the mob sent him around to give the place a going-over and see there wasn't anything there that might break security."

Abbie looked at her sidecar with revulsion. "Do you think he's poisoned us?"

"He isn't the killer," I said. "The killer is somebody outside either mob, that's pretty sure by now. And if he was the one who shot at me Wednesday night, he had a perfect chance to finish the job after Ralph left Friday morning."

"Then what's the problem?"

"The problem is, who do you suppose he's calling right now?"

"Oh, my Lord," she said, and spun around on the stool. "There's always a beige wall phone in places like this," she said.

"I already looked," I told her. "This is the exception to the rule."

"Unless—" She hopped down off the stool and walked around behind the bar, saying, "Sometimes they put it under— Here it is." She lifted a beige phone and put it on the bar.

"Gently," I said.

"Naturally."

Slowly, inchingly, she lifted the receiver. I could suddenly hear tinny voices. Abbie lifted the phone to her ear, put her hand over the mouthpiece, and listened. Gradually her eyes widened, staring at me.

I made urgent hand and head motions at her, demanding to know who it was, what was going on. She made urgent shakes of the head, letting me know I'd have to wait. But I kept it up, and finally she mouthed, with exaggerated lip movements, *Frank Tar-bok*.

"Oh," I said, aloud, and she frantically shook her head at me. I clapped my hand over my mouth.

But oh. Oh and oh and oh. Even thinking it, even being sure of it, I'd been hoping against hope that I was wrong. Because if I was right, we were on the run again, and this time with absolutely no place to go at all. No place at all.

Abbie carefully and wincingly hung up the telephone, put it quickly away under the counter, and hurried around to sit down beside me at the bar again, saying under her breath. "He doesn't want any trouble here, his wife doesn't know anything about anything. He's supposed to get us out of the house and take us to a rendezvous. A house in Babylon."

"Then what?" I asked, though I didn't really have to.

"Tarbok started to say something about the waterfront

being a handy place," Abbie said, "and Golderman broke
in and said he didn't want to know anything about anything like that."

I remembered what a short time ago it had been that
Tarbok and I had shaken hands in solemn partnership.
Well, that duet had gone off-key in a hurry.

We heard the door open at the head of the stairs.
Getting off the stool, I said, "When he's sitting down, you
distract him."

"What are you going to do?"

There was no time to answer. Golderman was coming
down the stairs. I shook my head and ran around behind
the bar. Scotch, Scotch. Here it was. Black & White, a
nice brand. A full quart.

Golderman was at the foot of the stairs. I gulped what
was left of the Scotch and soda in my glass, and was
starting to pour myself a fresh drink when Golderman
came over to the bar. "Well, well," he said. "You the new
barman, Chester?"

"That's me," I said. "What's yours?"

He sat down on a stool. "I'll just take my brandy, if
I may."

"Sure thing." I slid his brandy glass over to him. "What's
the situation?"

"Well, it's been taken out of my hands," he said. "The
captain's going to want to talk to you two. In the morning.
In the meantime, he refuses to let me keep you here."

"Oh, boy," I said.

"What does he expect us to do tonight?" Abbie asked
him.

"It just so happens," he said, "that my wife's brother
isn't home right now. He works for Grumman, they have
him and his whole family in Washington for three months.

I have the keys to his house, there's no reason you can't stay there tonight."

"Where's the house?" I asked. It was easy to resist the impulse to say something smart-alecky, like, "Oh, the house in Babylon?" Like him with Ralph in the closet. But all I had to do was forecast the dialogue from that point on, if I did such a thing, and the impulse got itself resisted.

"In Babylon," he said. "Not very far from here."

"Can you give me directions?"

"Oh, I'll drive you over," he said.

"I have my own car out front," I said.

"You'd better leave that here for tonight. The captain was explicit that I shouldn't give you two the opportunity to change your minds and take off again. I'll run you over there, it won't be any trouble at all."

"I hope there's no hurry," I said, lifting the bottle of Black & White. "I was just about to make myself a second drink."

"Go right ahead," he said.

Abbie got down off the stool and started walking away toward the other end of the room, saying, "Is that a color television set?"

Golderman swung around on his stool to watch her. "Yes, it is," he said, and I bonked him with the Black & White.

30

"We can't stay here all night," Abbie said.

I shut the last cabinet door. "Not a gun down here," I said. "And none on him. I thought cops were supposed to wear guns at all times."

"Not while they're at home," she said.

I went around behind the bar again and looked at him. He was tied hand and foot, he was gagged, and he was unconscious, and it all served him right. But if only he'd had a gun on him.

"Doggone it," I said. "That gun of yours might have been a pea-shooter, but it would have been better than nothing."

"Stop worrying about guns," Abbie said. "When we don't show up at that house in Babylon pretty soon, Tarbok and his men are going to come over to find out what's the matter."

"Yeah, and one of them will probably be carrying that gun of yours, and he'll stand very close and go *pit pit* and it's all over because we don't have anything to *defend* ourselves with."

"Where would one of *them* get it?" she said, frowning at me.

"Out of my pocket," I said.

"No," she said.

Why was she bothering me with things like that? I looked at her, exasperated, and said, "What do you mean, no?"

"None of those people took the gun," she said. "It was gone before you got to the apartment."

I stared. "Before?"

"Of course," she said. "When do you think I was looking for it?"

"I don't know," I said. "I thought one time while I was unconscious in the apartment."

"In the *car*," she said. "When you got yourself shot. I took off away from there, and every time I got stopped by a light I searched you some more. That's how I got so sticky."

"Never mind that part."

"Anyway," she said, "you didn't have it with you. I could have killed you myself, if you want to know."

"Not without the gun. Maybe it's in the car someplace, maybe it fell out of my pocket."

"I searched, Chet, I really and truly searched. That gun was gone."

"Well, I'll be damned," I said. I went over and sat down at the bar and pulled on my Scotch and soda. "Then who the heck took it?" I said.

Abbie came over and sat down beside me. "What difference does it make? The question is, what do we do now?"

"The question is," I insisted, "who took the goddam gun. I had it when I got to the poker game, I remember feeling the weight of it in my pocket when I was going up all those stairs."

She was beginning to get interested, too. "What about afterwards?" she said.

"I don't remember. But where did we go? I was in the car the whole time. Who could have taken it?"

"Somebody at the poker game," she said.

"Hmmm," I said. "It was hanging in the hall closet. Everybody got up from the table at one time or another. Yeah, that's when it must have been."

"That's the only time it could have been," she said.

"And I'll tell you something else," I said. "It was *your* gun that shot *me* in the *head*."

"What makes you say that?"

"Golderman told us they found the gun that killed Tommy. He also said it was an amateur. So where's an amateur gonna get another gun in a hurry when he decides he'll have to kill again? From the victim!"

"But why do you think it was the same gun?"

"First," I said, "because your gun was stolen the same night. Second, because the job was done by an amateur who wasn't going to have ready access to a whole arsenal of guns. And third, because Golderman told us I was shot by a smaller, lighter gun than the one used on Tommy, which is an accurate description of that gun of yours."

"But my gun always misses to the left, and he just nicked you on what was his right."

"Of course," I said. "It should have been obvious all along."

"What should have been obvious all along?"

"He was shooting at you."

31

"Now wait a minute!"

"Abbie, think about it. What did we tell the guys at that game? That you were Tommy's sister, and you came to New York because he was dead, and because you didn't have any faith in the police to find your brother's murderer you were going to look for him yourself. *You*, not me. All I ever said *I* was after was my nine hundred dollars."

She was shaking her head. "I wasn't the one who was shot, Chet, you were."

"Because your goddam gun shoots crooked."

"We aren't even *sure* it was my gun."

"I am," I said. "I'll tell you what I'm sure of. I'm sure I was shot with your gun. I'm sure the bullet was meant for you instead of me. And I'm one hundred percent positive that Tommy's murderer is one of the guys at that poker game."

"Hm," she said. She sat down on the bar stool beside me and swirled the remains of her sidecar in its glass. "I think you're right," she said at last.

"You don't know what a relief it is," I said, "to know it isn't *me* that guy is after."

"That's nice," she said. "It's a relief to know he's after me instead, is that it?"

"I know how that sounded—"

"Well, what I've got after me," she said, "is one poorly armed amateur, but what you've got after you, buddy, is two armies."

"Oh, for Pete's sake," I said. "We've been forgetting. One of those armies is coming *here*."

"Oh!" She finished her sidecar, and the two of us left the bar.

"Quietly," I whispered.

"I know, I know."

We tiptoed up the stairs. Detective Golderman's wife might not be in on her husband's nefariousness, but she wouldn't have to be in on it to take umbrage at two strangers knocking him out and tying him up and leaving him on the floor behind the bar in his downstairs play-room. So we moved slowly and silently up the stairs, and at the top I cracked the door open just a hair and peeked through the slit.

I saw nothing but a hunting print, but I did hear Mrs. Golderman humming to herself in the kitchen. I nodded back at Abbie, pushed the door open farther, and crept out.

She was humming one of those tuneless things, Mrs. Golderman, one of those things you hum when you're absorbed in a simple physical task that will take several hours, like stuffing a turkey or building a birdhouse. I don't say Mrs. Golderman was stuffing a turkey or building a birdhouse, but from the sound of her she was doing *something* that was going to keep her occupied for a while.

The two of us sidled up to the hall, inched the door shut behind us, and crept away through the dining room and the living room to the front door. I was about to reach for the knob when Abbie tugged my arm. I looked at her, and she pointed at the door of the hall closet.

Was she confused? I shook my head, and pointed at the front door.

She shook her head, and pointed emphatically at the hall closet.

I shook my head harder, and pointed very emphatically at the front door.

She shook her head hard enough to make hair fly, and pointed very *very* emphatically at the hall closet.

Oh, the hell with it. Nothing would do but I had to prove she was wrong. Then she'd come along quietly. So I went over and opened the hall-closet door and gave her a sarcastic smile and gestured to point out to her it wasn't the way out, it was a closet full of overcoats.

She nodded, and gave *me* a sarcastic smile and gestured to point out to me it was a closet full of overcoats.

Full of overcoats.

I blinked at the closet. "Oh," I said, out loud.

"Sst!"

I nodded, clamping my mouth shut, and we both listened for a minute. We could barely hear the humming at this end of the house, but it was continuing unabated.

Abbie poked through the closet and came out with a black-and-red-check wool mackinaw for me. I looked at it, looked at her, looked at it. She leaned close and whispered, "It's warmest. An overcoat won't do you any good, you don't have a jacket."

I nodded without pleasure and shrugged into the mackinaw while Abbie went through the closet some more, like one of those style-conscious women rejecting every dress in Lord & Taylor. Zip, zip, zip, pushing the hangers along one after the other.

Finally she settled, and I could see it was with vast reluctance, on a black cloth coat with a black fur collar. It had a tapered waist and silver buttons, and when she got it on, it looked pretty good on her. With the black boots it made her look vaguely Russian. More like the Cossack than his girlfriend, but that wasn't so bad at that, and when she found a black fur hat on the shelf and put that on I felt like leaping at once into one of those Russian dances where you end every line by throwing one arm up in the air and shouting, "Hey!"

I also felt like shouting hey and throwing one arm up in the air when she came out with a hat for me, though not exactly in the same way. It was orange, it had a little peak and earflaps, and it tied under the chin. Apparently

Detective Golderman spent his time in the woods hunting animals when not in the city hunting people.

I whispered, "I won't put that on!"

She whispered, "Then you'll freeze your ears off!" I think she said ears.

I whispered, "I'll carry it, and if it's really cold I'll put it on!"

She shook her head, probably thinking about the vanity of the male and other examples of the pot calling the kettle black, and I stuffed the offending cap into my mackinaw pocket.

From the same shelf that had produced the hats Abbie now brought out gloves. Hers were sleek and black and went halfway up her forearm. Mine were brown leather, a thousand years old, with the first finger of the right hand poking through. They were also a little too small.

Abbie whispered, "Ready?"

I thought of a sardonic answer, but I nodded instead. Then I opened the door, silently opened the outer door, and we went outside, and my ears fell off.

"Brrrr," I commented, and closed the door quietly behind me, and said, "Wait." I then took the cute orange hat out and put it on. I even tied it under my chin.

"That's darling," Abbie said.

"One word," I threatened. "Just one word."

"I promise," she said. "Come on."

We set off down the walk toward the cab and were about halfway there when the two cars squealed to a stop in the middle of the street and all the guys came boiling out of them.

32

All I hoped was that Detective Golderman's back yard wasn't a cul de sac. I grabbed Abbie's hand—I seemed to be doing that a lot lately—and we took off around the side of the house, headed for the back.

There was still snow in this part of the world. Not much, just enough to reach over my shoe tops and start melting in around my anklebone, soaking my socks and my feet. Not that I cared very much at that particular moment.

There was no shooting, and not even very much shouting. I suppose in a quiet neighborhood like that they would have preferred to take us without calling a lot of attention to themselves.

It was a cloudy moonless night, but there was enough spill from the back windows of the house to show me a snowy expanse of back yard leading to a bare-branched hedge that looked like a lot of scratched pencil marks dividing this yard from the one on the other side.

There was no choice, and when you have no choice it greatly simplifies things. You don't slow down to think it over at all, you just run through the hedge. It rips your trousers, it gashes your skin, it removes the pocket of your mackinaw, but you run through it.

It also takes your girl away from you. Abbie's hand was wrenched from mine, I tried to make a U-turn while running at five hundred miles an hour, I slid on the thickness of snow on top of grass, I made my U-turn while simultaneously going forward and falling backward, I landed on gloves and knees in the snow, looked up, and there was Abbie stuck in the hedge like Joan of Arc just before they started the fire.

"Chet!" she called, and reached her arms out to me.

Your feet are never there when you want them. Every time I got them under me they slid out again. I finally solved the problem by starting to run before I got up. I ran my feet up under my torso, made it through that chancy area of no balance, and ran into the hedge again, this time letting it serve as a cushion to stop me.

Abbie was beside me. A hundred people in tight black overcoats and black snapbrim hats were rounding the corner of the house. I grabbed Abbie's waving hands and yanked. Something ripped, Abbie popped out of the hedge, my feet went away again, and I wound up on my back in the snow.

Abbie kept yanking at my hands, keeping me from doing anything about anything. "Get up!" she shouted. "Chet, get up!"

"Leggo and I'll get up!"

She let go, and I got up. I looked across the hedge, and they were right there, on the other side of it. In fact, one of them made a flying leap over the hedge, arms outstretched, and I just barely leaped back clear of his grasping fingers. Fortunately, his toes didn't quite clear the hedge, so the beauty of his leap was marred by a nose-dive finish as he zoomed forehead first into the snow. The last I saw of him he was hanging there, feet jammed into the top of the hedge and face jammed into the ground, while his pals, ignoring him, pushed and shoved through the hedge on both sides of him, trying to catch up with their quarry, which was us.

And which was gone. Hand in hand again, we pelted across the snowy back yard, around the corner of the house and out to a street exactly like the one Detective Golderman's house faced on except that it didn't have my cab parked on it.

Abbie gasped, "Which way?"

"How do I know?"

"Well, we better decide fast," she said. "Here they come."

Here they came. There we went. I took off to the right for no reason other than that the streetlight was closer in that direction.

What was it now, a little after eight o'clock on a Sunday evening? And where was everybody? Home, watching television. Ed Sullivan, probably. That's what's wrong with America, its people have grown lazy, slothful, effete. They should be out in the air, out on the sidewalks, walking around, filling their lungs with God's crisp cool midwinter air, forming crowds into which Abbie and I could blend in comfort and safety. Instead of which that whole nation of ingrates was indoors sitting down with a can of beer in front of the television set, getting fat and soft while Abbie and I ran around in stark solitary visibility in the streets outside.

You want drama, America? Forget *Sunday Night at the Movies,* come out on the streets, watch the gangsters chase the nice boy and girl.

We ran three blocks, and we were beginning to gasp, we were beginning to falter. Fortunately, the mob behind us was in no better shape than we were, and when Abbie finally pulled to a stop and gasped, "I can't run any more," I looked back and saw them straggled out over the block behind us, and none of *them* could run any more either.

The one in front was doing something between a fast walk and a slow trot, but the rest of them were all walking, and the one at the end was absolutely dragging his feet.

So we walked. I had a stitch in my side myself, and I was just as glad to stop running for a while. We walked, and whenever one of them got closer than half a block away we trotted for a while. But what a way to escape.

Finally I said, "Doesn't Westbury have a downtown?" We'd traveled six or seven blocks now, three running and the rest walking, and we were still in the same kind of genteel residential area. There had been no traffic and no pedestrians, and looking both ways at each intersection I had seen no neon or any other indication of a business district. Sooner or later those guys back there were going to take a chance on opening fire at us and hoping nobody in any of these houses would notice, and for myself I believed none of them would notice a thing.

"There must be something somewhere," Abbie answered, in reply to my question about downtown. "Don't talk, just keep walking."

"Right."

So we kept walking, and lo and behold when we got to the next corner I looked down to the left and way down there I saw the red of a traffic light and the blue of a neon sign. "Civilization!" I said. "A traffic light and a bar."

"Let's go."

We went. We walked faster than ever, and we'd gone a full block before any of our pursuers limped around the corner back there. I looked back and saw there were only four of them now, and seven had started after us, so it looked as though we were wearing them away by attrition. I'd seen two quit earlier, falling by the wayside, sitting down on the curb and letting their hands dangle between their knees. Now a third must have done the same thing.

No. All five had been fine before we'd turned the corner, they'd been striding along like a VFW contingent in the Armed Forces Day parade. So where had the fifth one gone?

Could he be circling the block in some other direction, hoping to head us off?

"Oh," I said, and stopped in my tracks.

Abbie stared at me. "Come *on*, Chet," she said, and tugged.

I came on. I said, "One of them went back for a car."

She glanced over her shoulder at them, and said, "Are you sure?"

"I'm positive. The momentum of the chase kept them going this long, but sooner or later one of them had to remember they had wheels back there in front of Golderman's house. So one of them just went back for a car."

She looked ahead at that distant red light and distant blue light. "How much time do we have?"

"I don't know. He's tired, he'll be walking, it's about seven blocks. But we don't have forever."

"We should have gone zigzag," she said. "Turned a lot of corners. That way maybe they'd be lost by now, and they wouldn't be able to find their way back to the cars."

"Sorry I didn't think of it sooner," I said. "Do you know this is ridiculous?"

She looked at me. "What's ridiculous?"

"There are four guys back there who want to take us away some place quiet and murder us," I said. "Plus three others somewhere else behind them. And we're *walking*."

"So are they."

"I know it."

"So what's so ridiculous about that?"

"We're walking and we're having an argument," I said. "That doesn't strike you as ridiculous?"

"It would strike me as ridiculous if I tried to *run* at this point," she said.

I looked over my shoulder. "Get ready to laugh, then," I said. "Because one of them back there has his second wind, and we're about to run."

He'd gotten very close, much less than half a block away. About three houses away, in fact, so close that when we began to stagger into a sort of falling, weaving half-trot we could clearly make out the words he spoke, even though he was gasping while saying them.

We ran to the next intersection, and across, and I looked back, and he was walking again, holding his side. He shook his fist at me.

Abbie said, "Did you hear what he said he was going to do to us?"

"He didn't mean it," I said. "Just a quick bullet in the head, that's all we'll get."

"Well, that's sure a relief," she said, and when I looked at her to see if she was being sarcastic I saw that she was.

How far were those blasted lights? Maybe four blocks away. Thank God it was all level flat ground. I don't know about the mob behind me, but a hill would have finished me for good and all.

We went a block more and came suddenly to railroad tracks. Automatic gates stood open on either side. I said, "Hey! Railroad tracks!" I stopped.

Abbie pulled on me. "So what? Come *on*, Chet."

"Where there's railroad tracks," I said, "there's a railroad station. And trains. And people."

"There's a *bar* right down there, Chet," she said.

"And there's seven guys behind us. They might just

decide to take us out of a bar. But a railroad station should be too much for them." I looked both ways, and the track simply extended away into darkness to left and right, with no station showing at all.

"Which way?" Abbie said. "I suppose we have to do this, even though I think it's wrong."

"This way," I said, and turned left.

There was an eruption of hollering behind us when we made our move. We hurried, spurred on by all that noise, but it was tricky going on railroad ties and we just couldn't make as good time as before. We tried walking on the gravel beside the tracks, but it had too much of a slant to it and we kept tending to slide down into the knee-deep snow in the ditch, so it was the ties for us.

Abbie, looking over her shoulder, gasped, "Here they come."

"I never doubted it for a minute."

It was getting darker, away from the street. There should be another cross street up ahead, but so far I didn't see it. And in the darkness it was increasingly difficult to walk on the ties.

Abbie fell, almost dragging me down with her.

I bent over her, heavily aware of the hoods inching along in our wake. "What happened?"

"Damn," she said.

"Yeah, but what happened?"

"I turned my ankle."

"Oh, boy," I said. "Can you walk?"

"I don't know."

Light far away made me look in the direction we'd come from. "You better try," I said. "Here comes a train."

33

We stood in snow up to our knees in the ditch beside the tracks, Abbie leaning most of her weight on me. The train was taking forever to get here, just moseying along as though it was out for a little jog around the neighborhood, not going anywhere in particular.

At least the hoods had also stopped, and were also standing around in the ditch, watching the train. Four of them, all on our side of the track.

My feet were freezing. Abbie was protected by those boots of hers, but I was soaked and freezing from the knees down, and shivering from the knees up. And stupid from the neck up, since I had very obviously made a bad mistake coming in here instead of continuing straight on to that bar, where maybe I could have phoned the local police, or at least found a cab handy. Now Abbie could barely walk, we were moving deeper and deeper into the kind of darkness in which those four back there would have no problems about taking care of us for good and all, and to make matters worse, as the train ambled by them they began jumping up onto it, standing between cars or on the narrow platforms outside the closed passenger car doors.

"Abbie!" I shouted. "They're cheating!"

It was obvious what they meant to do. They'd ride the train up to where we stood, and then jump on us. Four against one and a half, which is about what we added up to, and the outcome was not in doubt.

"Oh, Chet. Chet, what are we going to do?"

None of them had gotten on the first car, or in the space between cars number one and number two. I said, "Honey, we've got to get on that train, too. It's our only chance."

"I can't *walk!*"

"You've *got* to! Come on, now."

I half-dragged her up the gravel slope, and saw the engineer of the train looking at us in open-mouthed bewilderment. His big diesel engine trundled by, and he looked down at the top of our heads, and I'm sure he kept looking back at us after he'd gone on by. I'm sure of it, but I didn't look to check. I saw a chrome railing coming toward us, and in a car farther on I saw the first of the hoods, with his gun out.

I had one arm around Abbie's waist, holding tight. She had both arms around my neck. I was about as nimble as a man in ankle chains wearing a strait jacket, but if I didn't connect right with that chrome handle it was all over.

Here it came. Here it was.

I stuck my free hand out, grabbed that bar, and held on.

The train took me away.

Funny how fast it was going all of a sudden. And my feet were dragging in the gravel, while simultaneously my arm was being pulled out of its socket. I pulled, and pulled, and pulled, and Abbie babbled a million things in my ear, and I finally got my right foot up onto that narrow ledge of platform, and then it was possible to get the rest of me up onto the train, and there I stood, with Abbie hanging on me as I held to the train by one hand and one foot.

Something went *zzzt*.

That louse hanging on the next car was shooting at us!

"Abbie!" I shouted. "They're shooting at us! Get in between the cars!"

"How?"

"I don't know! Just *do* it!"

So she did it, I don't know how. It involved putting her elbows in my nose, one at a time, and spending several hours standing on my foot—the one foot I had attached to the train—but eventually she was standing on something or other between the cars, gasping and panting but alive.

So was I, for the moment. There'd been several more *zzzts* and a *ping* or two, but the train was rocking back and forth so much it would have been a miracle if he'd hit me. I was a moving target and he was a moving shooter, and since we were on different cars our movements were not exactly synchronized.

Still, I wasn't all that happy to be out there in the open with somebody shooting bullets at me, no matter how much the odds were in my favor. Some gambles I'd rather not take. So I swung around the edge of the car and joined Abbie amidships.

It was very strange in here. We had three walls and no floor. A sort of accordion-pleated thing connected the end doorways in the two cars, so we couldn't get inside, but fortunately the ends of the cars were full of handles and wheels and ladder rungs to hold on to, and there was a narrow lip along the bottom edge of each car to stand on, so it was possible to survive, but very scary to look down between your legs and see railroad ties going by at twenty or thirty miles an hour under your heels. I spent little time looking down.

In fact, I spent more time looking up. A metal ladder

ran up the back of the car, and I wondered if we'd be safer on top than here. I called to Abbie, "Wait here! I'm going up!"

She nodded. She looked bushed, and no wonder.

I clambered up the ladder, my arms and legs feeling very heavy, and at the top I discovered that the top of a railroad car sways a lot more than the bottom does. It was impossible for me to stand, impossible to walk. So I inched along on my belly, and no matter how cold and windy it was, no matter how icy and wet my feet were, no matter how I ached all over, no matter how many people were after me with guns, I must say it did feel good to lie down.

Still, I was there for more than that. I crawled along the top of the car for a little ways, and it did seem safe up here, so I edged back and called down to Abbie to come on up. She did, slowly, with me helping her at the top, and when she was sprawled out on the roof, I yelled in her ear, "I'm going exploring! Don't move!"

"Don't worry." She shut her eyes and let her head rest on her folded arms.

I stuck my mouth close to her ear. "Don't fall asleep and roll off!"

She nodded, but I wasn't entirely convinced. I patted her shoulder doubtfully, and then took off.

It didn't take long to get to the other end of the car, and when I did, there was the pot-shooter, resting now between the cars. Waiting for the train to pull in at a station, no doubt. Then he and the others could just run along the platform to where we were, shoot us, and disappear.

Well, maybe, and on the other hand, maybe not. I pushed back from the edge and slowly sat up. I didn't

want to take my shoe off, wet and cold though it was, but
I didn't have much choice. So I took it off, and my foot
promptly went numb. I wasn't sure that was a good sign,
but it was better than the stinging ache I'd been feeling
up till now.

I lay on my belly again and crawled back to the end of
the car. He was still there, feet straddling the open space
as he faced outward. At the moment his head was bent a
bit because he was trying to light a cigarette.

Perfect. I put one hand on the top rung of the ladder
here to support me, took careful aim, and swung the heel
of the shoe around in a great big circle that started in
outer space and ended on the back of his head.

Lovely. He popped out like a grape seed out of a
grape, and landed in a snowbank. The last I saw of him
was his feet kicking in the air, black against the gray of
the snow.

One down. Three to go.

Sure.

I put my shoe back on and looked across at the next
car, trying to figure out how to get over there, and a head
popped into view two cars away. And after the head, an
arm. And on the end of the arm, a gun. It flashed, the gun
did, and I faintly heard the sound of the shot. It missed
me, but I wasn't encouraged. I quick hunched around
and started crawling back the other way.

Something went *p-tiying* beside my right elbow. I
looked, and saw a new scratch in the roof there.

He was getting too close. I hurriedly crawled back
to the pile of laundry I knew was Abbie and shook her
shoulder. "We've got to go down again!"

"Wha? Wha?" She lifted a shaky head and showed me
bleary eyes.

"One of them came up! Back there! He's shooting!"

"Oh, Chet, I'm so *tired.*"

"Come on, honey. Come on."

I herded her onto the ladder, with her about to fall twice, but the more she moved the more she woke up, and when she finally put her weight on the bad ankle on the ladder she woke up completely. She also let out a healthy yowl.

"That's right," I said. "Now get down and let me down."

"Oh, *wow,* that hurt."

"I'm sure it did. Go down, go down."

She went down, and I followed her. As my head was going down past the level of the roof I saw that guy back there on his feet. I stayed where I was, just high enough to see him. Now what?

He braced himself. He thought it over. He shook his head and got down on his knees. He shook his fist at himself and got up again. He braced himself. He ran forward. He leaped from the front of his car to the back of the next car. He made it, and the car he'd landed on jounced. He teetered way to the left, his arms pinwheeling. The car jounced again, and he teetered way to the right, his arms pinwheeling. The car wiggled, and he teetered every which way, arms and one leg pinwheeling. He got down on one knee, down on hands and knees. He'd made it. And the car waggled, and he rolled over onto his side and fell off the train.

"Well, I'll be darned," I said. I looked down at Abbie, asleep in midair between the cars. "We're going back up!" I shouted.

"Oh, *nooo!*"

"Oh, yes! Come on!"

She grumbled, she complained, she said unkind things,

but she came on, and when she got to the top, I said, "Now we go back down again."

She roused enough to stare at me. "Are you out of your mind? I hope they kill you, you crazy—"

"Listen to me. We're going down the other side. The last two are on this side of the train, so we'll go down the other side and jump off and they won't be able to see us go."

"Sure," she said.

"Just do it," I told her.

She did it. There was no ladder on this side, but there was a window ledge, there were handles and wheels, there were all sorts of things to climb on. As easy as falling off a building.

So we finally got back down again, both of us, and I spent some time instructing Abbie how to jump. I told her to stay loose, keep her arms and legs loose, don't stiffen up, roll when she hit, try to land in a snowbank, and all sorts of good advice like that. She nodded continually in a dull sort of way, meaning she wasn't hearing a thing I was saying. All I could do was hope some of it was seeping through into her subconscious and would show a result when we made our leap.

Finally I gave up on her and looked out from between the cars. We were on an overpass now, a deserted street below us. Beyond, the land fell away in a steep slope down from the tracks, with the rears of supermarkets and gas stations at the bottom.

"Up ahead," I said. "It's a snow-covered slope, it should be good for us. If there aren't a lot of old tin cans under the snow. When I give the word, you jump. And remember to jump at an angle, jump as much as possible in the same direction the train is going. And stay loose when you hit. And roll. You got that?"

She nodded. She was sound asleep.

Here came the slope. "Jump!" I shouted, and pushed her off the train. Then I leaped after her.

I must admit it was exhilarating out there for a second or two. In midair, sailing along high above the world, the cold wind whistling around my orange-capped head, a very Jules Verne feeling to it. And then the feeling became more physical as my feet touched the snowy slope and I discovered I was running at thirty miles an hour.

I can't run at thirty miles an hour, nobody can. I did the only thing I could do instead, I fell over on my face, did several loop-the-loops, and rolled madly down the hill, bringing up against somebody's trash barrel at the bottom. *Brrooommm,* it went, and I raised myself up a little, and Abbie crashed into me. And I crashed into the barrel again.

"Oh, come on, honey," I said. "Watch where you're careening."

"Growf," he said, and wrapped his hand around my neck.

It wasn't Abbie.

34

His hand was on my throat. My hand was on what I took to be his throat. My other hand was on what I took to be the wrist of his other hand, the hand in which he would be holding his gun if he was holding a gun. My head was usually buried under his chest somewhere, being ground into the ground. My feet thrashed around. We rolled and rolled, this way and that, gasping and panting, trying with only partial success to cut off each other's breathing, and from time to time we would bong one or another part of our bodies into that stinking rotten trash barrel. It got so I hated the trash barrel more than the guy trying to kill me. It got so what I really wanted to throttle was that trash barrel.

In the meantime, who was really getting throttled was me. We seemed to have stabilized at last, no more rolling, and unfortunately we'd stabilized with him on top. With his hand squeezing my jugular and my face mashed into his armpit, it looked as though I wasn't going to be getting much air from now on. About all I could do was kick my heels into the ground, which I did a lot of. I also tried squirming, but with very little success.

My strength was failing. I was passing out, and I knew it. I kicked my heels into the ground as hard as I could, but he just wouldn't let go. My head was filling with a rushing sound, like a waterfall. A black waterfall, roaring down over me, carrying me away, washing me away into oblivion and forgetfulness, dragging me down into the whirlpool, the black whirlpool.

He sagged.

His grip eased on my throat.

His weight doubled on my head.

Now what? I squirmed experimentally and he rolled off me, and suddenly I could breathe again, I could move again, I could see again, and what I saw was Abbie standing there with a shovel in her hands.

"Don't bury me," I said. "I'm still alive."

"I hit him with it," she said. "Is he all right?"

"I hope not." I sat up, feeling dizzy, my throat hurting,

and looked at my assailant. He was lying on his back, spread-eagled, sleeping peacefully. He was breathing. More important, so was I.

His legs were still on mine. "He's okay," I said, and pushed his legs off, and tottered to my feet. "Where's the other one?"

"Still on the train, I guess," she said. "I thought we were supposed to be getting away from both of them by coming over to this side."

"They must have figured that," I said, "and one of them climbed over. So they could watch both sides."

"So I didn't have to do all that climbing around."

"Did I know that? Come on, let's get out of here."

"Aren't you going to thank me for saving your life?"

"What?" I looked at the shovel, at the sleeper, and back at the shovel. "Oh, yeah," I said. "You did, didn't you?"

"Yes, I did," she said.

"Throw away the shovel and I'll thank you," I said.

She grinned and threw it away. I took a step closer and put my arms out and she came into them and we swapped breaths. Hers was very warm and sweet, and even through all our clothing she felt very soft and slender and delicious.

She broke first, and smiled at me. "That's nice," she said.

"Come back," I said. "I'm not done thanking you."

She came back.

I thanked her for quite a while, until she finally said, "Chet, this is lovely, but the truth is I'm cold. I'm freezing. And I think my ankle's swollen. And I'm exhausted."

I said, "When do you have to go back to Las Vegas?"

"Whenever I want."

"Do you think you could maybe never want?"

"You mean stay here?"

"In the vicinity."

"What about you in Vegas?" she said. "Nice and warm all the time, and you can gamble all you want."

"Not me," I said. "Look how much trouble I get in where I can only gamble a little. I'd better stay in a state where it has to be a sideline. Besides, Belmont opens in May."

"We'll have to talk about it," she said.

"Later on, right?"

She nodded. "Right."

"For now, we get you some place warm where you can sit down, right?"

"Oh, please, sir."

"Lean on me."

She did, maybe a little too much, and we staggered around the liquor store we'd landed behind and out to the street. And about a block away, on the other side of the street, was a big red neon sign that said BAR.

"Look, Moses," Abbie said, "it's the Promised Land."

I tried hurrying, but Abbie's ankle just wouldn't hold her any more, so finally I said, "Okay, let's do it the easy way," and I picked her up in my arms.

"Oh, what a grandstander," she said. "Now that we're almost there."

"You want to walk?"

"No!"

"Then be quiet."

I carried her across the street and into the bar, where the bartender and his three customers sitting at the bar all looked at us in deadpan disbelief. "She's my sweetie," I explained, and carried Abbie over to a booth and helped her sit down. Then I asked her, "What do you want to drink?"

"Whatever you're having."

"Scotch and soda."

"Fine."

I went over to the bar and ordered two Scotch and sodas. The bartender made them and set them down in front of me and I paid him. I put the glasses on the table while he got my change, and then went back to the bar, and he handed me my change and said, "I love your chapeau."

I looked at myself in his back-bar mirror, and discovered I was still wearing the orange hat. I'd forgotten all about it. I looked like Buddy Hackett being a Christmas elf. I said, "I won it for conspicuous valor."

"I figured you probably did," he said.

I took my change back to the booth, where Abbie was giggling behind her hand, and sat down. "Here's where you should of ordered a sidecar," I said.

"You do look kind of odd," she said.

"It keeps my head warm. Besides, it was a gift from a dear friend."

She got a tender look on her face and reached out to clasp my hand. "And you're a dear friend, Chet," she said. "I don't know what I would have done without you."

"Probably lived a lot quieter a life," I said. "But let me tell you, if you stick around I can't promise it'll all be as thrilling as the last few days."

"Oh, what a shame," she said.

I took a slug of Scotch and soda. "And it isn't over yet," I said.

"Why? What are we going to do now?"

"As soon as this booze gives me some strength back," I said, "I'm going over there and ask that very funny man behind the bar to call us a cab to take us back to New York."

"Why?"

"Because there's a poker game tonight," I said, "and one of the people sitting around that goddam table killed your brother. Not to mention winging me in the head while arming to kill you."

"I don't think you can be winged in the head," she said. "I think you have to be winged in the arm."

"I don't care," I said. "I was wung in the head."

"I thought you were," she said. She'd picked up the style from the bartender.

"And," I said, refusing to be sidetracked, "we are going to that poker game, you and I, and we are going to figure out which one of those lovelies it is. Just as soon as I have the strength to stand up."

35

I won't say climbing the stairs at Jerry Allen's place was the worst thing I went through that weekend, but it comes close. We'd spent a good forty-five minutes sitting in the back of that cab, relaxing, and we got out of it in front of Jerry's place feeling pretty good. Then we climbed all those stairs up to the fifth floor and we were dead again.

Abbie more than me, of course, because of her ankle. I'd had the cab stop in front of an all-night drugstore and I'd gone in and bought an Ace bandage, and I'd wrapped it around her ankle so that now she could walk on it at least, but it still slowed her down and drained her energy.

In the cab I'd offered to drop her off somewhere safe and go on to the game alone, but she'd said, "Not on your life, Charley. I want to be in at the finish." So here she was, hobbling up the stairs with me.

I wondered if they'd all be there. We'd discussed them on the way in, of course, the four of them, the four regulars, trying to figure out which one it could be, and we'd decided if one of them was missing tonight that was tantamount to a confession of guilt. But we'd thought it more likely the killer would try to act as normal as possible now, and so would more than likely show up.

So which one would it be? Jerry Allen. Sid Falco. Fred Stehl. Doug Hallman. There was also Leo Morgentauser, the vocational teacher, the irregular who'd been at the game last Wednesday and who surely wouldn't be here tonight. He'd known Tommy, in a business way, but very slightly. Maybe because he wasn't a regular in the game, I just didn't think he was our man. But if everybody else proved out clean tonight, I'd certainly go make a call on him.

In the meantime, it left four, and the most obvious right away was Sid Falco. But both Abbie and I had rejected him right away. In the first place, he wasn't an amateur, and Golderman had told us Tommy's killing had been the work of an amateur. In the second place, Sid wouldn't have had to steal Abbie's gun from me in order to have something to shoot me with. And in the third place, we just didn't like him for the job.

Then there was Jerry Allen, our host. Part-owner of a florist shop, a possible homosexual, a steady loser at the game, full of sad embarrassed laughter whenever one of his many bad bluffs was called. So far as I knew he'd never met Tommy, and I couldn't think of a motive for him, and I couldn't see him shooting anybody anyway. I particularly couldn't see him sitting at his kitchen table and carving dum-dum bullets.

Of course, the same was true of Fred Stehl. He was the one with the wife, Cora, who called once or twice every week, sometimes every night there was a game, for months, trying to prove Fred was there. What excuses Fred gave her a hundred and four times a year I don't know, but she obviously never believed any of them. Fred was a loser at the game, but not badly, and his laundromat had to be making pretty good money. He made bets with Tommy a lot, but where was his motive?

Of all of them, the only one I could see getting teed off enough at anybody to sit at a kitchen table and make dum-dum bullets was Doug Hallman, our cigar-smoking gas station man. But I couldn't see Doug actually shooting anybody. His hollering and blustering and loudness usually covered a bluff of one kind or another. When he was serious he was a lot quieter. If he ever decided to shoot somebody it would be a simple, clean, well-planned job, using one perfectly placed bullet which wasn't a dum-dum at all. Or at least that's the way it seemed to me.

So I'd wound up eliminating them all, if you'll notice. But doggone it, one of those guys had stolen Abbie's gun from me. It couldn't have been anyone else, that was the one fact we had for sure. The idea that I'd been shot by the same gun was an inference, but it was based on a lot of circumstantial evidence. The amateur standing of the killer, for instance, combined with the cops' having found the murder weapon that killed Tommy. And the fact that its aim was off, so that the shot that had hit me had probably been intended for Abbie, was another inference, but it followed logically out of the first one. And finally, that the person who shot at me—Abbie—us—whoever—was the same person who killed Tommy was yet another inference, but one I had no hesitation at all in making. So with one fact and three inferences we wound up with the conviction that one of the guys present at last Wednesday's poker game was the murderer. And then we went over them one at a time, and eliminated them all.

Hell.

We'd talked all this around and around in the cab, getting nowhere, and after we'd stopped talking about it I'd kept thinking about it and I still hadn't gotten anywhere, and as I stood now on the fifth floor of Jerry's building, gasping for breath and waiting for Abbie to catch up, I thought about it some more and I went on getting nowhere.

I also thought of something else. I said to Abbie, "Did I leave the meter running, do you know?"

She looked up at me. She had three steps to go, and she was white as a sheet. She breathed for a while, and then she said, "What?"

"The meter," I explained. "In the cab I checked out. The one we drove to Golderman's in. I wonder if I left the meter running."

"Oh." She shook her head. "I don't know."

"Christ, I hope I didn't."

She came up the last three steps and leaned against the banister. "I made it."

"I'll have to go out there tomorrow and get that cab," I said. "If everything's straightened out by then. What the hell am I going to tell the garage?"

"I don't know, Chet."

"You ready to go in?"

She nodded.

"Then let's go."

36

Jerry himself opened the door. "Well, look at you! We thought you weren't coming. And you brought the pro, too, how lucky. Come on in. Isn't that an interesting hat."

I'd forgotten about it again. I untied the lace from under my chin and took the damn thing off. "Just something I picked up," I said.

"Where? I might be interested."

"You can have this one," I said. "It doesn't go with my eyes."

"You're putting me on."

"No, I'm not. Here."

He took the hat, not sure I was serious. He said, "Are you serious?"

"Sure, why not?"

"Well, thank you. Your trousers are ripped."

That was that damn hedge I'd run through. "I slipped on the ice," I said.

"Isn't it awful? Abbie, what a lovely coat! But don't *give* it to me, for heaven's sake."

Abbie laughed. "Just to hang up for me?"

"Well, in that case—"

As he took our coats and hung them up, I looked at Jerry Allen and I just couldn't see it. Not Jerry. Jerry

wouldn't kill anybody, not in a million years. Scratch one.
Again.

We all went into the living room, where Fred Stehl
took one look, went, "Yip!" and threw his cards in the air.

"No applause," I said. "No demonstrations."

He put his hand to his heart. "I thought it was Cora,"
he said.

"After what she did the last time?" Jerry said. "And you
thought I'd open the door for her?"

"I know," Fred said. "I know. But boy, just for a second
there, wow. And Abbie, you don't look a bit like Cora,
honest to God."

"I hope that's a compliment," she said.

"Oh, it is," Jerry told her, and Fred nodded solemnly.

Fred? Fred Stehl, the henpecked laundromat man
with his glasses and his balding head? No. In his own
beer-and-undershirt way Fred was an even less likely
candidate for murderer than Jerry.

I looked around and all the regulars were here tonight,
Doug and Sid also sitting there, and besides them there
was a fifth man. Leo Morgentauser.

Leo? I frowned at him. What was he doing here, twice
in one week? He'd never done that before. That was suspicious, very suspicious. I said, "Leo, what a surprise. I
didn't expect you around for a couple of months."

"I called him," Jerry said. "When you didn't show up
I called a couple of guys, and Leo could make it."

"I won last time," Leo said, "and I still have some of it
left, so I thought I'd give you guys a chance to get it back."

"Well, that's good," I said, and it stopped being suspicious that he was here. Naturally the boys didn't want to
play four-handed, that's a terrible game, and naturally
Leo was one of the people they'd call, and since he had

won last Wednesday it wasn't unusual for him to say yes tonight. Besides, what was a poor but honest vocational high school teacher going to shoot a small-time bookie for? Leo had made his rare two-dollar bet with Tommy, but I knew Tommy would never have let him run up a big tab or anything like that, he wouldn't let anyone run up a tab too big for them to handle, and why would Leo shoot him? Why would Leo shoot anybody? No, not Leo.

There were two spaces next to each other at the table, so Abbie and I sat down there, Abbie on my left, and that put Doug Hallman on my right. He said, "What've you been up to, buddy? You look like you been mugged."

"I slipped on the ice," I said. "How you doing tonight?"

He had his inevitable rotten cigar in his face, and he puffed a lot of foul smoke in answer to my question, then amplified with, "Beautiful cards. Great cards. If we'd been playing low ball I'd own New York State by now."

I grinned at him, and tried to visualize him shooting Tommy. He knew Tommy the same way the rest of us did, but that was all. Because he played at being mean all the time, the tough grimy garage man, big and hairy, chewing his cigar, it was possible to imagine him with a gun in his hand, going *bang,* but it was not at all possible to imagine why he'd do such a thing. Very unlikely. I put a great big check next to his name in my head, with a little teeny question mark next to it.

The other side of Doug was Leo, and the other side of Leo was Sid Falco. Sid hadn't looked at anybody since we'd walked in, but had sat there studying the small stack of chips in front of him. Now, though, when Leo picked up the cards and said, "We ready to play?" Sid suddenly said, "Deal me out," and got to his feet. "I'll be back in a minute," he said, still not looking at anybody.

"Hold it, Sid," I said.

He did look at me, then, and I was surprised to see he was scared. He said, "What's the matter, Chet?"

"Sit down, Sid," I said.

He said, "I got to go to the bathroom."

I said, "You mean to go into the kitchen and use Jerry's other phone to call Napoli and tell him Abbie and I are here so he can have some people waiting outside for us when we leave."

Shaking his head from side to side, looking very nervous and embarrassed, blinking a lot, doing all the things he always does when he's trying one of his the-book-says-to-do-it bluffs, he said, "You got me absolutely wrong, Chet. I just got to go to the bathroom."

"Sit down, Sid," I said. "You can make your phone call in a few minutes, but right now sit down." I felt everybody else staring at me. Everybody but Abbie, who seemed to have fallen asleep again. I didn't blame her. I would have liked to fall asleep myself. I said, "Sit down, Sid, and I'll tell you and everybody else why I'm here now, and why I look like this, and why Abbie's sitting there with an Ace bandage wrapped around the outside of her boot. I'll tell you everything, Sid, and then you can go to the bathroom all you want."

Sid sat down.

I said, "The reason I'm here, Sid, is because somebody in this room killed Tommy McKay."

Sid stopped blinking. He looked at me cold-eyed. Everybody else went into shock for a second, and then I got a chorus of wha? and you're putting us on, and things like that. I waited for it to settle down, and then I said, "Sid, when you go to the bathroom, you're going to have a lot more to tell your boss than just where he can find

Abbie and me. You're going to tell him who killed Tommy McKay, and you're going to tell him about the lawyer I went to see on my way to town, and you're going to tell him about the letter I dictated to that lawyer, and you're going to tell him why his boys and Droble's boys both should lay off both Abbie and me permanently and forever. This is all going to be very interesting, Sid."

"Maybe it is," Sid said. He was very businesslike now, not doing a bluff at all.

I said, "All right. We'll start with Tommy's murderer. He's in this room."

Jerry Allen said, "Chet, what nonsense. For heaven's sake, what are you talking about?"

I stopped talking to Sid, and talked to Jerry instead. "When I came here last Wednesday night," I said, "I had a gun in my coat pocket. It was Abbie's, she'd given it to me to hold for her that afternoon."

"You took it," Abbie said sleepily.

"All right," I said, "I took it. The point is, I had it when I came here. When I left here it was gone. I didn't notice it until later, but the only place it could have been taken from my pocket was in this apartment, while my coat was hanging up in the hall closet. Somebody took my gun. Abbie's gun. Somebody in this room took it."

Doug said, "Chet, is this on the level?"

"Absolutely on the level," I told him, and I pointed at the wound on the side of my head. "You see that? I was shot at by that same gun."

Sid said, "You've got something wrong."

I looked at him. "I do? What?"

"I took the gun out of your coat," he said. "I was supposed to turn you over to a couple of guys after the game, and I was supposed to make sure you were clean. They told me they wanted to ask you some questions, they didn't say anything about bumping you off."

"That's what they wanted, though," I said.

"I found that out later," he said. "They told me the other at first because they didn't know how close friends we were."

"Not very close," I said.

He shrugged. "Anyway, you took off with the girl. I followed you, because maybe you were going to her place or something, but you gave me the slip. So I phoned my boss and he said they'd set things up another way and I gave him your home address."

"That was thoughtful," I said.

"He wanted to know. But the point is, I thought you'd got the gun back. I took it out of your coat pocket and put it in my coat pocket, and when I checked after the game it was gone. So I thought you took it back."

"I didn't," I said. I looked around, and everybody was staring at Sid now. So long as I was the only one who'd been talking crazy, they could all remain astonished spectators, but now that Sid had entered into a dialogue with me, the thing was turning real and they were beginning to realize they were in the middle of it. I said, "It looks as though this place was full of pickpockets last Wednesday night. Anybody got any ideas?"

Leo said, "I have the idea I should have stayed home tonight." He still had the cards in his hand, and he looked at them now, smiled grimly, and put them down.

Doug said to me, "Let me try and get this straight. You got yourself mixed up in Tommy's murder somehow, and got shot at yourself. And you say it was with a gun that was stolen off you while you were here at the game last Wednesday."

"Right."

"Why wasn't it with the same gun that killed Tommy? Maybe somebody here copped your gun, but didn't have anything to do with shooting at you."

"They found the gun that killed Tommy two days before I was shot at," I said.

"The cops found it?"

"Yes."

"So much for that," Doug said. He shook his head. "I pass. It wasn't me and I don't know who it was."

Jerry said, "It wasn't you, Doug? You have a pretty mean temper sometimes. And you did know this man Tommy, I believe. You couldn't have gotten angry at him over something—"

"I could get angry at you," Doug told him. "I could get angry, Jerry, and pull your head off you, but I couldn't go shoot people." He held up his hands, saying, "If I ever kill anybody, Jerry, this is what I'll use. And you'll be the first to know."

Leo said, "Doug's right, Jerry. You're much more the revolver type than he is. You might get into a pet and blast somebody with a gun."

"Me?" Jerry absolutely squeaked. "I don't even *own* a gun! I didn't even *know* the man who was killed! *You* knew him!"

Doug said, "Hold it. Let's not go pointing the finger at each other. That won't get us anywhere, it'll just get us mad."

"I disagree," I said. "Maybe it will get us somewhere. Why don't we all say what we think, and argue it out, and see if we can come up with something? Because I'll tell you the truth, I have absolutely no way to narrow it down. I know it has to be somebody in this room, I know it can't be anybody not in this room, but that's as close as I've been able to get it. Except I've eliminated Sid. But the rest of you—"

Sid smiled thinly, and everybody else objected at once. Leo succeeded in getting the floor at last, and said, "Why eliminate Sid? From the way you two have been talking, you and Sid, he knows as much about this as you do. And he's apparently connected with some underworld figures some way, I get that much from the conversation. Why wouldn't that make him your prime suspect, ahead of the rest of us?"

"He didn't have to shoot at me," I said. "No matter what he says now, he knew his boss was sending people to kill me. Professionals. So why should *he* bother to shoot me? Also, it made his boss very unhappy when Tommy was killed, and Sid wouldn't have dared do anything to make his boss unhappy. Right, Sid?"

"Close enough," Sid said.

Leo shook his head. "None of us knows anything about this, Chet. How can we talk sensibly about it? If one of us makes a suggestion, you tell us five more facts you already knew and we didn't which shows the suggestion is wrong. That's futile. What you ought to do is take your suspicions to the police."

"Of course," Jerry said. "Instead of coming here disrupting things, why not go to the police? Tell them what you think, what you know. Let *them* work it out."

It was Abbie who answered this time. "We can't go to the police," she said.

Doug said, "Why not?"

"Because," she said, "there are two gangs of crooks after us. Not one gang, two gangs. If one of them doesn't get us, the other will. Neither Chet nor I can live a normal life while they're still after us. And part of the reason they're all excited and upset is because of Tommy McKay's murder. If we could solve that for them, and also this business about the lawyer Chet mentioned"—I was glad she'd picked up on that, since I'd just made it up and we hadn't discussed it in the cab— "they'd leave us alone."

Fred, leaning forward with a worried expression on his face, said, "You mean your lives are in danger?"

"That's putting it mildly," I said. "We've been shot at, strangled, threatened, chased, I don't know what all. There are people out in the world with guns right now, and they're looking for Abbie and me, and they want to kill us. And Sid there wants to go make a phone call and tell one bunch of them where they can find us."

Fred shook his head. "I can't understand that," he said. "How did you get so involved?"

"I was trying to get that nine hundred thirty dollars I was owed," I said, "and Abbie wanted to do something to avenge her brother, since he was her last living relative."

Doug said, "Did you get the money?" He held one of my markers.

"No," I said. "They refused to pay off, in fact."

"That's too bad," Doug said.

Fred said, "How can you think about money at a time like this, Doug? Chet, do they really want to kill you?" He couldn't seem to get it into his head.

"Yes," I said. "They really want to kill me. Abbie, too. Ask Sid."

Fred turned his head and looked at Sid, who said, "Chet's right."

Fred said to him, "And it would help him if he found out who killed Tommy McKay?"

Sid shrugged. "It's possible. I wouldn't know about that."

I said, "The funny thing is, I think I know who it is. And yet I don't believe it."

Everybody looked at me. Abbie said, "Who?" Leo said, "Why don't you believe it?"

I answered Leo. I said, "One of the things I wanted to do here was throw this mess on the table and just watch reactions, see how different people acted. I figured maybe the killer would act different from everybody else, and I'd be able to spot him."

Leo said, "And did he? Have you spotted somebody?"

"Yeah," I said. "But I don't believe it. There's something wrong somewhere."

Abbie said, "For Pete's sake, Chet, who is it?"

"It's Fred," I said.

37

Nobody said anything. Fred frowned, looking troubled and worried and sad but somehow not like a murderer, and everybody else looked alternately at him and at me.

Leo broke the silence at last. He said, "Why do you think it's Fred?"

I said, "Because he jumped a mile when we came in here, and then covered it up by saying he thought Abbie was Cora. But Abbie doesn't look at all like Cora, and Fred just saw Abbie four days ago and knew she might be coming back tonight. And because Cora didn't call last Wednesday and I bet she doesn't call tonight, and that's because she knows what happened and she's agreed to let

Fred go on with his normal life as though nothing had happened, to cover up."

Leo said, "That isn't very much, Chet."

"I don't have very much," I said, "I admit that. But I have a little more. When I started talking, everybody got excited. Everybody but Fred. Jerry accused Doug, Leo accused Jerry, Doug got mad, Leo accused Sid, everybody was full of questions and excitement and disbelief. Everybody but Fred. He just sat there and didn't say anything for a long while. Until I made it clear that Abbie and I were now murder targets ourselves and the one who'd killed Tommy was indirectly responsible. Then he asked questions, hoping to get answers that would make it less tough. All he is is worried and troubled and sad, and everybody else is excited and irritated and surprised."

Abbie said, "But why do you say it doesn't seem right?"

"I don't know," I said. "There's something that just doesn't jibe. Fred's reactions are wrong for him to be innocent, but somehow they're wrong for him to be guilty, too. He should be tougher if he's guilty. I don't understand."

Fred gave me a wan smile and said, "You're pretty good, Chet. I don't know how you did that, but you're pretty doggone good."

Jerry gaped at him. "You mean you *did* do it?"

"No," Fred said. "I didn't shoot Tommy. But I did shoot you, Chet, and God, I'm sorry. I didn't want to hit anybody, I aimed between you and Abbie. When I saw I'd hit you I almost died myself. Christ, I've always been a pretty good shot, I don't know what went wrong."

"That gun shoots off to the left," I said. "You should have taken it out on a practice range for a while."

"It must shoot way the *hell* to the left," he said.

"It does," Abbie said.

Sid said to him, "You took the gun out of my pocket?"

Fred nodded. "I was going through Chet's and Abbie's pockets," he said. "I wanted to see if they had any clues or evidence or anything about the murder they weren't telling us about. I felt the heavy thing in your pocket, and took a look, and there was the gun. I knew you had something to do with the underworld, so I figured it was your gun, and I swiped it. I didn't know it belonged to you, Chet."

"To me," Abbie said. "Where is it?"

"In the Harlem River," Fred said. "I thought I'd killed Chet for sure, so I got rid of that gun right away."

I said, "But you didn't kill Tommy."

He shook his head. "No, I didn't."

"Then why do all this other stuff? To cover up for the real killer? But who?"

Fred just smiled sadly at me.

We all stared at him, and it hit all of us simultaneously, and six voices raised as one to cry, "CORA!"

Fred nodded. "Cora," he said. "Chet, you saw her right after she did it."

I said, "I did not."

"Sure you did. She was coming out of the building when you were going in."

I frowned, drawing a blank, and suddenly remembered. "The woman with the baby carriage!"

"Sure," he said. "Cora's a smart woman, Chet. She saw you through the glass, and she didn't want to be recognized, and there was a baby carriage in the hallway, so she figured that would make a good disguise, and with the two of you meeting in the doorway, you holding the door and the baby carriage in the way and all, her keeping her head down, she got away with it. She went right through and you never even noticed."

I said, "A day or two later I saw a sign in the entrance-way there about a stolen baby carriage, and I never connected it at all."

Abbie, in an outraged tone, said, "Cora? I don't even know who she is!"

"She's Fred's wife," I said.

"But that isn't *fair*," she said. "How can I solve the murder if I don't even know the murderer, if I never even met her? The woman never even put in an appearance!"

"Sure she did," I said. "She walked right by me with a baby carriage."

"Well, she never walked by *me*," she insisted. "I say it isn't fair. You wouldn't get away with that in a detective story."

I said, "Why not? Remember the story about the dog who didn't bark in the night? Well, this is the same thing. The wife who didn't phone in the night."

"Oh, foo," Abbie said, and folded her arms. "I say it isn't fair, and I won't have any more to do with it."

Jerry said, "Never mind all that. Fred, why on earth would Cora *do* a thing like that?"

"You're the one she punched in the nose," Fred reminded him. "She's a very violent woman, Cora. She'd been on Tommy's back not to take any bets from me, and she found out we were still doing business, and she went down there to really let him have it, and she took the gun along to scare him. She wasn't even sure she'd show it to him. But he apparently had something on his mind—"

"That's an understatement," I said. "His wife was running around with another man, and he was running around with another boss."

"Well, anyway," Fred said, "she showed him the gun. Then, instead of getting scared, he made a jump for her, and she started shooting." To me he said, "It's an old gun of mine, I've had it since I was in the Army. I do pot-shooting with it sometimes. That's why I didn't believe it when I saw I'd hit you the other night, because I knew I was a better shot than that."

"Why did you do it?" I said.

"I wanted to convince you it was a gang thing," he said. "I was afraid you two would find out the truth if you kept poking around. If you kept thinking about the case, Chet, you might suddenly remember the woman with the baby carriage. I didn't know. I figured if I took a shot at you, to miss, it might scare you into laying off. Or anyway convince you the mob was behind the killing."

Nobody said anything then for a minute or two, and then Leo said, "Where's your wife now, Fred?"

Fred looked embarrassed. "You won't believe this," he said.

Doug said, "Try us."

"She's in a convent," Fred said.

Everybody said, "What?"

"It preyed on her mind," he said. "So Friday night she packed her things and went to a convent. She says she's going in for good."

Abbie, returning to us after all, said, "Why didn't she go to the police if she felt so bad?"

"I didn't want her to," Fred said. "I feel responsible for the whole thing, damn it. I knew Cora hated me gambling, but I went right ahead and did it. So finally she blew her top and your brother got killed, but I'm just as much to blame as she is, and I just couldn't stand to see her go to jail for it."

Abbie said, "A convent's better?"

"Yes," he said. "And believe me, I hated the idea of coming here the last two times, but I figured I had to, to keep up appearances. I figure this is my last game."

I said, "Fred, are you telling me *Cora* took my money? To make up for *your* losses?"

"No," he said, and almost looked offended. "A lot of people were in and out of that apartment, Chet. Who knows whose sticky fingers carried that cash away. Cora's hotheaded, but she isn't a thief."

"Only a murderer," Abbie said.

Fred sighed. "I'm sorry about this," he said. "Whatever you want me to do, Chet, that's what I'll do. You want me to make a statement to the police? I don't want you and Abbie getting killed over this. Enough has happened already."

"More than enough," I said. I looked at Abbie. "What do you think? Is a convent punishment enough?"

"It would be for me," she said.

I said, "We don't care about the cops anyway. It's the mobs that worry us. Just so they know the story, that should satisfy us. Okay, Abbie?"

She hesitated, but I knew she couldn't retain the white-hot desire for vengeance against a woman who'd already turned herself in at a convent. "Okay," she said.

"Good." I turned to Sid. "You've got the story straight?"

"I've got it," he said.

"Okay. You go make your phone call now. And first you tell them what really happened to Tommy McKay. And then you tell them about the lawyer I stopped off to see on my way in here, and you tell them I dictated a long letter to that lawyer to be opened in the event of either my or Abbie's death, and you tell them that lawyer went to school with John Lindsay, and you tell them we want to be left one hundred percent alone from now on. You tell them we don't intend to make any waves, and we don't want any waves making on us, if you get what I mean."

"I've got it," he said.

"And you also tell them," I said, "to be sure things are squared with Golderman."

He frowned. "I don't know Golderman."

"You don't have to. Just tell them. And tell them to pass the word to Droble and his clowns before they screw things up. *And* tell them I want my doggone nine hundred thirty dollars."

Was he grinning behind that poker face? I don't know. "I'll tell them," he said.

"Let me think," I said. "Oh, yeah. And get word to Golderman to go outside and see if I left the meter running, and if I did, to turn it off, and I'll be out tomorrow for the cab."

"You'll be out tomorrow for the cab."

"Can you remember all that?"

"Of course," he said.

"And I'll tell you something *I'm* going to remember," I told him. "*I'm* going to remember that you were willing to turn me over to people to murder me."

He shook his head. "What would have happened if I said no, Chet? They would have killed me instead. You're a nice guy and I like you, but I can get along without you. I can't get along without me for a minute." He got to his feet. "I'll make that call now," he said, and he left.

There was a little silence, and then Fred said, "What about me, Chet?"

"You can do what you want, Fred," I said. "I don't hold a grudge against you. I'm glad your aim wasn't any worse than it was, that's all. But I'm not going to turn you over to the police. You can go or stay, it's up to you."

"Then I believe I'll go," he said, and got wearily to his feet. "I don't have much chips here," he said. "Just toss these in the next pot." He walked around the table and stood in front of me. "I'm sorry, Chet," he said. "I honestly am."

"I know you are."

Hesitantly he stuck out his hand. Hesitantly I took it. Then he nodded to Abbie, nodded to the table at large, and left, very slope-shouldered.

Leo had the cards in his hand again. He said, "I know momentous things are happening all around me, but I don't get to play poker that often. Are we ready?"

"We're ready," I said.

"Good," he said. "Five-card stud, in the lady's honor," he said, and started to deal. When he got to Sid's chair he said, "What about Sid?"

"Deal him out," I said.

DON'T LET THE MYSTERY END HERE...
Try These Other Hard Case Crime Books
By the Author of
SOMEBODY OWES ME MONEY

361

by DONALD E. WESTLAKE

The men in the tan-and-cream Chrysler came with guns blazing. When Ray Kelly woke up in the hospital, it was a month later, he was missing an eye, and his father was dead. *Then things started to get bad.*

From the mind of the incomparable Donald E. Westlake— Mystery Writers of America Grandmaster and Academy Award nominee for the screenplay of *The Grifters*—comes a shocking story of betrayal and revenge, an exploration of the limits of family loyalty, and how far a man will go when everything he loves is taken from him.

PRAISE FOR '361':

"My personal favorite of [Westlake's] hard-boiled period and, to my mind, the first book in which he found a voice that was uniquely his."
— Lawrence Block in
MYSTERY AND SUSPENSE WRITERS

"Classic hard-boiled style…prose so clean it's like Hemingway threw away his thesaurus."
— Booklist

"Neat and tight, like a well-delivered right cross."
— Steve Vernon

**To order, visit www.HardCaseCrime.com or call
1-800-481-9191 (10am to 9pm EST).**

Each title just $6.99 ($8.99 in Canada), plus shipping and handling.

More Great Suspense From
Donald E. Westlake's Legendary Alter Ego

Lemons
NEVER LIE

by RICHARD STARK

When he's not pulling heists with his friend Parker, Alan Grofield runs a small theater in Indiana. But putting on shows is expensive and jobs have been thin, which is why Grofield agrees to listen to Andrew Myers' plan to knock over a brewery in upstate New York.

Unfortunately, Myers' plan is insane—so Grofield walks out on him. *But Myers isn't a man you walk out on…*

RAVES FOR 'LEMONS NEVER LIE':

"This first-rate hard-boiled mystery…reads like Raymond Chandler with a dark literary whisper…of Cormac McCarthy."
— Time

"The prose is clean, the dialogue laced with dry humor, the action comes hard and fast."
— George Pelecanos

"Lemons Never Lie is a delight— a crime story that leaves you smiling."
— Washington Post

"The best Richard Stark ever."
— Paul Kavanagh

To order, visit www.HardCaseCrime.com or call
1-800-481-9191 (10am to 9pm EST).

Each title just $6.99 ($8.99 in Canada), plus shipping and handling.